# *The* DOG PARK MURDERS

# *The* DOG PARK MURDERS

ANGELA BARKER

HARLEQUIN

HARLEQUIN®

Recycling programs for this product may not exist in your area.

ISBN-13: 978-1-335-00173-3

The Dog Park Murders



Special thanks and acknowledgment to Stefanie London for her contribution to this work.

Map Illustration by Paula Miquelarena



Harlequin Enterprises ULC
22 Adelaide St. West, 41st Floor
Toronto, Ontario M5H 4E3, Canada
www.Harlequin.com

HarperCollins Publishers
Macken House,
39/40 Mayor Street Upper,
Dublin 1, D01 C9W8, Ireland
www.HarperCollins.com

Printed in U.S.A.

26 27 28 29 30 LBC 5 4 3 2 1

*To Frankie, solver of the mystery of the delicious-smelling takeout bag*

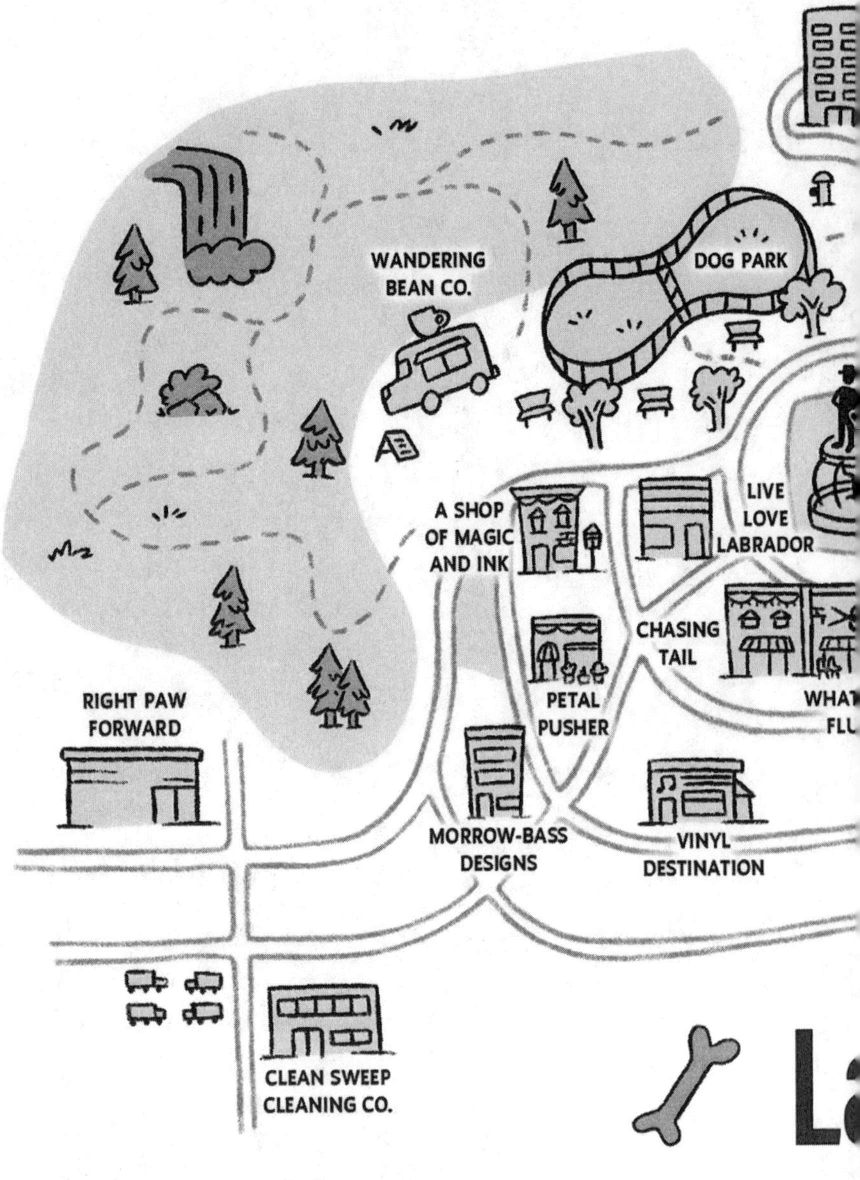
WANDERING
BEAN CO.
DOG PARK
A SHOP
OF MAGIC
AND INK
LIVE
LOVE
LABRADOR
CHASING
TAIL
PETAL
PUSHER
RIGHT PAW
FORWARD
MORROW-BASS
DESIGNS
VINYL
DESTINATION
CLEAN SWEEP
CLEANING CO.

# orador Falls, MA

# *Prologue*

**SPOTTING THE MURDERER** on a television show was easy. Sixty minutes—forty-five if you accounted for commercials—left little time for subtlety. That meant the bad guy always had a tell. Or they were too wide-eyed, too concerned, *too* innocent. The lady doth protest too much and all that. Sometimes the killer was obvious simply by being around too much, like a bad smell that wouldn't dissipate. But in real life, would it be so easy to spot a killer?

She hoped not.

It wasn't like this was going to become a habit. One murder was enough for her. One means to an end, one problem solved, one story over. She wasn't greedy or violent . . . usually.

*So long as nobody figures out what I've done . . .*

Sweat trickled down the length of her spine as she shifted her weight on the hard plastic chair. Her stomach growled. They'd left her sitting in the police interview room for nearly an hour already. Was that a tactic? Were they watching her in the little camera that sat perched like a bird in the high corner of the room? Or were they simply overwhelmed? Labrador Falls hadn't seen a murder in a long, *long* time.

And she'd changed that.

But as far as she was concerned, it was an act of public service.

The clock on the wall ticked so loudly it made her eye twitch. She wiped her palms down the front of her thighs, trying to get them clean and dry before the detective came in. If he shook a clammy hand, that would surely be a strike against her name. How did one *not* look like a murderer, exactly? She should be calm. Cooperative.

*Nothing to see here, Officer.*

She forced herself to relax back against the chair and take a deep breath. Then she folded her hands neatly in her lap, closing her eyes and thinking about her happy place—a tropical beach with dogs playing on the sand, a fruity drink in a pretty glass by her side, and the warm sun beating down on her bare limbs. A place where *he* would never set foot.

To be fair, he would never set foot anywhere ever again. Would never be able to ruin anyone's life the way he'd ruined hers.

That very thought made her relax.

Outside the shuttered interview room footsteps grew louder, the dull thud of rubber-soled boots against scuffed linoleum deepening with each step. It was now or never. Showtime. She would be the perfect picture of a law-abiding town citizen with a squeaky-clean record and nary a skeleton in her closet. Nobody saw her, of *that* she was certain. And there would be no proof, because she was smarter than that.

And like every smart person who'd done something bad, she'd made sure there was someone else to take the fall.

# *Chapter One*

*Earlier . . .*

**"BRAD, CAN YOU . . . ?"** Juliette Macintyre grunted as she adjusted her position. Being bent over with her butt in the air while reaching at an awkward angle was making her thighs shake. Why had she skipped so many Pilates classes lately? She could have used a little more flexibility. And core strength. "I can't get between your legs properly if you stand like that."

This was the second time she'd seen Brad, and even though the first time had been a bit of a disaster—took *far* too long to finish the job, in her humble opinion—she'd decided to give him another chance. If she was being honest, he was one of those all looks, no brains kinda guys. All the women at work thought he should be a model with his piercing blue eyes and shaggy golden hair, but Juliette was sure if there was a single brain cell rattling around in his head then it was one more than he regularly put to use.

"Just stop licking for a second." She gently pushed his head away. "Maybe we need to try a different position."

Brad glanced over his shoulder, tongue lolling out of his mouth.

"Good boy." She gave the dog a pat and gently nudged him toward the wall before returning to brushing his coat out with a slicker brush. "You know, I always thought Brad seemed a funny name for a dog."

Why *did* people give human names to their dogs? It was weird. Why not give them a quirky name that showed the dog's personality? Clearly there were plenty of folks who thought differently if What The Fluff's client list was anything to go on. Just today she'd groomed a cocker spaniel named Kenneth. And one of their longest standing clients had three dogs all named after the women in *Sex and the City*—but only Miranda, Carrie and Charlotte. For some reason, Samantha didn't get a doggy namesake.

By the time Juliette finished her appointment with Brad the Labrador-Great Dane mix, it looked like a fur tornado had blown through the room. Little tufts rolled across the floor like canine tumbleweeds. But the mess would have to wait until after a much-needed lunch break. Pet grooming was a physically demanding job and What The Fluff was *the* premiere pet grooming salon in Labrador Falls, meaning not a day went by where they weren't fully booked. Juliette often worked late—squeezing in folks who couldn't get an appointment in the standard hours—because her people-pleasing tendencies made it hard to say no.

*Don't you mean impossible?*

Look, taming the people-pleasing beast was a work in progress, okay? And now she had even *more* responsibility on her shoulders. For the next three weeks Juliette was running What The Fluff while her boss, Bonnie, went cruising around the Caribbean drinking margaritas and hitting on men half her age.

This was the perfect opportunity to prove—mostly to herself—that she was responsible enough to run a business. Bonnie had been pushing her to step into a partnership role for some time, but it seemed like *a lot* of responsibility. Too much responsibility. Now, however, she didn't have a choice. It was either run the salon in Bonnie's absence or let the dogs of Labrador Falls go shaggy and unkempt. She couldn't have that.

But was she *really* ready? Had she learned enough to do a good job? Would people around here finally look at her with a gleam of respect in their eyes instead the usual undisguised distaste?

*Wouldn't that be nice?*

Juliette locked up the salon, flipping over the sign on the front door so it read Be Back in Thirty Minutes. What was she worried about? Bonnie had taught her everything she needed to know.

Like that huskies would try to burst your eardrums singing the song of their people.

Or that a Shiba Inu would never do what you ask them to on principle.

And that Chihuahuas were the ones most likely to snap your hand off, if you weren't careful. Juliette knew better than to be fooled by their sweet little faces. They were tiny, adorable demons.

*See? You got this.*

Maybe the unwanted responsibility was actually a blessing in disguise. After all, she'd spent years trying to be her best, most perfect self in the hopes of convincing people around here that she was a good person. Not a disgrace, like her dad. And if Bonnie trusted her to run the salon—and Bonnie was loved by *everyone* in town—then that said something good about her, right?

Juliette tipped her face up to the sky, looking for a sign among the silver-tinted clouds, but all she saw was a cloud shaped like a weird five-legged giraffe and another that looked vaguely like a male appendage.

Were dick clouds a good sign? It was hard to be sure.

Stomach grumbling, Juliette headed toward her favorite lunch destination, Brewed Awakening. The café sat next to What The Fluff on the eastern side of the town square, bracketed by a walkway. Gold, orange and brown leaves skittered across the cobblestones as she walked, filling her with a sense of anticipation. Was it basic to say that fall was her favorite season? She loved all the key things about it, like UGG boots and cable-knit sweaters and cinnamon-scented candles and watching reruns of *Gilmore Girls* and . . . Okay, maybe she *was* a little basic. So what? Life was about enjoying whatever you liked, regardless of what stupid people on the internet had to say about it. And they could pry her pumpkin spice latte from her cold dead hands.

Not that she would get a pumpkin spice latte from Brewed Awakening, mind you.

The grumpy, stubborn owner of the café *hated* all things PSL. In fact, he offered no "flavors" of any kind. And don't even *think* about asking for a matcha or a mocha! He'd direct you to the Starbucks one town over. Really, he could be so gruff it was amazing he had any customers at all.

But as Juliette pushed open the door to Brewed Awakening, the scent of roasted coffee beans and freshly baked pastries hitting her nose, she spotted the owner, Joel, leaning against the bar, the sleeves of his checked shirt rolled up to reveal strong, muscular forearms and a broody expression narrowing his warm, burnt caramel eyes. Okay, maybe there was *one* reason this place was so popular.

Two, if you admitted that the coffee was *so* good it didn't really need any syrup.

"Hi, Joel," Juliette sing-songed as she waltzed up to the counter. "Isn't it lovely outside? It's gotten so crisp in the mornings! I'm so excited fall has finally arrived. You know, this is my favorite time of year."

Joel dragged his eyes away from the window, which faced out to the town square, and flicked them over Juliette before he reached for a white cup stamped with the café's logo—a coffee bean with a sunburst behind it. "Double shot latte and a cinnamon bun?"

Amusement tugged at the corner of her lips. She'd gotten progressively more "perky" with him since she'd started coming to his café, at first telling herself it was because of convenience—it *was* next door to work after all—but eventually admitting it was because she enjoyed trying to wind Joel up.

The guy was a certified brick wall, and not *only* because it looked like you could rest a felled tree on his shoulders. He resisted Juliette's attempts to befriend him the way a basset hound resisted getting off a couch. Therefore, it had become a challenge to see if she could get him to laugh or crack a smile. But she'd been coming to Brewed Awakening the whole year the café had been open and hadn't made an ounce of progress. He still moved their interactions along as quickly and efficiently as possible, as if small talk was a bullet to be dodged. None of her attempts to learn more about him had yielded anything except the occasional canned answer, which she was pretty sure was fake.

Who the hell moved all the way across the country to a non-touristy small town in Massachusetts (a place once described by a city visitor as, quote, "butt fuck nowhere") where most people were old enough to be your parents, if not your *grandparents*, simply because you felt like a change of scenery? Juliette called bullshit. He was running from something—she'd bet every dollar in her bank account on it.

"A cinnamon bun sounds wonderful," she said, pouring a little extra honey on her words and leaning against the counter to see how he'd react.

Joel eyed her warily, like she might bite him. Ha! Not likely. Juliette's twin sister had once said she had "golden retriever energy" and though her tone had implied it was definitely *not* a compliment, Juliette certainly took it as one. Goldies were among her favorite dogs—gentle, loyal, always ready to make a friend. How could anyone consider that an insult?

"Here or to go?" Joel asked, reaching for a pair of silver tongs and avoiding eye contact as usual.

She really *should* get it to go—there was paperwork to be done and she could eat while she worked. But without Bonnie to share the load, she was run off her feet and went home exhausted each night. Five minutes to sit with a coffee and a sweet treat sounded like bliss.

"I'll have it here," she replied with a decisive nod. "You know, we have even more in common now than we did before."

Joel put the cinnamon bun on a plate and slid it across the serving counter toward her, one eyebrow arched. "What exactly did we have in common before?"

"Well, we're both small-town folks who love dogs." Juliette picked up her plate.

Joel frowned. "I don't like dogs."

Juliette wrinkled her nose in confusion. "But you built that whole doggy pet garden for them."

She pointed toward a small outdoor space beside the café, which was securely fenced in. It was little more than a courtyard where the previous owner had kept a few rickety chairs and tables on gravel. But Joel had turned the place into a pet oasis with lush grass, water bowls, hooks for leashes and two nicely painted picnic tables. A window allowed customers to order their coffee while staying outside with their pet, and a jar of healthy dog treats sat on the counter that was *always* full. The pet garden was extremely popular—on the weekends it was packed with two- and four-legged customers.

How could someone who'd put in so much effort claim not to like dogs?

"It's good business." Joel gave a dismissive shrug, like it was the most obvious answer in the world.

"You built them a literal white picket fence," Juliette pointed out. He'd built it himself, too. With his own two hands!

"To avoid getting sued if someone's dog runs into the road while they're eating," he countered.

She wasn't buying that—the fence was too nice. Too much care had gone into it for it to be called a legal ass-covering activity.

"What about the dog treats?" She gestured to the glass jar, where a cute handwritten tag hung from the neck, a hand-drawn pawprint decorating the corner.

He looked at her like she was slow on the uptake. "It makes the customers happy, so they keep coming back."

All this time the sweet gesture she'd thought was an indication of Joel being a good human was just . . . Capitalism? The espresso machine hissed as he adjusted the steaming wand before dipping it into a jug of milk. His strong hands cradled the silver jug, using his palms to gauge the temperature of the milk, rather than a thermometer. Usually watching him make coffee would have her feeling all fluttery inside, but today she was too baffled to be attracted to him.

"But *nobody* hates dogs," she scoffed, refusing to accept his stance. "They're the purest beings on earth. They're happy and they love unconditionally and . . . well, they make the world a better place."

Joel wrinkled his nose. "They smell."

Juliette's mouth opened and closed like a goldfish. She was actually stunned—who in their right mind didn't like dogs? Even single-brain-cell-Brad was lovable in his own special way. Moreover, how had she gotten Joel so wrong? He was grumpy, sure. But she'd always sensed a good-heartedness in him. Could she be wrong about that, too?

"I mean, men smell . . . but some of us still date you instead of spending the evening with a good book."

The words slipped out before she could think about what they revealed. Like that her love life *absolutely* consisted of dates with fictional men rather than real ones.

*To be fair, fictional men are tough to beat.*

Much to her surprise, the comment wrenched a quiet chuckle from his lips. The sound was warm and comforting and delicious, like a slice of spiced apple pie. It didn't sound like the chuckle of a dog hater.

Flushing, Juliette clutched the plate containing her cinnamon bun closer to her chest. "Actually, the reason I mentioned us having something in common was because we're both running businesses now. My boss has gone on vacation and she's left me in charge of What The Fluff. I guess that's not entirely the same as *owning* a business, but I take it seriously when someone asks for my help and I want to do a good job. I *will* do a good job."

Ah, a classic case of word vomit. It was Juliette's go-to move when she got nervous which, admittedly, was better than *actual* vomit, but still—

*You're doing it in your brain now, too.*

Joel's eyes crinkled slightly in amusement, but he didn't say anything. The silence made her words feel even more ridiculous.

"I'm going to sit there, okay?" She pointed to one of the empty tables, desperate to extract herself from the awkward exchange. That was enough failed friend-making today. Sometimes a girl had to know when to quit.

"I'll have April bring your coffee out." His eyes were already back on the espresso machine.

Usually him avoiding eye contact carried a distinct air of "I wish you'd go away." This time, however, it felt more like he was trying to hold his laughter in. Typical. Being the butt of someone's joke wasn't new territory, especially when it came to men. Just call her Juliette "Too Much" Macintyre. Too talkative, too eager, too darn earnest. Not to mention she tried too hard to get people to like her. If only she could stop caring what they thought.

But that was like wishing the sky was green or a cat was a dog.

Only a miracle would change her people-pleasing ways. But until she finally separated herself from her family's dirty reputation, she was compelled to keep trying to win everyone over. All she wanted was for people to see her for *her*.

**"GIRL'S GOT IT *BAD*!"** April came up beside Joel to grab Juliette's drink and her elbow dug into his ribs. "Even Serenity noticed it when she came in yesterday. What did she say? Oh yeah, Juliette is *thirsty* for you."

Joel flashed her a scowl. Not that it worked to get April to mind his personal space—the woman wouldn't know boundaries if they slapped her in the face with a wet towel. It was lucky she was the hardest worker Joel had ever met, or else he'd fire her to be rid of the constant chatter. What was it with small-town folks talking all the damn time? It was *incessant*.

What he would give for a solid twenty-four hours where everyone was mute.

"She talks a lot," Joel muttered, hoping April might get the hint. She didn't.

"You either do the talking, or people talk *about* you." She shrugged. Her short purple hair flopped over one eye and she raked it back with her fingers. "That's how it goes around here."

April didn't exactly fit the small-town stereotype with her funky hair that changed hue on a weekly basis, glinting nose ring and her plentiful tattoo collection. The only thing about her that fit right in with the rest of Labrador Falls was that she owned a dog—a little brown spaniel named Bagel whom she often walked through the town square on her way to the dog park. But other than that? Well, it wasn't hard to imagine she'd been the target of judgment over the years.

Lord knew what people said about him behind *his* back.

Joel was an anomaly in Labrador Falls. The people who lived here were either born here or came from close by. At most, they'd come from Boston, looking for a slower pace of life or more affordable living. He wasn't aware of anyone who'd moved here from the other side of the country, like he had. That made people . . . nosy. They always asked why, and Joel always gave the same answer—change of scenery, looking for the right opportunity, enjoying the variability of a full four seasons over the dogged California heat.

He could see in their faces that they didn't buy it, but that was the only answer they were going to get.

"Juliette knows it, too," April added, her nose wrinkling. "Their family name was mud for a long time. Still is."

What kind of mud could possibly stick to someone as upbeat and smiley as Juliette? Surely she was the popular girl at school, someone with loads of friends and a slew of horny teenage boys lining up to take her to prom. Whatever happened, it must have been something bad.

*If you don't want people sticking their noses into your business, then don't do the same to anyone else.*

He tapped the milk frothing jug gently against the counter to get the bubbles out before he started pouring, cradling the cup in one hand and working the jug back and forth to create an intricate design on the top of her latte. He always tried to do something different—some days it was palm leaves, other days it was stemmed flowers. If he was feeling fancy, he might bust out a swan or a seahorse. It was a rare creative outlet for him and he was always perfecting his technique. Today he was distracted, though, and the leaf design came out looking a bit blobby. He frowned.

"I probably wouldn't ask her about it, though. I imagine it's a sore point." April was still there. Still talking. "But you should ask her out. Like, on a date. I'd bet she'd say yes."

Joel grunted and placed the coffee cup on a saucer, sliding it carefully toward April. "Remember that part in your employment contract where it said absolutely under no circumstance were you to give your boss dating advice?"

"Oh come on. Don't tell me you've taken a vow of celibacy or something." April grinned and picked up the cup. "People will be devastated."

Unfortunately, single men under thirty-five were an endangered species around here. But Joel wasn't interested in changing his relationship status. The single life was the life for him. Commitment and happily ever afters? Leave it to Hallmark. Far as he was concerned, romance was a marketing ploy used to sell people shit they didn't need. Maybe it was time to invest in a fake wedding ring and a story about a wife who lived in Canada, working with penguins or polar bears or something. Maybe then people would leave him alone.

"Coffee's getting cold," he grumbled, rinsing out the milk frothing jug. "And I'm paying you to work, not manage my love life."

"Sure thing, boss." April nudged the swing door with her hip and headed out into the café.

He watched as she delivered the latte to Juliette's table and the two women chatted amicably. Labrador Falls was a true small-town cliché like that—everybody knew everybody from school or work or some social club he had no interest in joining. They did those small-town things like drop casseroles at each other's houses and shovel the snow from each other's driveways and smile for no good reason. Joel preferred to do things by himself.

And smiling only encouraged people to ask questions, so he kept that to a minimum, too.

Juliette laughed at something April said, and the sound carried clean across the café, like tinkling bells. She was a real Disney princess type, that one. In looks, with her big brown eyes, flawless fair skin and long, silky dark brown hair, and in her demeanor, too. She was always friendly, doing kind things and trying to charm everyone. He wondered if she had woodland creatures doing her housework or a couple of dwarves living with her.

*Want to audition for the part of Grumpy? You'd be a perfect fit.*

Cute as she might be—and *boy* was she cute—Joel knew better than to look twice at any woman, let alone one like Juliette. She had marriage and babies and fifty-year anniversary written all over her, even if April *did* hint at something mysterious in her past.

*Stop thinking about that. It's none of your damn business.*

The last thing he needed was romantic trouble—he'd had enough of that to last a lifetime. An image of the letter waiting in his office flashed through his mind. The Los Angeles return address, the fancy schmancy business insignia printed on the envelope, the impersonal nature of it all. The seal remained closed, despite the fact that it had arrived two days ago. It was only a matter of time before a phone call followed.

God, he hated phone calls.

And he was going to avoid this one as long as he possibly could.

# *Chapter Two*

**"YOU SAID *WHAT?*"** Juliette's twin sister, Norah, let out a deep, raspy laugh that sounded as though it went all the way down to her belly.

*I mean, men smell . . . but some of us still date you instead of spending the evening with a good book.*

"Don't make me repeat it," Juliette groaned. She was *still* red in the face.

The two women were sitting in the front of Juliette's sunflower yellow Toyota Yaris, which looked like a supersized toddler's toy, and were currently on their way to the dog park. This wasn't common, since neither of them actually owned a dog. But Juliette occasionally fostered animals from the local shelter when they got too full or when they had a dog who wasn't coping in the shelter environment. Today was the latter.

Norah, on the other hand, was reluctantly house-and-dog-sitting for Juliette's boss, Bonnie, while she was away on her cruise. The reluctant part was more related to the dog than the house. But given Bonnie was like a surrogate grandmother to both women, Norah—who usually tossed the word *no* around like confetti—could never seem to say it to Bonnie.

"Besides, who doesn't like dogs?" Juliette said, feeling defensive. This wasn't exactly a hot take. "If that's not the biggest red flag I've ever seen, then I don't know what is."

"You don't know his history," Norah countered. She sat in the passenger seat, feet up on the dashboard no matter how many times Juliette had asked her not to. Like usual, she was dressed in head-to-toe black. "Maybe he got bitten when he was a kid."

"I guess."

"Or maybe his next-door neighbor had a dog that used to bark and keep him up at night," Norah added as Juliette pulled to a stop at a red light. "Or maybe he befriended a sweet old lady without knowing one day she would go on vacation and ask the unsuspecting victim to look after her dog who, despite looking cute and cuddly, is actually a devil spawn. Or is that just me?"

The twins turned to look at the small pile of white fluff dotted with beady black eyes who was currently huddled into a doggy car seat behind them. The dog glared at Norah and Norah glared back.

Marshmallow the Pomeranian—aforementioned devil spawn—wasn't the only occupant of the back seat. Juliette had also picked up her newest foster pup, Digger, and the Jack Russell currently had both front paws slapped against the window while he vibrated with excitement, tail a furious blur as the view rolled past outside. He was the cutest little thing—small but sturdy terrier body covered in a rough coat of white fur, with rich tan ear and eye patches along with one over his right shoulder and another at the base of his tail. He had a sweet face, adorable ears that flopped over into cute triangles and an excitable, affectionate demeanor that immediately endeared him to her.

On the other side of the back seat, Marshmallow looked on warily, eyes narrowed. Apparently, she did not find him so endearing.

"I take it last night didn't go well," Juliette said, cringing behind her sister's back and then returning her gaze to the front just in time for the light to go green. To say Marshmallow and Norah were not getting along was putting it lightly. Like, a piece of one-ply toilet paper lightly.

"She bit me while I was sleeping," Norah said, indignant. Her dark hair was piled into a messy bun on top of her head and bruise-colored smudges circled both her eyes. She was wearing a sweatshirt that said Bite Me, with two vampire fangs underneath. The irony. "While I was absolutely defenseless and causing her no harm at all, mind you. That's pure evil."

"Okay well, dogs aren't *evil*." Juliette glanced at Marshmallow in the rearview mirror and would swear the little white dog was quietly plotting their demise. She reminded her of Brain in that cartoon, *Pinky and the Brain*. "But this one . . . comes close."

Norah folded her arms across her chest and shot her sister a judgmental look. "I still can't believe you agreed to foster a dog after rejecting my pleas for help!"

Norah had been desperately trying to convince Juliette to take over the Marshmallow dog-sitting duties ever since Bonnie mentioned it. But Juliette had steadfastly refused, saying that if Bonnie had wanted *her* to do it then she would have asked. Not that she wasn't relieved as hell. Marshmallow was . . . Well, let's just say that Juliette hadn't secretly nicknamed her Satan's Cotton Ball for nothing.

"I'm sleeping with one eye open from now on," Norah added.

"She probably misses her mom," Juliette offered, her gaze drifting to the rearview mirror to make sure Marshmallow didn't try to ninja attack Digger in the back seat. Marshmallow looked up and caught her gaze, eyes narrowed as if to say, *the second you turn your back, I'll strike. Stay vigilant, Bitch.*

"What if we swapped dogs? I could take Digger and you could take Marshmallow," Norah said, as if having a stroke of genius.

"Nice try, but I'm only fostering Digger. Hopefully he'll be off to his forever home in a flash."

"Why did his previous owners give him up? He seems so sweet."

"Apparently because he dug up one of their prizewinning petunia bushes." They'd called him Digger and then tossed him aside when he dug something up? The nerve! "The people were from out of town. Probably because they were too ashamed to dump him at a shelter where someone might recognize them."

What lies had they told their family and friends?

*Oh he's gone to live with my sister. She just* adores *dogs.*

*The breeder who sold him begged to have him back so he could be with his brothers and sisters. How could we possibly say no?*

*We're devastated that he ran away.*

It was reprehensible how some people treated animals like a five-dollar T-shirt from some fast fashion company, produced to be worn once and then thrown into a Goodwill bin. Like their lives didn't mean anything. Like they didn't have feelings and emotions and wouldn't wear the scars of such abandonment for the rest of their lives.

*Projecting, much?*

"That really sucks," Norah said, her shoulders slumped. "Poor little guy."

"If you can have that kind of empathy for Marshmallow, then things will work out fine," Juliette pointed out.

Norah sighed. "I don't even know *why* I let you convince me to come here. The dog park contains three of her most hated things: dogs, parks and humans."

"Might be quicker to list what she *doesn't* hate," Juliette quipped and Norah shot her a dirty look. "Seriously though,

Bonnie brings her here occasionally. Maybe she'll tire herself out so much that she sleeps through the night without trying to kill you."

"One can only hope. Otherwise, it's been nice knowing you."

Juliette chuckled as she pulled the car into an empty spot outside the dog park and went to fetch Digger from the back. As soon as she opened the door he tried to leap out of the car, forgetting he was still attached by a safety strap and making a cute little noise of frustration like he was saying, *what's the holdup, lady? Can't you see there's a park right here? It's playtime! Let's. Freaking. Go.*

"No need to rush, little guy." She unhooked him and clipped his lead into the harness she'd taken to the shelter for his pickup, all prepared for foster dog mom duties.

Her apartment was well stocked for such occasions—harnesses and collars in several sizes, water and food bowls, toys, blankets, as well as a supply of dog food at the ready. No way would she turn down a foster placement because she wasn't prepared! Norah thought it was weird to own all that stuff when Juliette never talked about adopting any of her foster dogs. But adoption was very permanent. It was a big decision.

One people took too lightly in many cases if the full shelters were anything to go on.

Once they were safely inside the small dog area of the park, Juliette released Digger and he took off like a bullet. Maybe that would have been a better name for him. Bullet. She laughed as he raced toward two other dogs, running frantic rings around them before charging off to the far corner of the fenced-in area, his small legs a blur beneath him.

Marshmallow, on the other hand, stayed exactly where she was as Norah unclipped her.

"Go on, it's playtime." She made a shooing motion with her hands, but the dog simply sniffed at her.

*Don't shoo me, peasant. I do what I want.*

"I can't even with this dog." Norah shook her head.

Juliette stifled a smile, because the dog was *so* much like Norah it was almost comical. They were both feisty, stubborn and *hated* being told what to do. No wonder sparks were flying.

But then, miracle of miracles, Marshmallow trotted off, waiting long enough that the twins knew she was doing it of her own accord. Norah rolled her eyes.

"Hey, have you heard from Bonnie today?" Juliette asked. "She promised to text once she made it on the cruise ship. I messaged her on my lunch break, but I haven't heard back."

"I bet she's busy having the time of her life. She made a joke about finding herself a boyfriend, so perhaps she's working on that."

Juliette snorted. "Bonnie's *always* on the hunt for a new boyfriend."

It was a running joke, though neither of the twins had ever seen her with a man. Bonnie was in her seventies, and she'd never married nor had kids. What was unusual, however, was that she didn't seem to have *any* family at all. No brothers or sisters, no cousins. No stories of an ex. It was one reason they liked to check in on her regularly. Nobody else was doing it.

"I hope everything is okay," Juliette said, watching Digger race around.

"Everything is fine," Norah assured her. "She'll be back in three weeks with an epic tan and a million funny stories. What you should really be worried about is if *I* make it that long. Twenty-one days is a lot of time for Marshmallow to hatch a murder plot and hide the body."

"You're *so* dramatic."

"Wait and see," Norah said. "Mark my words, there will be an attempt on my life. If I suddenly stop answering my phone, just know the dog did it."

**HALF AN HOUR LATER,** Digger was panting and spent, but happy. Juliette hadn't even needed to throw a ball for him, since he'd only wanted to run and run and run. After being stuck in the shelter, it probably felt like heaven to be in the open air. Her heart squeezed as Digger came trotting over, tongue hanging out of his mouth and eyes a little droopy.

"Good workout, huh?" Juliette crouched and he came willingly, nosing her palm as if looking for a treat. "Did your previous owners reward you like that? I have some treats at home."

At the *T*-word, his ears perked up.

"Well, you can have one when we get back if you're a good boy." She ruffled the fur on his head and then clipped the leash onto his harness. "Which I suspect you will be."

Two warm brown eyes stared up at her and she could practically see the golden angel's halo floating above his head. *I'm always a good boy. Cross my heart.*

Who in their right mind would give up such a sweet little bean? Hopefully the shelter could find him a nice forever home. He deserved that much.

On the way out of the dog park, Juliette and Norah bumped into Corinne, a longtime client of What The Fluff and a good friend of Bonnie. Her stunning Afghan hound, Brigitte, walked daintily by her side. The animal was a Victoria's Secret model in dog form. Tall, especially next to her petite owner, with long, gleaming champagne-colored fur and a slender, regal face. Juliette had groomed Brigitte for the last three years, taking over from Bonnie when the dog's maintenance got too much for her arthritic hands.

"Juliette! Fancy seeing you here." Corinne smiled. "And Norah, I haven't seen you in ages."

Corinne, as usual, was dressed as if she was hoping to score at an over fifties' nightclub in a leopard-print sequin top with a pair of shiny leather pants that were so tight Juliette was concerned for her internal organs. Her hair was styled short and spiky, dyed the exact same shade as a red Crayola.

"How's Brigitte doing?" Juliette asked, leaning down. The dog swished her fabulous tail, perfectly patient as Digger had a curious sniff around her. Marshmallow, meanwhile, kept her distance, looking up at Brigitte as if the bigger dog were a particularly impressive statue.

"Oh, you know my baby, she's always an angel." Corinne stroked the dog's head affectionately. Brigitte, unlike Marshmallow, was only a challenging groom because she had a lot of fur. But temperament wise? The dog was a delight—friendly, calm, took instructions well. No wonder she'd been a prizewinning show dog in her younger years. "Aren't you, sweetheart? Such a well-behaved girl."

"See," Norah said to Marshmallow. "You could learn a thing or two."

Marshmallow glared up at Norah. *Bite me.*

"Hey, Corinne, I don't suppose you've heard from Bonnie today?" Juliette asked.

"No, I've been so busy with work lately that I haven't spoken to her for a little bit. Hasn't she gone away on that cruise—"

At that moment, a man stalked over to the group, his face beet red, forehead shiny with exertion. He was tall, slim and had a shock of thick, dark hair with a widow's peak and a distinctive white streak through the front that gave off strong Dracula vibes. It was a weird contrast to his outfit, which could have been worn on the cover of Rich Yacht Dudes Monthly. He was Corinne's soon-to-be-ex-husband, Maurice Allsop. Most people around town knew of Maurice—because . . . well, he was loud and obnoxious. So, it was hard to ignore him.

"Where have you *been*?" he demanded, cutting Corinne off mid-sentence. Digger skittered behind Juliette's legs, ears flattened out to the sides. "You were supposed to drop Brigitte off at my place at 6 p.m. sharp."

"I thought I would bring her to the park first." Corinne straightened her spine, though the embarrassment radiating off her diminished any attempt to appear confident. "The 6 p.m. drop-off is a guideline, not an ironclad rule."

Nobody was surprised when gossip streaked around town that Maurice and Corinne had separated. Juliette tried to see the best in people, but why *anyone* would marry Maurice was beyond her realm of comprehension. He was always blustering and talking down to people. Especially women. Yet he'd managed to convince *three* to walk down the aisle with him.

None of it stuck, however, and now poor Brigitte was the baloney in a custody battle sandwich.

Maurice held up his phone with the time showing. "It's 6:15 and you've only just arrived. How much longer were you planning to eat into *my* time?"

"How do you know I've only *just* arrived? Have you been following me?" Corinne glared at her soon-to-be-ex-husband as she pulled Brigitte closer. The dog immediately lowered her snout and eyes to the ground, and Juliette's stomach flipped. "Are you *stalking* me?"

"Don't be ridiculous, Corinne." Maurice rolled his eyes, though a vein pulsed in his neck. "Why would anyone bother to stalk you?"

Corinne bristled, her cheeks doing their best job of matching her Crayola red hair. "Well, *you* were late bringing Brigitte over to my place last time. I'm simply reclaiming the time *you* stole from *me*." If only the ground would open up and swallow them whole. Public arguments were the worst. So embarrassing.

"This is why I left you, Corinne. You're petulant." Maurice took a step forward, reaching his hand out as if planning to snatch the leash from her. "And I'm concerned that you're not giving my precious baby the care she needs."

"Brigitte is *our* dog, Maurice." The red spikes of her hair seemed to quiver with anger. "And I take very good care of her. You know that."

"Not as good as I do." He reached for the leash and Corinne backed up, but he was faster. He grabbed hold of the corded strap and pulled, causing Brigitte to yelp as she was yanked forward.

"That's enough!" Juliette stepped forward. It was one thing for two adults to argue, but the second it got physical and risked hurting someone, *especially* an animal, she couldn't sit idly by. "Don't yank her like that."

"You of all people should know when to mind your own business." Disdain coated his words. Maurice made no effort to hide that he thought she was trash. That her whole family was trash. "So don't tell me what to do with my own dog."

Just as Juliette felt Norah's body coil up, she grabbed her sister's hand and squeezed. The last thing they needed was Norah throwing a punch and ending up in the back of a police car, because that would only further cement their reputation as bad eggs. And Maurice was right; she *did* try to mind her own business.

But she wasn't a doormat, either. Her father might not have been perfect, but he taught her that much.

"Let go of that leash before you hurt someone," Juliette said, her voice calm but firm.

"Stay the fuck out of it." The vein on his neck pulsed harder and his knuckles turned white where he gripped the leash. His eyes seemed a little wild and something acrid wafted from his breath. Whisky? Something stronger? Juliette recoiled.

Maurice tugged on the leash again, harder this time, and Corinne relented, releasing Brigitte, who skittered over to him, frightened and whimpering.

Oh he did *not*! Juliette's desire for people to like her momentarily vanished.

"I should report you for animal abuse," she said sharply. Having groomed her share of rescue pets, she'd seen the aftereffects of abusive behavior more times than she'd ever wanted to, which, frankly, was zero.

Beside her, Norah stiffened and the air suddenly became charged. Labrador Falls's police chief was heading straight toward them, exiting from the big dog park. His Belgian Malinois, Hook, was at his side, eyes alert, dark ears pricked as if assessing the situation. The dog always seemed prepared to jump into action, as if there were a spring coiled tightly inside him, and the chief was much the same—always on duty, even when he wasn't.

She glanced at Norah, whose lips had turned up into a sneer. *Don't you dare*, Juliette mouthed. But Norah's eyes were steadily burning a hole into the Chief's head as though she wanted to pop it like a grape with telekinetic powers.

"What's going on here?" Chief Dooley asked. His thick, silver hair—the years having zapped its original coppery red—was neatly styled, as were his civilian clothes. That was the chief in a nutshell. Not even the hair on his head nor the cotton of his shirt would defy his orders to stay tidy at all times. "Who's being accused of animal abuse?"

"This woman is threatening me," Maurice said, jabbing an accusatory finger at her and barely missing her nose. "She's inserting herself into my personal family business and then she threatened to report me for animal abuse for no good reason."

"I have *very* good reason," Juliette argued, turning to Corinne for support. Women had to stick together against men like Maurice, right? But Corinne looked mortified and her spiky hair seemed to wilt under the chief's gaze. "He was manhandling poor Brigitte. He hurt her!"

"I did nothing of the sort."

"Corinne?" the chief asked, his voice firm. "What happened?"

"I was late bringing Brigitte to Maurice's house," she replied, squaring her shoulders and attempting a smile, which turned into more of a grimace. Beyond where they stood, several people were huddled together and looking over without any attempt to disguise their gawking. Typical. If this went on too much longer someone would open a popcorn stand. "It's no big deal."

Fantastic. Now the chief would *definitely* think Juliette was butting in without reason. So much for sticking together.

"Didn't seem like that a second ago when he was degrading you in front of everyone. Too bad being a dick isn't a crime around here," Norah piped up, and Juliette frowned, wishing her sister got the message to stay quiet. They didn't need to *both* be in trouble.

"We're done here," Maurice said, turning on his ugly brown boat shoes as if he knew no one would have the nerve to stop him. "Don't be late again, Corinne."

He stalked away from the dog park, leaving his ex-wife standing there, her hands wringing in front of her while she studiously avoided Norah's disbelieving stare. Since Brigitte was so well-trained, she followed her owner without hesitation, which didn't support Juliette's assertion that Maurice was hurting the dog. At her feet, Digger stretched forward to have a curious sniff at Hook, but Juliette gently eased him back, feeling the suspicious eyes of the police chief on them.

A feeling with which she was *far* too familiar.

"There's a lesson in this. You shouldn't insert yourself into other people's personal situations," Chief Dooley said, nose wrinkled as if there were a stench coming off her. "Both of you, more than anyone, know how that can lead to dire consequences."

Despite the bonfire of shame heating her face, Juliette leveled a stare at the chief and tugged on her sister's hand. "Come on, Norah. Let's get the dogs home."

The chief's eyes burned a hole in her back as they walked away. Jerk. No matter what they did, she and Norah were tarred with the sticky brush of badness. They were criminals, even before they'd committed a crime. Bad influences, even before they'd taken a breath. It was almost like a foregone conclusion that they would screw up, and the chief watched closely, waiting for one wrong move. One slipup. One toenail out of line. But as far as Juliette was concerned, the chief would die waiting.

She would *never* give him the satisfaction of doing something wrong. And one day people would know her for *her.* Not for the bad stuff Dad did, not for the fallout that crushed them and not for the rumors which grew legs of their own and walked all over town.

No matter what it took, she would prove them all wrong.

# *Chapter Three*

**THE FOLLOWING MORNING** Juliette awoke with hair stuck to her face, a drool patch on her pillow and the general feeling of being hit by a FedEx truck. It was a good thing her eyeballs were still attached to their sockets, because it seriously felt like they were at risk of dropping out of her head and rolling through the Labrador Falls town square.

"You're lucky you're adorable." She yawned as she clipped a pink-and-blue leash bearing the What The Fluff logo onto Digger's harness, the ring of which was poking through a bright yellow raincoat. It was slightly too big for him, but it was all she had. "Did you really need to play tug-of-war at three in the morning?"

Digger stared up at her, head cocked. *Well yeah. When* else *do you play tug of war?*

After putting him to sleep in a cozy basket in her bedroom, he'd drifted off like a little angel. Ha! That was nothing but a false sense of security. He'd woken her up at midnight, barely an hour later, crying by the side of her bed. Then he was up again at 3 a.m. with a chunk of her duvet in his mouth, growling and yanking on it like he was trying to drag her from a burning building. *Then*, after she cajoled him back to sleep, he awoke at 4:30 a.m., pawing through her laundry basket like he was trying to dig to Australia.

Now it was 6:30 a.m. and sleep was in her rearview mirror. Thankfully Norah was staying at Bonnie's place because that girl was *murderous* if she didn't get a solid night.

If there was any hope of keeping Digger calm through the workday, he needed a chance to get that Jack Russell energy out before What The Fluff opened.

"Come on. Let's see if we can wear that battery down a bit."

Fall was a Jekyll and Hyde season around here. The good days were crisp and sunny and tinted with the glorious burnished shades that made her heart sing. The bad days . . . well, they were soggier than a bowl of Frosted Flakes that had sat too long in milk. Today was, unfortunately, the latter. Silver-and-dark-gray clouds patterned the sky, and raindrops splattered against her hood as they exited her apartment. But Digger forged ahead, unperturbed by the weather. His tail was in the air, feet trotting in a happy staccato as if simply being outside was all he needed in life. He stopped every so often to sniff at a plant or to chase the scent of an animal, and she had to pull him away from a tree when he caught sight of a squirrel and went into full terrier mode.

"What have you got against squirrels, huh?" she asked as they walked into the town square. Digger looked over his shoulder as if to say, *Have you seen those things? Their tails totally look like toys! They're practically designed for me to chase them. It's hardly my fault.*

She couldn't really argue.

Juliette checked her phone to see if any texts had come in overnight. There was one from Norah with a funny photo of Marshmallow staring at her from across the room and another from her close friend Alexa that had arrived at 2 a.m. Alexa was the reason Juliette had her Do Not Disturb set every single night, because her friend was a scatterbrained night owl prone to blowing up WhatsApp at the most ungodly hours.

But still nothing from Bonnie. A hard little lump lodged itself in her chest.

*You're being paranoid. Bonnie is busy feasting on margaritas and shrimp cocktails.*

Then why did it feel like something was about to go horribly wrong?

The dog park was on the other side of the town square, and it was quicker to cut through the middle than go around. Most of the shops were dark at this early hour, except for the bakery, which was already bustling with staff though it wasn't yet open. The scent of fresh bread mingled with the petrichor of rain, perhaps two of her most favorite smells in the whole wide world. Digger seemed to like the smell, too, because he tugged in that direction.

"We can't go there, buddy. It's not open yet." She directed him across the square, noticing that there *was* one other shop with the lights on—Brewed Awakening.

With everything else still dark, the light inside the café shone brightly, making it look like a diorama. A sneak peek into a private moment. Joel sat at a table with one hand scrubbing over his face and a piece of paper in the other. It looked like a letter. Surely it couldn't be financial troubles. Finding a table at Brewed Awakening on the weekend was like panning for gold. And that was saying a lot, since loads of customers got their coffee to go. In fact, April had mentioned recently they were thinking about hiring another staff member to help out.

So what else would have Joel scrubbing like he was trying to erase something bad right out of his brain?

Intriguing as it was, she resisted the urge to knock on his door. One, Joel wouldn't tell her anything. That guy was harder to crack than a macadamia nut. And two, it looked like the light mist of rain would soon turn into something heavier. Which meant she had to get one Energizer Bunny to the dog park, stat.

Just as she was about to guide Digger away, Joel looked up and his eyes caught hers through the glass door. There was something sad about his expression. Something far more vulnerable than she'd *ever* seen in any of the times she'd walked into his café, where he wore a brusque mask of efficiency and focus. This was a Joel she'd never encountered before. Tentatively, she raised one hand in a wave, but he'd already risen from his chair and disappeared further into the café, letter in hand.

What was *that* all about?

But there was no time to speculate, so Juliette forged on, stepping carefully on the slick cobblestones. Light crept over the horizon, the purple of dawn bleeding into inky night wherever the clouds weren't blotting out the sky. As they approached the dog park, an eerie feeling manifested, like a cold hand curving over her shoulder. Whereas the town square was lit by ornate iron streetlamps and the glow from the bakery and café, the path leading away from the square felt darker and more isolated. Only one lamp at the corner of the parking lot created a pool of sickly, yellow light, flickering intermittently, and beyond it the shadows stretched and warped.

The feeling of being watched skittered over her skin. She glanced around, fingers gripping Digger's leash as her eyes combed through the darkness, but she and Digger were alone.

The parking lot was empty, except for a single car—a shiny black Mercedes sedan with fancy chrome wheels. Labrador Falls was SUV country. Practical cars and trucks ruled the day, since folks cared more about getting their dog into the back seat and off for an adventure than worrying about getting scratches on expensive leather.

Digger trotted happily ahead, unaware of the discontent humming in the air like electricity before a storm. Labrador Falls was a safe town, of course. But bad things could still happen in good places. To good people. Juliette quickened her steps. Best to get Digger into the park and then back out as quickly as possible.

They approached the fencing that divided the small dog and big dog areas. Both sides were empty. Who would leave their car here if they weren't using the dog park?

Digger danced around her feet and whined, eager to be freed from his harness. Rain continued to patter against Juliette's hood but there was also another sound. Shuffling. Or dead leaves crunching. The feeling of being watched intensified and Juliette whipped around, her heart a pounding fist.

"Is someone there?" she called out, clutching Digger's leash tightly.

A shadow moved and she froze on the spot, her eyes searching through the hazy darkness, trying to turn fuzzy shapes into sharp ones. Was that a person crouched down? Shit. There was no one around. If she screamed for help . . .

Her breath hitched and then released. It was just a trash can with the lid askew, the shape seeming like a crouched body. Something darted out from behind it and raced away, making a chittering noise as a distinctive striped tail disappeared into the darkness. Digger yanked forward, barking at the fleeing creature. A raccoon, nothing more. A nervous laugh bubbled up out of her throat and she shook her head.

"That's what I get for watching those awful horror movies with Norah." She put her hand on the gate, ready to press it open. "I don't understand why she likes that stuff. Blood and guts and jump scares? No thanks. Give me a Hallmark 'happily ever after' any day."

But before she opened the gate, something caught her attention. Through the gaps in the black wire fencing she could see a dark lump on the ground in the big dog area. It looked like a bundle of clothing. Or was it trash? Juliette took a step forward and squinted. It almost looked like . . .

"Oh my God." She rushed forward, startling Digger, and charged through the gate into the big dog area, his little legs speeding up to keep pace.

It wasn't a bundle of clothing. It was a person!

"Shit. Shit. Shit." Juliette hurried over, her free hand reaching for her cell phone in case she needed to dial 911. Had some poor person collapsed all on their own with no one to help them? But where was their dog? "Hello? Are you hurt?"

No response. The rain came harder, streaming down Juliette's hood and soaking the strands of hair the wind had pulled free, lashing them against her face. Overhead, thunder cracked, causing Digger to yelp and surge forward, bringing Juliette with him. Her sneakers skidded on the wet ground and she lost her grip on the phone, the device bouncing away from her and disappearing into the grass. She crouched, searching for it, all the while trying to keep hold of the panicking Digger and frantically thinking about how to help this poor person.

They still weren't responding.

When her hand grasped the hard case of her phone, she finally looked at the crumpled body again. There was a good reason they hadn't responded. Their eyes were open but unblinking, lips parted and blue as a bruise, a distinctive widow's peak carving a sharp vee into an unnervingly pale forehead.

It was Maurice Allsop.

He had a dog leash wrapped firmly around his neck and he was, without a doubt, dead.

And if that wasn't bad enough, the leash wrapped around

his neck matched the one Juliette gripped tightly in her hand—pink and blue with the distinctive logo of What The Fluff dotted all over it.

**JOEL WAS AN** early bird.

Not because he thought about getting the worm—those days were behind him and hustle culture was bullshit, anyway—but because he'd spent so many years on call that mornings always came as a relief. Better to be fully awake, instead of only partially asleep.

Plenty of other businesses around Labrador Falls didn't open until later, and the peaceful stillness before the rest of the town awoke was golden. The quiet was a comforting blanket over his world. How could anyone *not* love early mornings? The light was soft and buttery, the trees whispered and dead leaves brushed over the cobblestones as a breeze carried them to their next destination.

Most of all, it was the lack of talking. Ahh, what bliss.

But today his peaceful morning routine was ruined by a couple of things—starting with the letter. It had been staring at him whenever he walked into the café's back office, sitting there on his desk like a hairy tarantula. Then came the phone call, which he ignored, and the subsequent voicemail with the irritatingly professional tone.

*"Hello, this is a message for Joel Cunningham. My name is Stacy Novak from Novak and Johnson Family Law Attorneys. I'm calling in regard to—"*

He knew exactly why they were calling and exactly what the letter entailed, despite not having opened it. Letters and phone calls he could handle. Hell, one might even say ignoring them was his specialty. But it was the text message that got him. An old name from a new number.

Hi Joel. It's Marissa. I suppose you've got the letter by now. I hope you won't make things difficult. I just want this to be over.

*She* hoped he wouldn't make things difficult. *She* just wanted things to be over.

It was a miracle he hadn't thrown his phone into the exposed brick wall behind the seating area. Maybe he should have moved further away from California than the East Coast. Like Australia. Or better yet, the South Pole. Hell, maybe he should start saving for intergalactic space travel. Had someone figured out how to start a colony on Mars yet?

Marissa. The wife he'd pledged his life to in front of their family and friends. The one he'd nursed back to health after a car accident almost stole her from him. The woman he used to wake up next to with her elbow in his ribs, always wondering how someone so small could take up so much space in a king-size bed and laughing because he wouldn't have it any other way.

He crumpled the letter and tossed it into the trash, shredding the envelope for good measure.

It wasn't a surprise that she wanted a divorce—that day had been coming for some time now. But the revelation that had followed cracked his already scarred heart in two, splitting the pieces apart like tectonic plates.

*I've met someone.*

Was that before, during or after the time he spent looking for her, frantic when he'd found her drawers empty one day? It wasn't only that she'd left him.

She'd thought he was a killer.

Joel cringed as a warning spike of light shot through his eyeball right to the back of his skull, and he pressed the heel of one hand to his eye. Nope. Not now. Not today.

The migraines had started after the fire, along with panic

attacks and insomnia. The Three Stooges of trauma. Since being in Labrador Falls, his symptoms had eased, but experience told him if he didn't get some painkillers in the second he felt an aura coming on, he was toast. Those fuckers knocked him out for a solid twenty-four to forty-eight hours if he didn't act fast.

He retrieved the bottle of painkillers he kept at the café and washed a couple down with his coffee, which had gone stone-cold. There was no point wallowing or feeling sorry for himself. And he would get back to Marissa and her fancy pants lawyers at some point, but it would be on *his* time. On his terms.

After all the pain she'd put him through the last few years, he wasn't exactly eager to say, "how high?" when she asked him to jump.

Joel collected a tray of freshly baked cinnamon rolls, which had been dropped off by the wonderful baker who made them for the café each morning, and he carefully set them into the glass-fronted cabinet. Outside the rain pelted down harder and his mind flashed to Juliette. She was out there with some little white dog, and his heart twinged, hoping they weren't stuck out in the open. But he shook the feeling off—she was a grown-ass woman and she could take care of herself in the rain. And the dog.

But just as Joel was doing his best *not* to think about the way Juliette had looked at him through the glass door earlier—and how it made him feel all kinds of things that were fraught and dangerous—a scratching sound yanked his attention to the present. He stood alone in the café, with over an hour to go until opening, and could hear every creak of the building, every whistle of the wind and . . . yeah, it was definitely a scratching noise.

Squinting, he tried to focus on the sound to see where it was coming from.

To his complete surprise, when he walked over to the shuttered pet garden ordering window, a customer sat outside. Not a paying customer, mind you. The four-legged kind.

He slid the window open and poked his head out. The dog's body was pressed as close to the building as possible to get out of the rain. There was only a small overhang and it wasn't doing much to protect the animal from the elements. But she didn't bark, didn't whine. Didn't make a single sound. In fact, she barely made eye contact with him.

The beautiful creature with her long, champagne-colored fur was instantly recognizable. Her owner, Maurice, was a regular and often brought her to the café, ordering a double espresso and sitting outside while the dog sat obediently by his side. She never twitched a muscle without her owner's command, and Joel had often wondered if anything was going on in the poor dog's head, or if she wasn't even allowed to have doggy thoughts of her own until her owner said so.

"What on earth are you doing here, Brigitte?" he asked, glancing around. There was no sign of Maurice anywhere. Nor of his soon-to-be-ex-wife, Corinne. Hmm, maybe he should ask Maurice about the intricacies of getting divorced. The guy was a pro by now.

Brigitte looked up at him, liquid brown eyes pleading, though she remained still and silent.

It was strange to see a dog wandering around town on their own, but especially strange for it to be *this* dog. Maurice had told him one time that Afghan hounds were one of the most expensive breeds in the world and he had paid a small fortune for her as a puppy, because she had a decorated and prestigious show dog mother. The whole conversation had grossed Joel out a bit.

"Maurice?" he called out of the window, and the dog perked up at her owner's name. But the man himself was nowhere to be found. "Ah, shit."

Joel headed outside, rounding the corner of the café into the fenced-off pet garden. Rain splattered his head and shoulders, running in rivulets down his neck and soaking the thick wool of his chunky, cable-knit sweater. Brigitte was practically glued to the wall.

"Come here, girl." He motioned for her to come forward, but she didn't move. If he stayed out here much longer he'd be soaked through and so would she. Maybe he needed to use the stern-sounding voice he'd heard Maurice use with her. "Brigitte, come!"

The forceful command seemed to work and she trotted forward, though her nose was lowered, either because she hated the rain or thought she'd done something wrong. As she got closer, he hooked a finger into her collar and she allowed herself to be led into the café. Once inside, she sat and looked at him, as if awaiting another command. It almost made him laugh. He wasn't used to a dog like that, so well-trained and well-behaved.

An image flashed into his mind, a wet nose being shoved into his palm, a chocolate tail wagging frantically and sending a coffee cup flying.

He shook his head. "Are you hungry, girl?"

Joel dug his hand into the jar of dog treats. They came from a local pet boutique, Chasing Tail, which coincidentally was run by Corinne. The second the lid came off, he could sense Brigitte's anticipation. Her eyes were locked on his, and there was the barest little swish of her champagne tail against the floor.

Ah, so she *was* a real dog after all. Not just a command robot.

He brought the treat over to her and held it out, but the dog didn't move. If anything, she seemed to still entirely, becoming statue-like and staring *just* to the side of the treat, but not directly at it.

"Shouldn't you be trying to snatch this right out of my hands and chowing it down so fast it'll land mostly unchewed in your stomach?" He wrinkled his nose in confusion. "You're a very strange dog."

Brigitte glanced at him and then whipped her eyes back to their straight-ahead position. Her paw twitched, lifting off the ground for the barest moment before coming back down.

"Shake?" he tried, wondering if she needed to complete some tasks before accepting her treat. The dog glanced down at his hand, as if waiting for something to happen. He held it out and the dog delicately raised her paw and placed it on his palm. "Good girl."

But when he held the treat closer to her, she still wouldn't eat it. Maybe that also required a command.

"Take it," he tried, but Brigitte still didn't move. This time, however, she looked as though she was leaning to the left. "Spin?"

She spun around in a perfect, graceful circle and sat back down.

"Gee, they make you work hard for a single treat, don't they?" he muttered, waiting for another cue from the dog. "High five?"

He held up his hand and Brigitte stretched up and tapped his palm with both her paws.

"Good girl," he praised, and her tail swished. Okay, got it. The girl was praise motivated. What else could she do? "Drop."

He pointed to the floor and she lay down, her eyes trained on his.

"Up." She sat back up. "Speak."

She let out a single clear bark, and it almost surprised Joel to hear such a deep sound come out of her, when she was usually silent.

"Such a good girl." He ruffled the top of her head and held the treat out again. "Take it."

This time she reached forward and gently took the treat from his hand, dropping down and happily munching away.

Now that the dog was safe and had something to keep her busy, the next step was finding out why she was wandering around on her own. Joel grunted his displeasure. Getting involved in other people's lives and problems was *never* a good idea. A, they might feel like they owed him a favor (and everybody with a brain cell to spare knew favors were shackles) or B, they might be inclined to ask for further help. Both were terrible outcomes.

But he wasn't about to let the poor gal sit outside in the rain.

"You stay here a bit. I'm going to see what's up, okay?"

He wasn't concerned about leaving her unattended for a few minutes, because she was likely more trustworthy than most humans. Throwing on his jacket and pulling the hood up over his head, he headed outside to see if he could locate Maurice or Corinne in the town square. It seemed unlikely the dog had simply wandered off on her own, but you never knew.

However, there was almost no one outside. It still wasn't close to opening time for the majority of businesses here, aside from the bakery. The square sat deserted, bathed in glossy wetness and shadowed by the clouds.

His next port of call was What The Fluff—because if anybody knew what to do with a lost dog, it would be Juliette. He jogged over to the obnoxiously pink building and knocked on the front door. Nothing stirred inside. Cupping his hands against the glass, he peered into the darkened interior, but it seemed as though nobody was there. Juliette must have been going somewhere else with the little white dog.

The whooping sound of an emergency vehicle snatched his attention before he made it back inside the café. Down the pathway leading to the dog park, blue-and-red lights flashed and his heart sped up, old memories stirring from within the depths of his brain.

The wail of sirens. The spike of adrenaline. The scorching heat and smell of smoke. Creaking wood. Panic.

Swallowing, he jogged toward the scene. An ambulance sat with the back open while an EMT milled about, talking on a cell phone, though it didn't appear that anyone had been loaded onto the stretcher inside. Two police cars were nearby, and one officer rolled yellow police tape across the gates at the dog park. The rain had momentarily stopped, as if pausing so people could do their jobs.

A murmuring crowd gathered—folks bundled up in scarves and coats, dogs held close or kept beside them. They'd probably been on a walk and seen the lights, like he had. He was about to ask someone if they knew what was going on when he stopped in his tracks, the words sucked right out of his throat.

It was Juliette, and she was being loaded into the back of a police car.

# *Chapter Four*

**JULIETTE FOLLOWED DETECTIVE** Dooley toward the front doors of the Labrador Falls police station, Digger clutched to her chest. The little dog wriggled, squirming this way and that, resisting being confined. But if she didn't hold on tight, she might simply float away. Right now, she needed the feeling of something real, something warm. Something *alive*.

Maurice was dead.

She'd stumbled across a dead body. A corpse.

It was like being shunted into an episode of *CSI* or *NCIS* or *LAPD* or one of those other shows with an acronym for a name. How could this be real? Something acrid rushed up her throat and for a hot second she thought she might vomit all over the detective's back. That would *not* be a good look.

And if this whole thing wasn't bad enough, she had to be *here*. With *him*.

Detective Dooley was none other than Chief Dooley's son. And yes, the family connection had to be the only reason he'd climbed the ranks within local law enforcement, because the guy was as sharp as a bowl of Jell-O. A true nepo baby. In fact, in high school it was common knowledge he used his father's position to threaten teachers who didn't give him a decent grade. He'd been an all-round bully who'd tortured Juliette and

Norah, doing his utmost to make sure everyone hated them as much as he did.

A shame, really, since the Macintyres and the Dooleys had been the best of friends before it all fell apart.

"I don't suppose you remember the way," Detective Dooley said, throwing a smug glance over one shoulder as the glass doors slid open, a gust of warm, stale air blowing out.

She ignored the comment. He might have gotten her mixed up with Norah, because Juliette wouldn't bite at such an obvious piece of bait.

Stepping inside the station was like stepping back in time. Plastic chairs sat in rows in the reception area and a young officer in uniform staffed the front desk, helping an older woman with paperwork. Posters clung to the walls, some of them yellowed and curling at the edges, warning people not to drink and drive, and telling everybody to wear their seat belts. Some of them were *old*, if the mustaches on the police models were anything to go on. The room looked gray and run-down, a hairline crack shimmying up one wall and the overhead fluorescent lighting flickering weakly as if begging to be put out of its misery. Behind the front desk was a collection of headshots showing the current team of police working at the station, with Chief Dooley's photo biggest of all, a shiny gold plaque beneath his visage.

Juliette had a sudden memory of being a little girl, playing My Little Ponies with Norah on the floor while Mom whispered at them not to make too much noise. They'd spent a lot of time here, as kids. Too much time, probably.

Detective Dooley led her through the reception area toward one of the interview rooms. She wasn't here as a criminal. A bad guy. Yet the officer behind the reception desk and the older woman both glanced at her, eyes narrowed in suspicion. The woman was the grandmother of one of her old schoolmates, who'd suddenly stopped allowing Juliette and Norah to come play in their pool with the rest of the kids.

*I'm not in handcuffs*, she wanted to scream. *I'm here to help!*

A man was dead, and even if Maurice could be a jerk, he deserved justice. That was right, wasn't it? People who did bad things paid the price. Lord, if anyone knew that, it was the Macintyres. One bad decision and your grandkids' grandkids would be shouldering that social burden.

"In here," Detective Dooley said, holding the door to an interview room open but not moving out of the way, so she was forced to squeeze past him.

He was built like a wine barrel, thick, sturdy and slightly round in the middle. Despite being a skinny, freckle-faced redhead when they were kids, he'd grown into an intimidating presence. And whereas his father had an air of control and discipline, Shane Dooley was a hornet. Ill-tempered and fiery, with a mean streak as wide as a country mile. She did *not* want to get stung.

Juliette entered the room, still clutching Digger to her chest. The warmth of his little body and the wiry texture of his hair was a much-needed comfort right now. He must have sensed something weird was going on, because the wriggling had stopped, though his head swung around while he took in the change of scenery. Not that there was much to see. The interview room could easily double as a sensory deprivation chamber. Bland white walls, a basic table and more of the same plastic chairs. There was a whiteboard in one corner, the contents mostly wiped off save for a swirling red smear where the letters B-E-R-S remained to one side.

Detective Dooley closed the door behind him and gestured for her to take a seat. He sat opposite to her, pulling a notepad and pen out of his pocket and placing a small recording device on the table. "Tell me again what happened this morning, from when you left home."

Juliette outlined her walk to the dog park, noting that she went through the town square. She mentioned the lone car in the parking lot and how she thought she heard a noise at the dog park, but it turned out to be a raccoon. Of course she didn't tell Detective Dooley that she was scared—he didn't need to know that little tidbit.

"Then something caught my eye," she continued, her voice turning squeaky. Not to mention her palms were doing their best to outdo the great falls that gave Labrador Falls its name. "I went to investigate and found that Maurice had . . . died."

Saying it out loud felt surreal. Like a script. A piece of fiction. A lie. She blinked, fighting back a wave of tears at the memory of his open, unblinking eyes and the angry purple skin around his neck. She'd never seen a corpse before. It was so strange and awful.

"You look like you're about to cry," Detective Dooley said without an ounce of compassion. "Any reason for that?"

She sucked in a shaky breath. "A man is dead. It's sad."

"So you're not crying because you had any particular personal connection to him?" Shane Dooley's eyes narrowed, and it felt like she was being picked apart. She *hated* that feeling. It was just like that day in the main hallway of her high school, when all hell broke loose and news spread that her dad had done something bad. The way the other kids had looked at her, people she'd previously been friends with immediately distancing themselves.

*Criminal*, they'd said. *Your dad's going to jail.*

"I'm not crying at all," she replied stubbornly. Digger's head swung from the detective to her and back again as if watching a ping-pong match. His body huddled tight against her.

"Ah, so you're not *that* sad he's dead." The detective scribbled in his notebook, the scratch of his pen condemning her.

"No, that's not . . ." She gritted her teeth. Why was he

doing this? She was supposed to be giving her statement, not being turned around in circles by his questions. "It's sad that a man has died and even worse because it was murder."

"Ah, so you *know* it's murder." The detective's eyes were practically gleaming, as if he thought he'd lured her into some grand trap.

"Do you think he tripped and fell and the leash wrapped magically around his neck?" She knew mentioning the leash was a mistake the second the words came out of her mouth.

"Yes, let's talk about the leash for a moment." He leaned back in his chair, crossing his beefy arms over his chest. From this angle his neck looked so thick there was no definition between it and his head. It made him look like a giant red-headed thumb. "The crime scene folks will investigate things, of course. But I'd like to hear your view on how you think a leash from *your* workplace came to be wrapped around Maurice Allsop's neck."

The freaking leash. She had no earthly idea!

It was a merchandise sample she'd convinced Bonnie to order a while ago, thinking it might be fun to have some branded items to sell to loyal customers—an extra revenue stream *and* free advertising! But they'd ended up being too expensive to make any profit on and Bonnie had decided not to go ahead with a full order. Juliette had taken one sample home for herself and the other sample had been chucked in a drawer at work.

But who could have accessed What The Fluff to steal the leash and use it as a murder weapon? With Bonnie being away on her cruise and Juliette running the place by herself, there was nobody else with a key.

This did *not* look good.

"I don't know," she replied, knowing it was the wrong thing to say. "Maybe someone snuck in and took it while I was occupied with a client?"

"Have you noticed anything else missing recently?"

"Well, no," she admitted.

Detective Dooley nodded. "Let me see if I understand. You think someone snuck into your place of business to steal a dog leash, but they didn't touch anything else of value like, say, the money you keep in your till?"

"Most people pay by card these days," she tried, but the detective wasn't buying it. This conversation was going down a path she didn't like one bit.

"I have to ask, Juliette, do you have any reason to want Maurice Allsop dead?" He leaned forward and Juliette clutched Digger tighter. The little dog squirmed.

She swallowed. "No, I don't."

"Even though you were arguing with him publicly last night? And don't try to deny it, you know that account comes from a very reputable source."

"Your dad?" she asked, unable to help the slight sneer in her tone. He was riling her up and the panic was setting in. Detective Dooley was *not* treating her like a witness.

"That's Chief Dooley to you," the detective replied stonily.

"For the record, I wasn't going to deny anything. But if one little argument was cause for murder, we'd have a lot more dead bodies in Labrador Falls, don't you think?" Her heart was pounding now, the sense of being trapped making her twitchy. She glanced at one of the walls. Was it closing in? Sure felt like it.

"I don't care about other arguments. I care about *this* argument. You threatened to report Maurice for animal abuse and less than twenty-four hours later he turns up dead."

Why had she opened her big mouth? All the times she'd told Norah to keep quiet and save the peace, now she was here, suffering for not following her own advice. Served her right.

*Everything will be fine. You didn't do anything wrong, so they won't be able to find evidence to pin on you.*

"It was a misunderstanding," she said. "I promise."

"Easy to say that now that he's dead." The detective scribbled something else in his book, the pen looking comically small in his meaty paw—almost like a Grizzly trying to use chopsticks. "Where were you last night . . . after your altercation with Maurice?"

"I dropped my sister off at the place she's house-sitting and then I went home."

"Did you leave your home again that evening?"

"Not until I took Digger out for a walk this morning like I told you."

The detective looked up from his notes. "Can anyone corroborate that?"

Why did this have to happen when Norah was staying at Bonnie's? Not that she would have helped too much, since Norah worked her cleaning job at night, anyway. At least they wouldn't be able to pin anything on her. She cleaned offices and they usually had cameras. But that left Juliette with nothing to support her claims.

*Damn your nonexistent dating life! This is what you get for preferring fictional men.*

"Unless you take the word of a dog?" She attempted a smile.

Digger looked up at her incredulously. *Don't involve me in your criminal dealings, I'm innocent!*

"I'll assume that was an attempt at humor." The detective bowed his head back to his notes.

"Sha—Detective Dooley, I'm here to give a statement about what I saw this morning. I have no other involvement in this matter." She straightened her spine, willing herself to remain calm and collected. Panicking would only make her look unstable. "I want justice for Maurice as much as anyone else. So if I can help the Chief solve this crime then—"

"*I'll* be solving this crime," he cut in. There was a look of hardened resolve in his blue eyes. Suddenly he didn't seem like a simple bully anymore. He looked like someone who would bring her whole world crashing down if it served him even for a single heartbeat. "I know you civilians think I got here because of my family name. That I got a leg up or favoritism. But I didn't. So when I put someone behind bars for this, everyone will know I *earned* my place here and that I deserve this job."

The way he said *someone* with such unwavering eye contact made Juliette's breath hitch.

A detective with a chip on his shoulder who needed to prove himself was already dangerous. A detective with a chip on his shoulder who needed to prove himself *and* who was gunning for her was the worst-case scenario. If Shane Dooley had even the slightest opportunity to use her to further his own career, he wouldn't hesitate. She knew that down to her bones.

Juliette might not have committed murder. But she wouldn't put it past him to make the evidence say so.

*Sound like anyone you know? Karma has come to collect.*

"I'm afraid I have nothing else to tell you," she said, standing up. Her hands were trembling so much that Digger practically jostled in her arms. "Unless you have any more questions for me, then I'll be going."

"Thank you for your statement, Ms. Macintyre. We'll *absolutely* be in touch."

## *Chapter Five*

**JOEL HAD ALWAYS** thought the old saying "nothing was certain except death and taxes" should be amended to "nothing was certain except death, taxes *and* gossip"—especially if you lived in a small town. And while a dead body in any small town was a big deal, here in sleepy Labrador Falls murder was *extra* unusual. From what he'd heard—against his will, admittedly—the last murder to occur in Labrador Falls was in 1965 over a land dispute. Two brothers, farmers, and a heated exchange resulting in the misfiring of a gun. Not exactly the same thing as someone getting strangled in the middle of the night in cold blood.

At least, that's what everyone assumed.

Thankfully one of the police officers at the dog park had recognized Brigitte immediately and agreed to take her home safe and sound. Good thing, because *that* was a level of responsibility he could do without. What a shock it must have been for Corinne to have someone turn up on her doorstep with her missing dog and news that her ex was dead.

"People are saying Juliette Macintyre did it." April appeared next to him, her hair freshly dyed an orange that sat somewhere between Fanta and high-vis traffic cone. The way she changed colors it was a miracle she had any hair left at all. "She had a *huge* fight with Maurice at the dog park last night. I saw the whole thing! I was there with Bagel and she was *pissed*. Now he's dead. Then she 'conveniently' finds the body the next day. Seems sus, don't you think?"

The very idea of Juliette strangling a man seemed almost . . . funny. Not in a ha-ha kind of way. But more that he couldn't really imagine it at all.

"You're kidding, right?" Joel snorted. "I once saw her catch a fly between a glass and a napkin, and release it outside. No way she killed someone."

"Women can snap, Joel. They put up with the patriarchy their whole lives and then boom!" April tossed her hands up for effect. "One dude says the wrong thing and it's good night Irene. Or good night Ivan . . . or something. You know what I mean."

"Message received." Joel looked at her warily while holding the silver milk jug up to the espresso machine's foaming wand. The milk swirled inside. "If you wake up feeling murderous one day, please call in sick. I'd rather cover your shift than end up dead."

April grinned. "And here I was thinking that nothing could possibly scare you."

"I know better than to not take a woman at her word," he replied sagely. His two younger sisters had him intimately acquainted with the consequences of pissing them off. Just thinking about the girls—who were now in their late twenties and very much women—made him smile. One thing that sucked about living so far away from family was not getting to see his sisters every week, like he used to.

But their prodding and poking had become too much.

*Marissa can't blame you for what happened.*

*You can't hide away from the world forever. You have to start living again.*

*You're a good person, Joel. You did the right thing.*

It got too much in the end. They wanted the best for him,

but he didn't have any fight left and he couldn't dodge the questions anymore. Moreover, he couldn't face seeing that house—what was left of it—every time he turned right at the bottom of his street. At least here, he could lick his wounds in a place where nobody stared at him with pity whenever he left his house.

"Even if Juliette didn't kill Maurice, she's not going to have a great time with the cops," April barreled on, scribbling on two takeout coffee cups. Apparently, they were back to talking about the murder. Joel had a feeling it was going to be like this for a while, at least until the cops had someone to pin it on. "That neanderthal Shane Dooley will have her in cuffs the second he gets a chance. He *hates* the twins. I would not want to be in her shoes, let me tell you."

"I heard Maurice was strangled with a pair of pantyhose." An older woman wearing a pair of red glasses and a matching slash of lipstick leaned over the counter to join in the gossip, her eyes gleaming with salacious intent. "And not the regular ones, either. The *lacy* ones."

She said the word *lacy* as though it were a particularly offensive descriptor.

"Maybe they were having an affair and it turned violent," she added, nodding so that her curly salt-and-pepper hair bounced in agreement.

Joel wrinkled his nose. Maurice was old enough to be Juliette's father. Not to mention that he'd heard the man mocking some of Brewed Awakening's younger female clientele for taking photos of their lattes—calling them vapid and classless. Maybe April's assessment about a woman finally cracking after dealing with misogynistic assholes wasn't too far off. At the very least, Maurice didn't seem like someone Juliette might be attracted to.

*Why? Because you know she has a crush on you and you try to be as far from guys like Maurice Allsop as possible?*

He went back to making coffee. What was the point in speculating? The police would do their job and any evidence would eventually come to light. But even as he thought about it, his chest hummed with discontent. Joel knew firsthand that it didn't always work like that—because cops were people and people weren't infallible. He'd met plenty of good cops over the years and even a handful of excellent ones.

But he also knew some people went into that profession for a less than altruistic reason: because they liked power.

And here, in a small town like this, biases and grudges and personal conflicts could color an investigation like streaks of paint. He'd seen it before. An arson investigation in a town like this, where an innocent man went to jail and a firebug went free, only to start another fire that claimed the lives of three people. Lives that could have been saved if vendettas hadn't gotten in the way.

"Well, *I* heard Maurice talking recently about how someone broke into his house!" Another woman—he was pretty sure her name was Carol or Caroline or maybe Carol-Lynn—joined Red Glasses. "I bet both those Macintyre girls know how to pick a lock."

Red Glasses nodded emphatically at Probably Carol. "Crime begets crime."

"Well, *I* heard Juliette has a list of all the people who've wronged her," said another customer, behind them. "Maybe Maurice won't be the only victim."

"The easy way to stay off such a list is to treat people the way you wish to be treated," Joel said, giving the three women a pointed glance. April ducked her head and scurried off to deliver some pastries to one of the tables, and Probably Carol harrumphed. Mercifully though, it seemed the women received the message and didn't continue to gossip about the murder.

*Lecturing customers isn't good for business.*

True. But people didn't come to Brewed Awakening *for* him,

they came in spite of him. Because the coffee was so good they'd put up with someone only giving the bare minimum of human interaction. In any case, Joel was under no illusion that this silence would last long. Gossip was the lifeblood in any small town, and information traveled between people like a brain signal traveled along nerves. The lives of these people grew more intertwined with every generation, and that was precisely why Joel planned to stay here a few years and then move on.

He wasn't going to get woven into the fabric of this place. Or any place, ever again.

While he worked his way through the line of coffee cups awaiting his attention, the café suddenly went silent. It was almost eerie how the fervent chatter hushed in an instant, like someone had stuck plugs in his ears or a cone of silence over his head. Life could never be that merciful.

He looked up. Juliette stood in the doorway, the small white dog from earlier clutched to her chest, her gaze sweeping cautiously around the silent café, while every set of eyes stared back in her direction. It was like someone had hit pause. The only sign that time still crept ahead was the deepening flush that crawled up her neck to pool in her cheeks. Shaking her head, she turned on her heel and walked back outside. Instantly, the café erupted in chatter.

*"Did you see the look on her face?"*

*"Can't trust that family."*

*"Maybe she's covering for her sister. That one's a loose cannon."*

Joel turned to April. "Can you take over for a minute?"

Her eyebrows shot up so fast it was a miracle she didn't launch her eyebrow ring into space. "Uh, sure thing, boss."

Joel jogged out of the café to follow Juliette, knowing he was fueling the fire back inside. But something compelled him to check on her. Because that moment—the wall of silence she'd faced, knowing that *everyone* had been talking about her a second ago—he'd experienced it firsthand. It still lived rent free in his dreams, even all these years later.

A quick sweeping glance around the town square told him Juliette wasn't outside. She couldn't have disappeared that easily, and he'd bet she'd slipped inside What The Fluff, although the sign was still flipped to Closed, swirling pink letters telling him to come back soon. He knocked, but there was no response. The salon, like the café and most of the other businesses here, was glass fronted. But the interior remained in semidarkness with the lights off and little sunshine from the gloomy day.

Joel cupped his hands to the glass for a better look. The salon's decor was . . . Barbie soup. Every shade of pink imaginable, glitter and sparkle, velvet chairs and that kind of over-the-top faux luxury that made him cringe. On the wall was a picture of a fluffy white dog—not the one Juliette had been carrying around—sitting on a jewel-studded cushion and wearing a tiara. The place appeared empty. But then he spotted a tail wagging from behind the reception desk. A hand snuck out and scooted the dog out of view.

Was Juliette . . . hiding?

A second later, the dog's face poked out from behind the counter before it was yanked back.

"Juliette?" Joel knocked again. "I know you're in there."

Nothing.

"I'll give you a free cinnamon roll if you come out and talk to me."

Part of a face and some long, dark hair peeked out. Ah, he *knew* that would get her. The woman had a weakness for sweet treats. The little white dog came tearing out from behind the counter, then skidded into the door and bounced off. Giving itself a little shake, the dog slapped its paws up against the glass, tail wagging. Meanwhile, Juliette got to her feet and dusted off her knees before coming over to unlock the front door.

"Quick, get in before anyone sees," she said, urging him inside. The dog danced around his feet, face eager and begging for attention.

*Please pat me! Come on, man. Just one little pat. You know you want to!*

Juliette ushered him and the dog into the back, where the grooming room was located. It was a small but organized space, with an open shower stall and a table with a harness attachment above it sitting beside a wall-mounted dryer. There were several caddies and sets of drawers housing equipment and tools. The room was spotless. Not a hair in sight and the silver hardware gleamed. Juliette clearly had a fastidious cleanup routine.

"Why were you hiding behind the front counter when you could have hidden out here?" he asked. "This is a much better hiding spot."

"I panicked, okay?" She pushed a strand of dark hair out of her face. Her long ponytail was lopsided and starting to come undone, and one of her earrings was precariously close to falling out. Joel wasn't sure he'd ever seen Juliette looking disheveled before, and while this was kind of low on the disheveled scale—in his mind, from mismatched buttons to longstanding pasta sauce stains—it was *very* out of character for her. "It's been a hell of a day."

"So I heard."

That was apparently the wrong thing to say, because her mouth pinched. "What did you hear exactly?"

"Uhh . . ." Shit. *Don't mention the gossip. Don't mention the revenge list. And* definitely *don't mention the lacy pantyhose.* "I heard you were the unfortunate person who found Maurice Allsop's body."

*Solid recovery.*

"I did." She swallowed and looked down, a haunted expression flashing across her face.

The urge to bundle her up in his arms was so strong he had to look away. Nobody should have to experience that—it was traumatic, even for those with training. But for Disney princess types who probably thought the view through her rose-colored glasses was the real deal . . . it must have really shaken her.

"Why are you here?" she asked. Then she was distracted by the dog trying to chew on a cord. "Digger, no!"

"I uh . . . I more than heard what happened this morning. I saw it." Joel stepped out of the way of Digger, who was trying to yank a cord out of its socket. Juliette retrieved it from his mouth and found a toy for him to chew on. She did it with patience, even though the dog looked like a real handful. "I was at the park."

He left the rest unsaid: *I saw you get into the back of a police vehicle.*

"Oh." She averted her gaze. "Right."

"I wanted to see if you were okay."

He already regretted coming here. It was so unlike him to get involved in anyone else's business, especially something that had every chin in town wagging. He knew better! But the moment she'd walked into his café and everyone had made her turn tail, the empathy for her plight had hit him like a ton of bricks. Funny how old instincts could kick in and override sensibility under the right circumstances. The instinct to protect. To save.

*That's not who you are anymore.*

Maybe he should leave. This was a stupid idea. Juliette had family, she had friends to rally around her . . . he assumed. She didn't need him. And he was only inviting trouble getting embroiled in her business.

"Oh I'm *fine*." Rather than the tears he'd expected, there was a fire in her eyes. "I'm going to figure out who killed Maurice Allsop and show that bully, Detective Dooley, who he's messing with."

Somehow, this reaction was worse than tears. Because tears could be easily solved—a cinnamon roll, calling a loved one, a good nap, a cup of coffee. But fire . . . well, fire could destroy everything.

"I'm sick and tired of everyone in this town assuming the worst about me." She grabbed a rag and started buffing at some invisible spot on the silver grooming table, her vigorous movements causing the whole thing to shudder. "I never did *anything* wrong. I certainly didn't murder anybody. And if Shane Dooley thinks he's going to stick my head on a proverbial spike to further his own career, then . . . then . . ."

She was so worked up the words sputtered, getting tangled up in her anger.

"Then he's going to be *very* disappointed." She was scrubbing the table even harder now. "And as for everyone else in this town—they're wrong about me. They're just plain wrong. I'll show them."

Digger looked at Joel warily as if to say, *You know it's bad when she starts cleaning like dirt is her mortal enemy.*

"Giving yourself RSI isn't going to help." Joel reached out and gently retrieved the rag from Juliette's hand. "And the police will do their job and find the evidence that points to the real killer."

"You don't understand," she said, shaking her head. "The police here . . . they're not like in the cop shows. You know the ones, where the main character is a bit messed up and probably has some kind of bad habit like drinking too much or gambling or something, but underneath it all they're a good person and they always catch the real bad guy. The police hold grudges, here. They're biased. They'll use any chance to get back at my family."

Her voice climbed with each word and there was a wildness in her eyes. A panic.

"The detective will look for *anything* to tie me to this, and if he can't find it, he'll make it up. He'll *make* me into a murderer."

"You really think the police would fabricate evidence?"

"As revenge? Yeah, I do." She nodded emphatically.

*Why?*

The question was like sugar crystals melting on the tip of his tongue—so tempting, so enticing. Juliette was an enigma. A woman who seemed sweeter than apple pie but clearly had history with the police. It didn't fit.

"Revenge?" he asked, shaking his head. "What do you mean?"

"My dad used to be a police officer," she said. "But he . . . he got mixed up in something bad. Now everybody hates my family. *Especially* the Dooleys. So I have to figure out what really happened to Maurice or else I'm cooked."

Joel wasn't naive; he knew bad cops existed. Hell, more than one Netflix documentary had been made on this exact topic and they usually involved all the same elements: a small town, personal grudges, law enforcement staffed with people who'd been there a long time. And Juliette seemed to truly believe the police would try to frame her for murder.

Knowing her father was a disgraced police officer . . . well, that certainly fortified her concerns.

"Don't you think they'd be more interested in catching an *actual* killer?" he asked.

"Yeah, sure. But does every murder case get solved?" she asked, not even waiting for him to answer. "No, it doesn't. And if the person who killed Maurice knows that my family has a long-standing beef with the police force here, what better way to save themselves? That has to be the reason a What The Fluff dog leash was used. The murder weapon is tied directly to me, Joel. This is *bad* news."

Well, shit. She wasn't wrong about that.

He wasn't going to dwell on the slight bit of relief he felt, knowing the lacy stockings were nothing but baseless gossip.

"See?" she said, gesturing to him when she caught his perplexed expression. "If I sit on my hands and they *don't* figure out who did it, then I'm exactly what they need. The perfect scapegoat."

At ground level, a soft whine came from Digger, who was almost squirming with the need for someone to play with him. Poor dude was probably picking up on Juliette's anxiety. Joel had a strong urge to scoop him up, to offer some comfort to the little animal, but he immediately suppressed that feeling. He was already so far outside his set of personal rules that he wasn't going to pile on by letting himself get smitten with a dog. Juliette did it instead, cradling the terrier to her chest. Instantly, he quietened down.

"Maybe you should hire a lawyer," he suggested.

"And won't that look guilty as hell?" She shook her head. "No way. I might as well paint *I'm a killer* down the side of my car and drive around town blaring death metal."

"Then what are you going to do? You can't go out there and question people."

He didn't want to stereotype, but Juliette looked like she could step right into a Hallmark movie . . . and Joel knew far more about Hallmark movies than he would *ever* admit. His mom loved them and after his dad died, Joel used to put them on to cheer her up, even though they were saccharine and unrealistic. Seriously, how many big city women *really* shunned their careers to fall in love with a checked-shirt-wearing handyman? Not many, he would guess.

And the worst thing about the main characters in those movies was the very thing that worried him about Juliette—naivete. They trusted too easily, handing out smiles like they were balloons at a parade. People like that got chewed up and spat out. They got squashed by reality. The last thing he wanted was for her to go from being a Hallmark character to that girl in the horror movie who runs down into the basement instead of going out the front door.

*And you care, why?*

Human decency. That sounded legit, right? It was nothing to do with *her*, per se. This could be any person about to make a boneheaded move. He had a duty of care to point out the obvious.

"Why can't I question people?" she asked, bouncing Digger gently in her arms like he was a baby.

"Because . . ." Joel tossed his hands in the air. How else could he explain such a simple argument? "It's obviously dangerous."

"Doing nothing is dangerous," she argued. "And if both options are bad, then I'd rather err on the side of taking action than sitting on my backside waiting for fate to save me."

Joel looked at Juliette. Juliette looked at Joel. She didn't blink.

Oh boy, she was a stubborn one. He knew that already from her relentless attempts to befriend him every morning in the café. But this . . . this was something else.

"So you're going to march around town with a magnifying glass and go all Scooby-Doo on this situation?"

"Exactly. I'll speak to people, look for clues. Anything I have to do to get out of this." She jostled the dog in her arms, who looked over at Joel with concern.

*If she starts trying to use me as a cleaning rag, you'll save me, right? Buddy? Pal?*

The thought of Juliette running all over town in her perfectly neat outfits and her perfectly glossy ponytail, poking around in people's business while there was a murderer on the loose was enough to send a shiver down his spine. The girl was going to get herself hurt, or worse. Killed.

He couldn't have that on his conscience. There was already enough blood on his hands.

"Juliette, I don't think—"

"Excuse me if this sounds rude, but I didn't ask for your opinion," she said. Her words didn't contain any prickle or sting or even indignation. They were stated clearly and evenly, drawn like a line in the sand. She wasn't going to be swayed. "I didn't ask you to come here and give your two cents."

"Why did you come to the café before?" he asked.

"I haven't eaten anything all morning and I'm starving," she admitted. "But the second I walked in there, I knew everyone was gossiping about me. They were, weren't they?"

What the hell was he supposed to say to that? There was no point denying it, but admitting it felt like kicking Juliette when she was already down, and he didn't want to do that, either.

"People are always talking here and most of it is drivel, so I don't tend to listen much," he said.

A wry smile curved the corner of her lip. "Including when *I'm* talking?"

"Don't ask questions you don't want the answer to," he said drily. "And, for the record, I don't think it's safe that you're going out questioning people about their motives and such. If this person killed once, they could kill again."

"Don't suppose you know someone who would consider being a bodyguard for hire?" she asked, offering up one of those deadly hopeful smiles. The kind of smile that could shackle a man to his tombstone far too early.

*Don't do it, man. You know she's trouble.*

"I'll be going, regardless," she added, that stubborn streak rising strong again.

He let out a breath and raked a hand through his hair. He knew what he *should* do—the smart thing to do—which was to walk away and forget he'd ever had this stupid, impulsive urge to look after her. If she wanted to get herself into strife, that wasn't his problem. But even as he thought the words, they clashed with something deep inside him. The *old* Joel. The one who believed in right and wrong, who believed in looking after the folks in his community, the one who rushed headlong into things without fear for his body, mind, or his heart.

The Joel he'd thought was long dead.

And it was that Joel, resurrected from purgatory deep inside him, who sighed and said, "If you're going out clue hunting, just come and get me first."

"Great! We should probably exchange numbers then."

God. She was relentless, this woman.

He handed his phone over and the smile that blossomed on her face was both beautiful and terrifying, because it made the tiniest little thump in his heart, and that was a feeling he never wanted to experience ever again.

## *Chapter Six*

**"YES, I UNDERSTAND.** That's no problem," Juliette said into the phone. "Okay, bye."

That was the *third* What The Fluff client to cancel so far. They were dropping like flies! Juliette looked up at the whiteboard that listed all her appointments for the day and erased another name with a heavy sigh. It wasn't surprising, but it still hurt. Not only because she knew that Bark Wahlberg was already three weeks past due and probably had some matting behind his ears. But also because it meant less money in the bank account for Bonnie.

Technically it was less money for *her*, too. The month before Bonnie left for her cruise, she'd made a big song and dance about signing paperwork that would name Juliette a partner in the business, so she could run it while Bonnie was away. It seemed overkill for a three-week vacation. Juliette didn't want profit sharing for that time since she was just doing her job, but Bonnie had been so insistent that Juliette eventually caved.

The chain of text messages stared back ominously from her phone screen.

**JULIETTE:** Hi Bonnie, hope you boarded the ship okay. Have an amazing time and find yourself an ocean romance. And don't forget your sunscreen. Every two hours, remember? And stay hydrated after drinking all those margaritas!

**JULIETTE:** Hi Bons, just checking in again. Let me know how the trip is going so far. Can't wait to hear all about it!

**JULIETTE:** Hi Bonnie, can you please reply and let me know you're okay. I guess service on the boat is spotty, but when you land at one of your stops just shoot me a text. Please. You know how I worry.

She chewed on the inside of her lip, gnawing at a sore spot she'd been working on the day before. When she really got anxious, she chewed until the skin bled and she gave herself a painful little ulcer. She could already hear Norah scolding her—it was a terrible habit.

*Life would be easier if you stopped worrying about every little thing, Jules. Chill out.*

Was this one of those "every little things"? Probably. Maybe Bonnie cheaped out and didn't pay for Wi-Fi on board the cruise liner and hadn't had a chance to hotspot off someone or grab free Wi-Fi at one of the ports. It had only been four days since she left, and one of those was her flying down to Miami and seeing a friend before she boarded. A picture of two ice-cream cones held together was the last Juliette had heard from her.

A text popped up from Norah, with a picture of her cuddling Digger on the couch while Marshmallow glared at them from across the room. She wasn't starting work until later in the day and had agreed to take Digger so Juliette had one less thing to stress her out at work. Turned out it probably wasn't even required, if her dwindling schedule was anything to go on.

Before she could worry further, the front door to What The Fluff opened and in walked her 1 p.m. client. Juliette almost sighed in relief.

"Hi, Mrs. Carver." She offered up her most sunny smile. "Good to see you."

Cecelia Carver hovered inside the door of What The Fluff, her two miniature poodles at her feet. Butterscotch (the apricot poodle) strained on his leash, tugging forward with eager boisterous energy, while Cookie (the cream poodle) sniffed the air and was her usual calm self.

"Is Bonnie not here?" she asked. Her sunglasses were still perched on her nose, the rhinestones blinking accusingly. Mrs. Carver *loved* a rhinestone—bedazzled onto her jean jacket, studding her pearly pink manicure and clustered onto the plastic flowers dangling from her ears.

The woman needed a flash warning before she entered a room.

"Bonnie is away on a much-needed vacation," Juliette replied, trying to keep her smile going, though it felt like someone had coated her face in plaster. Her muscles were stiff, her smile brittle. "As I mentioned when you booked your appointment two weeks ago."

It wasn't like Juliette hadn't groomed the poodles before. Bonnie had been cutting back a lot in recent months, opting to manage the front desk and answer the phone and sweep up while Juliette did the actual grooming.

What did the woman think? That Juliette was a crazed murderer about to lunge at her with a pair of grooming shears?

*Don't ask that question out loud.*

"Oh that's right, I do remember." Mrs. Carver nodded. Cookie looked up at her mother trustingly while Butterscotch continued to yank forward. "Well . . . Let's start with Cookie."

Juliette held both hands out but Mrs. Carver only handed her one leash. Usually Juliette took both dogs back together, since they could become anxious if separated. But Mrs. Carver bent down and scooped up Butterscotch, who wriggled and tried to swipe his pink tongue along her cheek.

"I'll hang on to Butterscotch until it's time to switch," she added, going to sit in one of the chairs.

Well, knock her over with a feather. Usually Mrs. Carver couldn't wait to hand over her precious little fluff balls so she could head next door for a latte, taking slightly blurry photos for her "foodie" Instagram, CeeCee's Cravings. The posts were always punctuated with a nonsensical string of emojis and random capitalization.

> Loved the Lattes at brewed Awakening Today! 😻 👯
> 🥵 😈 🍪 🩶

For a while there everything had the eggplant emoji on it because she was in a "purple phase" but that stopped abruptly one day. Her daughter must have told her what it meant.

"No problem." Juliette took Cookie's leash and led her back to the grooming room, her smile dropping the second she turned around.

How was she going to explain this to Bonnie? If the customers kept canceling—like she suspected Mrs. Carver would have if she'd remembered that Bonnie was on vacation—that would really impact the business. It might open up a gap for someone *else* to start a grooming business and lure all of Bonnie's customers away! What then? Juliette would be out of a job and Bonnie was too old to start another business. They would be desolate. Nobody else would hire Juliette, especially if everyone thought she was a murderer.

Maybe she would end up going to jail and this would all be moot anyway.

"Stop it," she hissed to herself under her breath. "This isn't helping."

Cookie looked up at her as if to say, *You know talking to yourself is the first sign of madness, right?*

Was giving dogs imaginary dialogue the second? If so, she was screwed.

She lifted Cookie into the silver basin where they washed the smaller dogs. Cookie immediately skittered toward the edge, throwing her paws over and trying to escape.

"Oh no you don't." Juliette held her gently with one hand while she turned the taps to get the water going. Cookie whined and looked toward the door. "I know, I'm sorry Butterscotch can't keep you company today. Your mother thinks I'm homicidal."

Juliette reached for the detachable nozzle and checked the temperature of the water before starting to wet down Cookie's coat. The poor girl didn't love being bathed, but she was a sweet thing and didn't protest too hard, even though she was shaking a bit.

"Aren't you a good girl?" she cooed, moving the nozzle over the dog's body and making sure everything was evenly dampened. "Not like your little brother, he's a real chaos monkey."

She massaged shampoo into Cookie's fur, making sure to use a special tear-free version around the eyes so it didn't sting, and then rinsed everything off. Grooming always put Juliette into a state of flow because it allowed her mind to quiet down. Some groomers liked to listen to music while they worked, but Juliette preferred the sounds of her job. The *whoosh* of the water from the basin nozzle, the skittering of doggy toenails as she lifted her client onto the grooming table, the *clink* of the harness getting clipped in. Most of all, she loved the happy little grunts she was rewarded with when she gave the dogs exactly what they wanted.

For Cookie, it was a scratch right under the chin.

Juliette breezed through the stages of grooming, getting lost in her work. Brushing and combing and fluffing. Then it was time to work on her favorite bit—the *artistic* bit—shaping the coat. Poodles had a number of different cuts, and Mrs. Carver preferred the lamb cut for both her dogs. That meant the dog's face, tail and feet were shaved down, with the rest of the coat left full. It was cute and low maintenance.

She switched to a pair of scissors, shaping Cookie's fur to get the most out of her lines, doing what Juliette jokingly referred to as the "hedge trimming" portion of the groom. She was so deep in the flow, she almost missed the hushed voice coming from the front of the salon.

"Yes, I'm here now . . . no I thought the *other* one was doing it."

Without the hum of clippers or the satisfying snip, snip, snip of scissors, the conversation carried through to the back room. What The Fluff wasn't big—just a front area for customers to wait and the back grooming room plus one tiny bathroom. They didn't even have an office.

"I wasn't going to leave them . . . you know what people . . . did it."

She'd lowered her voice, perhaps noticing the grooming room had grown quiet. Juliette released Cookie from the harness and set her down on the floor, clipping her leash back on and completely skipping the part where she usually sprayed the dog with a sweet-smelling pet-safe cologne. She tiptoed to the edge of the grooming room and pressed herself against the wall, straining to listen.

"You know those dogs are worth a fortune. She was probably intending to sell it." Mrs. Carver's voice was raspy. There was a pause for a few seconds. "That's what I heard. That she tried to steal the dog and he caught her and they had an altercation."

*That's* what people were saying? What a ridiculous theory.

But there had been some panic around "dognapping" in the last few years, since a report from the American Kennel Club claimed instances of the crime had risen over 20 percent in North America. People became paranoid about the safety of their furry best friends, though to her knowledge the closest they'd come to anything like that in Labrador Falls was the time two owners accidentally mixed up their Japanese Spitzes at the dog park.

Seriously, those dogs looked like they came off a production line. So a simple mix-up was hardly a surprise.

"I don't know about that but I'm not taking any chances. If she *is* selling off dogs to some backyard breeding ring, then I won't put my precious babies at risk."

Backyard breeding ring? What the hell? Juliette *abhorred* unethical breeding. In fact, she wasn't very pro-breeding at all, always encouraging people to adopt from the shelter where possible.

Squaring her shoulders, Juliette marched Cookie out to the front of the salon, looking Mrs. Carver right in the eye as the woman scrambled to end her phone call.

"Here's your precious baby, safe and sound," she said through gritted teeth.

"Ah I just remembered that I actually have to . . . wash my car." Mrs. Carver dumped a handful of green bills onto the reception desk. "I'll rebook Butterscotch."

And with that, she snatched the leash out of Juliette's hand and dragged both dogs outside, letting What The Fluff's front door swing shut behind her with a bang. Two people outside watched Mrs. Carver darting away from the salon and then looked through the glass at Juliette with suspicious eyes. They bowed their heads as they walked away, probably speculating that she was a murderer or a failed dognapper or something else equally horrible.

She needed to solve this murder and clear her name, stat. Or else she was going to ruin Bonnie's business in the process.

**JOEL BARELY HAD** time to regret offering to chaperone Juliette on her clue hunting mission before she came calling. As soon as Brewed Awakening shuttered its doors for the day, she was there with her chin raised, a backpack slung over one shoulder and a little white dog at her feet. Her T-shirt said, Nancy Drew Fan Club.

Joel opened the door and let her inside quickly, before anyone mistakenly thought he was open. It had been a long workday, what with having to listen to everyone gossiping about the murder. He shouldn't be complaining—his seats were even fuller than usual—but the whole thing had worn him down and made him grouchy.

*Don't you mean* grouchier.

God, his internal monologue was a sarcastic jerk sometimes.

*Sometimes?*

Shut up.

"I like the Nancy Drew T-shirt," he said. "Very subtle."

Juliette shrugged. "I would have worn my 'I got 99 problems but homicide ain't one' T-shirt, but it was already in the wash."

In spite of his shitty mood, Joel found himself laughing. Okay, so this Disney princess had a bit of an edge. Good to know.

"I've made a plan for how we're going to tackle this murder investigation," she said, slinging off her backpack and dropping into one of the empty seats. The little dog—Dizzy . . . no, Digger—sniffed around, coming close to Joel, his wiry tail wagging and a pink tongue lolling out of his mouth. He seemed as guileless and trusting as she did. They were a perfect match.

Joel lowered himself into the seat across from Juliette and watched in awe as she opened her backpack and pulled out what appeared to be a planner decorated with watercolor pen artwork and calligraphy. She opened it to a page that had *How to solve a murder* written in scrolling pink ink with a little glittery skull and crossbones next to it for good measure.

"I wonder if Michaels ever thought of amateur detectives as their ideal customer base," he quipped.

"Work was kind of slow today," she admitted, fishing a pen with lilac-colored ink out of an embroidered pencil case with her name on it. He would bet his last ten bucks that she was one of those girls in high school who made scrapbooks for their friend's birthdays and dotted the *i*'s in their name with little hearts or stars. It made him smile—his younger sister, Faith, was like that. "I had a few cancellations."

"That normal?" he asked.

"No." She shook her head. "Generally speaking it's quite the opposite and we have people begging us to squeeze them in."

"I see."

"Which is why this plan is so important." She tapped the notebook with the end of her pen. "Now, the first thing I did was ask the internet how to solve a murder and it had some very good suggestions. Number one, secure the crime scene and gather initial facts."

"You asked the internet?" He blinked. "How, exactly?"

"I made a post on Reddit," she replied. "I found a perfect sub-Reddit, actually. It was called R/HowNotToGoToJail. And I don't want to go to jail. It's a perfect fit. There was this one guy, he laid out a whole plan for me."

"Those are random internet weirdos that you're talking to. Hell, it might have been a bot." He blanched. "You can't take advice from a bot."

"There's no way it was a bot," she scoffed. "He was far too polite."

*I wonder if she thinks Clippy is a real person.*

"And you might be shocked to know this, Joel. But I have never solved a murder before. I need all the help I can get."

He would not be shocked. But it seemed there was no point arguing with her—the woman had made up her mind.

"Carry on," he said with a begrudging sigh.

"Since we can't secure the crime scene," she continued. "We have to move on to gathering initial facts. Which are, number one, Maurice Allsop was strangled to death with a branded What The Fluff dog leash."

Oh yeah, that. It was a damning fact and for a brief moment Joel wondered if maybe Juliette's wide-eyed naivete was a carefully constructed disguise. Could she possibly be a wolf in princesses' clothing? It would be the perfect cover for a murderer. Nobody suspected the ingenue. But he dismissed that thought as quickly as it came. Joel had a good nose for bullshit. Juliette was telling the truth—right down to the fact that she thought random weirdos on Reddit could help her solve a murder.

"Number two . . ." She tapped her planner again. "Maurice likely drove to the dog park, since I assume that flashy Mercedes was his."

"Then how and when did the dog get loose?"

"We haven't got to the questions yet. That's step 2 when we do the timeline." She looked at him like he should know this already. Apparently, he had not consumed enough Nancy Drew, Hardy Boys and reruns of *Scooby-Doo* when he was a kid. "Number three, he was currently going through a difficult divorce, which involved a custody battle over his dog, Brigitte."

"They were having a custody battle over the dog?" Joel snorted like it was a stupid, frivolous thing, but he knew dogs were part of the family and he'd seen people fight over far less. Still, if he wanted to keep Juliette at a safe distance through all this, then his dog-hating persona would be useful.

Better that she thought of him as a jerk than a good guy. It was safer that way.

"Don't they usually suspect the spouse?" he continued. "Or can't I ask more questions until you declare we've moved onto step 2?"

"We have to follow the process, Joel." She looked at him with absolute seriousness. "The last initial fact, as I see it, is that Maurice was a jerk."

"You think jerks deserve to be murdered?" Hmm, maybe it wasn't a good idea for her to think him a jerk, after all. Not unless he wanted to sleep with one eye open.

"Of course not. But someone who goes around town pissing people off is likely to end up with more than one enemy. That means we should brace for multiple suspects." She looked at him pointedly. "Now we can move on to step two, initial questions."

"The first being, *who* murdered Maurice?"

"Very good." She nodded like a proud teacher. Digger sniffed around Joel's feet and jumped up against his leg, two white paws landing on his shin and a pair of brown eyes looking up at him hopefully. The urge to pat was strong, but he resisted. Digger dropped back down and went to Juliette, who immediately reached down to ruffle his head. "Now we can add your other questions: How did Brigitte get loose? And, is the spouse—Corinne—involved?"

She dutifully wrote out the questions in her book. Her handwriting was curly and even, though he noted that she didn't put little love hearts or stars over the *i*'s. She did, however, neatly number the questions down the side of the page.

"I also want to know why Maurice was back at the dog park that night when Corinne had already taken Brigitte there earlier in the evening." She scribbled another question down, pen scratching across her notebook page. "Afghan hounds do need a fair amount of exercise, but I know that both Corinne and Maurice walk her early in the morning, too. It seems odd he took her back to the dog park only a few hours after she'd already been there. Maybe he was meeting someone?"

"How do you know Brigitte had been to the dog park, already?" Joel asked.

"I was there with Digger," she said. "I saw them."

Juliette's cheeks flushed as though there was something she wasn't saying—likely that she'd had an argument with Maurice, which he knew because April had told him. Joel got the distinct impression there was a lot more to her than met the eye. When he'd first encountered Juliette (and yes, *encountered* was the only correct word to describe the pink tornado of Type A energy that whirled around her) he'd written her off as a perky small-town class president type. Popular, confident, probably never had to struggle in life.

But the longer he knew Juliette, the more he felt that his initial assessment of her had been very off base.

She was a woman with a past. With secrets. Question was, did he want to know what was underneath her glittery pink surface or not?

# *Chapter Seven*

**AFTER JULIETTE HAD** dutifully written down all their questions in the "how to solve a murder" notebook, it was time to move onto step 3, gathering evidence and step 4, interviewing witnesses and persons of interest. Joel seemed to think adhering to a plan was strange, but Juliette didn't agree. Plans were tethers that kept you grounded when life felt overwhelming. They were guardrails to keep you on the path toward your goals and stop you wandering off in the wrong direction.

Most importantly, they made her brain feel quiet. Because she was *way* less likely to make a mistake if she had a plan to follow.

"We don't even know if the dog park has been opened up again," Joel said as they walked past the parking lot where Juliette had gotten into the back of the police car yesterday.

The telltale yellow flutter caught her eye up ahead. "Looks like some crime scene tape is still up."

When they arrived at the dog park, the big dog area was still sealed off, but the little dog area was open. Digger yanked forward on his leash, tail wagging so hard the whole back half of his body wriggled.

*Come on, let me in! We're so close. It's zoomies time.*

Juliette pushed the gate open and walked in, with Joel close behind. Nearby, a couple walking a boxer grumbled about not being able to use the park. Juliette gave them a reproachful look. A man was dead! Not being able to use the dog park was a very small matter, by comparison. And they couldn't know it, but if Juliette did a good job with her investigation, the dog park would be properly open again soon, for all dogs.

*Everything is riding on this. If you mess up, it's game over.*

"Let me give you the lay of the land," Juliette said as she bent to unclip Digger. He immediately raced off. "If we're going to be investigating these people, you need to know who's who in the zoo. The dog park is kind of like high school. There are cliques, there are social norms and there are unspoken rules."

Okay, maybe she was hamming it up a little. But she'd never seen Joel outside Brewed Awakening before, except that one time he avoided her while they were both in line at the supermarket. That was embarrassing—she'd waved and he'd turned to look in the other direction. So, seeing him out and about in the real world was kind of like watching a science experiment.

Joel seemed on high alert. Was it because there was a murderer on the loose, or something else? Maybe he had social anxiety. Or maybe it was just his misanthropic tendencies showing.

"Sounds delightful," he deadpanned, as though being out in society was about the worst thing he'd done in his lifetime.

"First things first, coffee and snacks." Juliette pointed to a bright blue van featuring a painting of a coffee bean with arms and legs and a slightly manic smile. It was currently closed. "There's the Wandering Bean Co. coffee truck. They make a decent coffee—though not quite as good as yours, in my humble opinion. They also do puppaccinos with homemade crushed dog biscuits sprinkled on top."

"Puppaccinos?" He scrubbed a hand over his face. "Ridiculous."

"As for the people of the dog park . . . there's some funny characters to watch out for," Juliette barreled on, pointing to an older woman with coiffed hair and bright blue eyeshadow all the way up to her eyebrows. "That's Ruth Goldstein, she's a stickler for the rules. If you even so much as *think* about not immediately latching the gate when you come in, she'll be all over you like a rash. Her favorite things in life are complaining about the temperature of her coffee and giving lectures. Not the educational kind."

Joel looked at her with a hint of amusement in his expression. Or maybe it was a trick of the light. Or some personal dark magic that dwelled in the slightly sad, downturned brown eyes that were the exact color of maple syrup.

*Would Nancy Drew be losing herself in his eyes? No, the hell she would not. She would be focused on her goal. Get it together, Macintyre.*

Clearing her throat, Juliette dragged her gaze back to the people of the dog park.

"That's Serenity McFarlane." Juliette pointed to a slim early-20s woman with blond pixie cut hair and an adorable long-haired chocolate brown dachshund. "She moved here the year before last. Apparently, her mom was born here and after she passed away, Serenity wanted to experience the town where her mom grew up. She's sweet but a bit woo-woo. She's into healing crystals and essential oils and will probably try to sign you up for an MLM."

"With a name like Serenity I'm not shocked." Joel scoffed. "What kind of name is that, anyway?"

"She introduced herself to me as Serenity Hope Rainbow McFarlane." Juliette giggled at the look of utter disbelief on his face. "Pretty sure that's not what's on her birth certificate, though. Rumor has it she legally changed her name."

"*To* Serenity Hope Rainbow?" Joel was aghast.

"I bet her real name is something really basic like Mary or Amanda or something."

"Who's next?"

"The guy in the leather jacket is Beau Gerrard. He runs a record store and used to be an actual legitimate rock star." Juliette pointed to a guy who looked to be early thirties and had shaggy blond hair and a pair of jeans that were torn to shreds. He was throwing a ball around with an exceptionally cute French bulldog. "Like, songs on the radio and Grammy awards and everything."

Joel watched her closely and Juliette cleared her throat. Even though Beau had grown up here it was a little hard not to be starstruck in the presence of someone famous—especially when she'd once had a poster of him in her locker at school.

"You know I'm only here to make sure you don't get yourself murdered, right?" he said. "I don't need to know about all these people. I don't *want* to know, either."

"You sound *just* like Norah." She chuckled. "I bet you two would get along great—two misanthropes hating on the world together."

"Sounds like you might have a reason or two to hate on the world."

Something about the way he said it made the monster stir in her belly, the one that always said shitty things to her.

*You'll never win these people over.*

*You'll always be an outcast.*

*Nobody will ever love you.*

Of course she knew it wasn't true—Bonnie had told her time and time again that ugly voice was fear trying to hold her back. But right now, without Bonnie close by and with the whole town looking at her like she murdered a man, it was hard to believe it.

"*Hate* is a strong word," she replied. "I try not to hate anything or anyone."

Joel stuffed both hands into the pockets of his jeans—perfectly faded Levi's 501s, not that she'd spent excessive time looking at his ass—and nodded, maple syrup eyes sweeping across the dog park. The sun was getting low on the horizon and a chilly breeze swept through, ruffling the thick strands of his dirty blond hair. Juliette wrenched her eyes away, flushing for an entirely different reason now.

"Let's—" Before she could even suggest that they go talk to people, Ruth Goldstein marched toward them, a tiny angry-looking dog trotting by her side.

Ruth was in her late seventies with a blunt graying bob and sharp brown eyes that pierced through you like she was aware of your deepest, most shameful sins. She wore her signature hot pink lipstick (that always ended up on her front teeth) and a pair of purple plastic cat-eye glasses, and she arrived in a cloud of eye-wateringly strong perfume.

"Well, well, well. I wasn't expecting to see *you* around here," she said. Unfortunately, due to Ruth having a lazy eye, Juliette wasn't quite sure who she was addressing.

Ruth's shih tzu, Robert, marched up to them with equal bossy energy, jutting his furry chin forward and showing off an impressive underbite that made him look like a Muppets Movie reject. He had long charcoal ears which were uncannily similar to Ruth's bob. It was almost like the dog had been created in her image . . . right down to the disdainful sniff he took in Joel's direction.

*Maybe I should set Robert and Marshmallow up on a date. They'd be a perfect match.*

"I take it you heard about Maurice's . . . passing," Juliette said.

"That man had it coming." Her electric blue eye shadow was creased and had gathered in the folds of her eyelids. "Do you know he left the gate open *twice* last week? I said to him, were you born in a tent, Maurice? Close the goddamn gate! He should know better than that. I mean, he's been coming here for years. There's absolutely *no* excuse not to follow the rules. Typical big dog people. They only think of themselves."

Joel raised an eyebrow.

"Don't you look at me like that, young man." Ruth waggled her finger at him. "I didn't kill him. I'd be more worried about your girlfriend here."

Juliette held up both hands. "Oh we're not—"

"Absolutely not." Joel's nose wrinkled. Ouch.

He didn't have to deny it *quite* so hard.

"Never, ever," Juliette added for good measure, folding her arms tighter across her chest.

"Ah, I see." Ruth looked at them over the top of her glasses and frowned. "I know what you young ones are like—you don't want the cow, just the milk for free."

"I'm *not* a cow—"

"She's not a cow." Joel shook his head.

"What do they call it? Friends with benefits." Ruth made a noise of disgust. "In my day, a man would do the honorable thing and ask for a woman's hand before getting it out of his trousers. Now you all organize your sex arrangements on your phones. This world is going to hell, I tell you. Nobody has morals anymore."

Juliette blinked. Joel looked at the ground. Even Robert seemed a little surprised by his owner's outburst.

"Do you happen to have any idea who *else* might have thought Maurice had it coming?" Juliette asked, figuring if she could get some information out of Ruth then she would let the cow comment slide.

"Why? So I can give you ideas of who to pin it on? I'm smarter than that, young lady. Now, if you'll excuse me, it's time for Robert's supper."

Ruth and Robert breezed out of the little dog area, leaving

a heavily scented trail behind them, the gate swinging closed so sharply it was lucky no one else was coming, or else they might have lost a finger.

"I stand by my decision to make sure you don't get murdered," Joel said, watching them go.

"You don't think I could take her?"

"Tough old broad like that? Not a chance, Sunshine. Not a chance."

He'd called her Sunshine.

Juliette immediately turned away, her face warming and, she was sure, beet red—which she absolutely did *not* want him to see. But damn if she wasn't going to hang on to that little moment next time she needed a smile. Which, given how her week was going, would probably be sooner rather than later.

The moment was shattered, however, when a shriek came from the other side of the small dog area. A streak of white blazed past and Juliette had a sinking feeling in her stomach. Ruth and her "getting the milk for free" tirade had distracted her momentarily, and she'd taken her eyes off Digger. He was currently running rings around a small chocolate brown miniature dachshund, kicking up dust with his energetic paws. The dachshund was rooted to the spot, looking terrified.

"Digger, stop!" Juliette said.

But Digger didn't stop. He would never stop. The dog lived by a credo of *I'll sleep when I'm dead.*

The dachshund whined and her owner, Serenity, tried to pick her up, but Digger's frantic running made it hard to grab the small, brown dog. Suddenly, Digger came screeching to a stop behind the dachshund, wiggled up the back of her and threw his paws over her shoulders, hinging his little hips back and forth. His mouth was open, tongue out, and he looked like this was the best darn day of his life.

"Digger. No!" Juliette rushed forward. Joel snorted but broke into a jog beside her.

"What was that about getting the milk for free?" he said.

"This is *not* funny."

Serenity shrieked and grabbed for her dog, yanking her out from under the enthusiastic Jack Russell. "My poor Nibs!"

Juliette skidded to a stop and crouched next to Digger, who looked annoyed that his fun had been ruined.

*Can't a dog enjoy himself with his lady friend, huh? What's wrong with a little romance?*

"We're going to talk about this later," she said under her breath. "You can't go around humping anyone you feel like. Not cool."

"You should watch your dog better than that," Serenity said, her tone softening when she saw Joel standing there. "Oh hi, Joel."

"Hi, Serenity."

He knew her. Why hadn't he mentioned it when she was doing her introductions? Was it her imagination or did his voice drop a few octaves when he said hello just then.

*Nancy Drew would be ashamed of you.*

Serenity wore an old hoodie with a cheerleading logo on the front that said Spirit Sirens, Scranton PA and a pair of mint green leggings so tight they could have been spray-painted on. The hoodie had been cut short to expose her toned stomach and she wore her socks pulled up to mid calf in that way all the younger girls thought was cool. Juliette had tried it one time and it made her legs look like tree stumps.

"I'm so sorry. Digger is a rescue and I'm fostering him at the moment, so I'm still trying to figure out all his quirks." Juliette gave Digger a little pat and stood back up. "I was watching him but then Ruth came over . . ."

"Say no more." Serenity's eyes didn't budge from Joel. "We've all been 'Ruthed' at some point. Even Nibs!"

Juliette was familiar with Nibs, since Serenity brought her in for grooming occasionally, though it was clear Serenity took her role as dog mom seriously and took excellent care of her at home, too.

"My sweet little girl is such a sensitive soul and she's easily triggered by male attention. I'm pretty sure she's a feminist. I'm so proud of her."

"Uh yeah, sure. That's wonderful." Juliette exchanged a look with Joel. She wanted to scream, *see? I'm not the weirdest person in this town!* "Hey, uh . . . so it's wild what happened to Maurice, right?"

Serenity's eyes widened and Juliette would swear her pupils dilated like she'd stuffed a load of cotton candy into her mouth and the sugar was lighting up her brain. At least, that's how cotton candy made Juliette feel. Judging by Serenity's physique *and* the fact that she was a super-fit Pilates instructor, she probably didn't indulge in cotton candy all that often. If ever.

But one man's trash was another man's dopamine. And like a lot of folks around here, Serenity's poison of choice was gossip.

"I mean, I haven't lived in Labrador Falls all *that* long compared to most people around here, but I realized pretty quickly if there was one person who might get murdered in this town, it would be Maurice. Not that I condone it," she added quickly, looking at Joel and practically fluttering her eyelashes. "I don't support killing animals for food, let alone murdering a human. Fun fact! Did you know that Worcestershire sauce isn't vegan because it contains anchovies? Even poor ugly anchovies deserve the right to live."

Joel's expression said that while this might technically be a fact, *fun* probably wasn't the descriptor he would use.

"Why would you guess Maurice might be murdered?" Juliette asked. Digger had raced off again, and she kept a studious eye on him this time, lest he try to hump anyone else. The last thing she needed was everyone around town thinking that in addition to being a possible murderer, she also supported nonconsensual humping.

"Not literally. But the guy had beef with everyone. Maurice was a stickler. Not for the rules necessarily, but for, like, how *he* thought things should be done. He was probably an Aries. Or a Scorpio." Serenity made a face and placed Nibs back down, where the dog looked around warily as if trying to assess if Digger was in striking distance. "Fire signs always have beef with people."

"I take it you're not a fire sign then," Juliette replied. Joel's eyes had glazed over as if the talk of star signs had literally shut off the part of his brain that allowed him to pay attention to the conversation.

"Uh, no way. I'm a Pieces, the best of all the water signs. Sensitive and caring, but still passionate." She said the last part a little louder, almost as if she hoped it would catch Joel's attention. It did not. "I'm a lover, not a fighter."

"Who did Maurice have beef with? I mean, other than his ex-wife. Ex *wives*."

"How much time have you got? He told one lady at the dog park that her poodle looked like an 'overused shower loofah' and then he picked a fight with someone else, saying their dog was poorly trained because it wanted to play with Brigitte. Oh, and then there was the time that he fully screamed at this poor woman in the street because her kid tried to pat his dog." Serenity ticked the infractions off on her fingers. "Then he fired his cleaning lady. And *then* he was going around telling everyone that Kacey, who runs the puppy academy, is a scam artist and that she doesn't train people's dogs properly and takes their money for nothing."

"That seems like a big accusation," Joel said, apparently having rejoined the conversation now that they'd moved on from star signs.

"Oh it was *huge*. Kacey was furious! And, like, I wouldn't mess with her. She comes to my Pilates class on Wednesday nights and she's strong. Stronger than most men." Serenity let out a giggle. "Well, not as strong as you, I'm sure."

Juliette rolled her eyes. Was this chick for real? Whatever happened to the art of subtlety? Or was throwing yourself at someone the same as those hiked-up socks? Good if you had confidence, not so great when you fed your insecurities and cuddled up to them at night like they were your pets.

And maybe, just *maybe*, there was a little part of her that was jealous at how everyone seemed so drawn to Joel despite the fact that he did *zero* to encourage it. The guy literally grunted at people on a daily basis, while she was over here busting her ass with smiles and niceties and trying to be perfect, perfect, perfect just so people wouldn't look sideways at her in the street. Maybe she was going about things all wrong.

"Any chance you know the name of the cleaner he fired?" Joel asked.

Juliette almost gasped. He'd engaged! He was trying to help by asking questions. So much for the whole "I'm only here so you don't get murdered" thing. He was interested in what happened to Maurice, she could tell. For some reason, it felt like a small victory. Joel *never* asked questions.

"I don't." Serenity shook her head. "I saw her at the wellness center once, but she wasn't in my class. I think she was there for a massage or something."

"Oh yeah," Juliette said, barely able to contain her grin. "Did I tell you that Serenity works at Live Love Labrador?"

Joel immediately got that glazed look in his eyes again. "Wellness" was probably up there with star signs in things he thought weren't worth his time. If he didn't believe in putting syrup in coffee, there was no way he'd be into a wellness center where they offered to clear your chakras with the healing magic of crystals for a princely hundred bucks a pop. Healing magic her ass. No way was a rock doing anything except looking pretty as a paperweight.

"That's right." Serenity beamed. "You should come by. I teach on Wednesdays, Thursdays and Saturdays. Oh, and I have a new class that incorporates aromatherapy and crystal healing and, like, energy redistribution and biohacking and stuff."

"Energy redistribution *and* biohacking, wow." Juliette nodded like she had any clue what those words meant.

Joel grunted. Ah, there was the grump she knew.

"Thanks." Serenity toyed with a strand of hair by her ear. "I'm pretty proud of it."

"Well, we should get going. Sorry again for traumatizing Nibs." Juliette bent down and extended a hand to the dachshund, who looked at her cautiously but then came over for a pat.

"It's okay. We'll discuss her trauma tonight." Serenity nodded. "We try to do a sharing session once a week with a pet therapist. It's been really helpful to understand her past issues before I adopted her."

Joel was already walking away. Apparently pet therapists were the line for him.

"Bye, Joel!" Serenity called after him, waving. "I'll come by the café and see you soon."

Juliette collected Digger and they jogged to catch up to Joel, who was striding toward the exit.

"Had enough already?" Juliette asked him, barely able to suppress a laugh when he shot daggers at her.

"Yes, but something tells me we've got a *long* way to go before we figure this out."

While the thought of having to trudge through a murder investigation to clear her name made Juliette feel sick to her stomach, there was a teeny, tiny little part of her that was excited to be doing it with Joel.

# *Chapter Eight*

**THE NEXT DAY,** Juliette's 9 a.m. appointment was a no-show. The client didn't even have the decency to answer the phone when she called, sending her straight to voicemail. Being canceled on was one thing. Being ghosted was another! Two more clients had *both* left messages before opening hours saying they wouldn't be coming in today—calling early enough to avoid talking to Juliette directly.

If it wasn't for Joel's employee April and her adorable German spaniel, Bagel, coming in for their regular grooming spot, she might as well have closed up shop for the morning. But that one appointment had only kept Juliette busy for so long.

Now it was eleven-thirty and she was so bored it felt like her eyes were going to pop out of their sockets. Salon so clean it sparkled? Check. Replenishment orders for cleaning products and salon-grade doggy shampoos? Check. Appointments confirmed for the rest of the day and tomorrow? A few answered, but most didn't pick up so that was only a partial check. One person answered but as soon as she introduced herself there was a weird fake crackling noise and the call mysteriously "disconnected" even though Labrador Falls usually had great cell service.

How much longer would people keep canceling? Did they really believe she was a dog napper? What if What The Fluff never recovered and Juliette had damaged her boss's business for good?

Not to mention, Bonnie *still* hadn't responded to her messages.

Her worries collided into one another, clumping together and growing like a snowball racing down a mountain. Her lungs squeezed tighter, tighter, tighter until her breaths came in strained little puffs. She pressed a palm to her chest and closed her eyes for a moment, taking a long breath and holding it for a few seconds before releasing slowly to a count of five. Juliette was no stranger to panic attacks. They'd plagued her teenage years after "the incident" with her dad, when the bullying had started. But despite getting good at staving them off with her breathing exercises . . . that would only work for so long.

The pressure was building. The scrutiny was intensifying. And if she didn't clear her name soon, then—

"Everything will be okay. This is just a blip." Right? *Right?* It had to be. People could only pelt her with baseless accusations for so long, couldn't they?

*You know the answer to that.*

"People are reacting to the shock of someone dying," she rationalized, pacing back and forth, arms wrapped around her stomach. "Things will go back to normal in a day or two. They have to! I mean, what are they going to do? Let their dogs turn into shaggy bushes? They'll have to come back. When they do, they'll see I'm not a bad person. Then the real murderer will get caught and everything will go back to how it was before."

Which admittedly wasn't perfect, but it was sure as heck better than this.

Digger looked up from where he was currently huddled in a basket behind the front desk, a red bandanna neatly tied around his neck, and eyed her warily. *Okay lady, if you say so. Sounds a little delulu if you ask me.*

Dammit. If the dog's voice was imaginary, why couldn't she

make it more supportive? That probably said more about her than she wanted to admit.

"No more wallowing." She gave herself a little shake. "And if I have to stay here doing nothing for the next three hours, my brain is going to turn into a potato. How about we go for a walk?"

At the *W* word, Digger shot out of his basket so fast he clipped one paw on the edge and went tumbling over the side, doing a barrel roll and popping up on all four feet, tail in the air.

*Ta dah! Nailed it.*

"Besides, if we're going to solve this murder, we need to be out there looking for clues," she added, already feeling better. Taking action was the best way to get in control of a situation—because you only failed if you gave up! It's why she still tried to win people over all these years later. It's why she persisted in trying to make friends with Joel. It's why she kept fostering dogs, even though it sometimes got her down to see how many poor little creatures needed a forever home.

Because *trying* meant she had another chance to make a difference.

Digger danced around Juliette's feet as she slipped her jacket on and gathered up her purse and scarf. Once he was securely in his harness and raincoat, they were off. First stop, Glow Up.

Whereas most businesses—including What The Fluff—leaned into small town kitsch, Glow Up looked like it had been ripped out of New York or London or Paris and plonked down somewhere it didn't belong. It had dark green marble floors, fluted wood cabinetry, and a blown glass light fixture that looked like floating iridescent bubbles. It wasn't just a candle store. It was an *experience*. Sometimes Juliette would pop in to feel transported somewhere far fancier than she could ever afford in her real life.

But mostly she popped in because Glow Up was run by her dear friend Alexa.

The store was unusually quiet when Juliette and Digger walked in. So quiet, in fact, Alexa was nowhere to be seen. In some places that might be a security issue since anyone could walk in and make off with the gorgeous handmade candles. But not here. People didn't worry about security in Labrador Falls.

*They might now.*

A second later, Alexa appeared from the back room, a cardboard box in her arms. Her long reddish-blond hair was arranged into a messy bun and she wore her signature red lipstick, which she'd been wearing daily since high school. Chronically averse to blending in—a product of growing up being the "dud child" compared to her musical prodigy younger sister—Alexa's outfits always commanded attention. Sometimes that command was spoken and sometimes, like today, it shouted.

"That's uh . . . a hell of a dress," Juliette said. Digger cocked his head like he wasn't quite sure what he was seeing.

The dress was strapless and fitted to the knees, where a stiff tulle ruffle jetted out. A large bow sat on one hip and the whole thing was made in a shiny red satin with sequined black polka dots that would have been impossible for anyone else to wear. But Alexa looked like an eighties prom queen living her best life.

"I found it at Goodwill for a steal. It was in the costume section, if you can believe it."

She could, actually.

"You know the eighties isn't my usual decade, but I couldn't leave it behind." She lowered the box with an *oof.* "What are you doing here anyway? I thought you'd be knee-deep in dog fur by now. Don't tell me Bonnie is back already."

"She only left a few days ago," Juliette replied with an amused smile.

Alexa was easily one of the smartest and most creative people she knew, but the girl lived in a bubble. When she was in product development mode, she would disappear into her studio and days would go by before anyone heard from her. In fact, more than once, the twins had gone to her house for a welfare check after a week of unanswered texts only to find her buzzing over some new scent she'd designed. That was Alexa to a tee—hardworking, but with a loose grasp on time and her cell phone.

"Oh right." Alexa nodded, though Juliette was sure that information had already flown out of her brain. Alexa crouched and gave Digger a little scratch, not even questioning who this new dog was or how long he was staying.

Digger stuck his head into the air and had a curious sniff. Each day Alexa featured one candle on a marble table at the front of the shop, burning it for hours so the scent wafted out and enticed people inside. Her scents ranged from sweet and familiar, like grandma's sugar cookies, to those lodged in memory—like the fresh pine of a Christmas tree or salt-drenched ocean air mixed with coconut sunscreen—to more unusual combinations, like zesty grapefruit and aromatic rosemary or ozonic notes and ambergris (which smelled great but was made from whale poop!)

Today was one of Juliette's personal favorites—she currently had a half-burned one in her bedroom that Alexa had gifted her for her birthday. It was called Thankful and it smelled like eating a slice of homemade pumpkin pie while sitting outside in the crisp fall air, watching the leaves glow and catching a hint of smoke from someone's woodfire.

"How's it going? Slow day?" Alexa asked as she began to unpack her box, lining up neat rows of candles in beautiful pottery jars that she'd thrown, fired and glazed herself.

"Well, everyone around here thinks I killed a guy to steal his dog *and* I'm running my boss's business into the ground . . .

so, you know, not exactly my greatest Wednesday ever." Juliette attempted a laugh. "Still better than the time we road tripped to the cape and got stuck in that awful motel during the hurricane."

"I *still* have nightmares about the stains on those walls." Alexa shuddered. "CSI would have had a field day!"

"Speaking of CSI," Juliette said. "I don't suppose you heard about my, uh, trip to the police station?"

Alexa frowned. "No."

"Tell me you heard about the murder, at least."

"Murder?" Alexa's head snapped up. "What murder?"

Juliette resisted the urge to roll her eyes. Alexa didn't care for gossip *or* what folks around town thought of her, so she went about her business oblivious. It had been that way since high school. When kids pointed and laughed at her vintage fashion and quirky mannerisms, she shrugged and got on with her life.

*You could learn a thing or two from her.*

"You must be the only person who doesn't know." Juliette filled her friend in on what'd happened, watching Alexa's face get madder and madder. "So yeah, Maurice is dead and Shane Dooley wants my head on a pike so he can leverage himself some respect."

"That . . . dickwad!" she sputtered. "I swear to God, that man lowers the bar of humanity on a weekly basis. In fact, I would go so far as to say his only purpose on earth is to provide an example of what *not* to become in life. If it wasn't for his father, he'd be cleaning gutters or washing people's armpits or something."

"You're singing to the choir, girl." Juliette absently picked up one of the candles on a small round table. The jar was a blue glazed ceramic with shimmering flecks scattered throughout and when she brought the candle to her nose, the scent of leather, paper, amber and cedar filled her nostrils. It smelled like an old library. Flipping it over to check the name, she smiled when she saw it was called Bibliophile. Nailed it. "I came over in case you'd heard anything that might point to who killed Maurice, but if you didn't even know he was dead . . ."

"It's usually someone close to the victim, isn't it? We all think of murderers as anonymous evil villains who stalk people in the night, but in reality only about 10 percent of murders occur where the victim didn't know their killer," Alexa said. Juliette raised an eyebrow. "I heard it on a podcast once. Chances are there's a murderer walking around town right now, and Maurice might have called them family or friend. At the very least, they were an acquaintance."

"That's comforting . . . not." Juliette frowned and looked down at Digger. The dog met her gaze.

*We both know who's likely to kill us . . . Marshmallow.*

At that moment, a darkly dressed figure darted into the store. It was Norah. It looked like she'd been . . . running.

"The apocalypse is finally here," Alexa quipped, nudging Juliette. "Norah has been exercising."

Norah's hatred of physical movement could be traced back to high school when their father forced her to join the track team in an effort to get her off the couch and away from her PlayStation. The plan had backfired, however, when Norah got dropped from the team for moonwalking across the finish line in last place as a form of protest.

"Rude." Norah flipped her off. "Aside from that, I come with news!"

"You heard from Bonnie?" That would be one major thing off her "things to worry about" list.

"Uh no, not that kinda news." She frowned and rubbed a hand along her jaw, showing off chipped holographic nail polish. "You *still* haven't heard from her?"

Juliette shook her head. "Not a single reply to any of my texts."

"Weird. She hasn't responded to me, either," Alexa chimed in, continuing to unpack her box of candles. The next batch were in smaller, squat jars with a rich black glaze. "I'd made her a custom scent a while ago and she loved it so much she asked for a whole batch. I offered to bring them by the house while Norah was house-sitting but she never got back to me."

The three women stood in silence for a moment. Something was wrong. Bonnie might be older, but she could blow up a group chat with the best of them. What Juliette would give now to see Bonnie's name pop up on her phone's screen.

"What if something's happened?" Juliette worried her bottom lip between her teeth. "Maybe we could find out the name of the cruise ship she's on and see if there's a way to contact them. Bonnie probably has brochures for the cruise at her house or a note in her personal diary or something."

"I'm sure she's fine," Norah said, with a much less convincing tone than the last time she'd spoken those words. "I thought you might want to know what I heard at work. It's about the murder."

Juliette's eyes widened. "Tell me."

"One of the ladies I work with, Patrizia, used to clean Maurice's house," she said. Norah juggled two jobs—working as a delivery driver and general gofer for the local florist during the day, and cleaning offices at night. But the company also did residential cleaning services, too. "She was fired recently. He accused her of stealing and they had a huge fight about it. Apparently the police were called, but there was no evidence of theft so they didn't follow it up. She was spitting mad when it came up at work and said, quote, 'I'm happy that fucker is dead.'"

That must be the cleaner Serenity had told them about!

"Any idea what she supposedly stole?" Juliette asked.

"A vinyl record." Norah shrugged. "No idea why anyone

would want that when they could take one of his expensive watches or designer shoes or something. Surely those things would be worth more."

"Depends on what vinyl it was," Alexa chimed in. "As far as collectibles go, it could easily be something of value."

Alexa would know—apart from making candles her hobbies included scouring flea markets and thrift shops for discarded treasures and collecting things from bygone eras. She had a vinyl player of her own and quite the record collection.

"Did you know the most expensive record ever sold was a one-of-a-kind recording by Wu-Tang Clan that went for over two million dollars in 2015?" Alexa added, her light eyes sparkling like they always did whenever she shared a random fact from one of her internet rabbit holes.

"Why do you know this stuff?" Norah asked, shaking her head.

"Beats me." Alexa shrugged. "Do you think I can remember the password to my online banking? Not a chance. But I can tell you Napoleon Bonaparte was once attacked by a swarm of rabbits."

The twins exchanged an amused glance. There was a reason Alexa was the undisputed trivia night queen of Labrador Falls.

"Well, Wu-Tang Clan and angry bunnies aside, Patrizia says she didn't steal anything. But apparently Maurice had been spreading the word that she couldn't be trusted, and suddenly other clients began requesting a different cleaner. Since then, she's been getting less shifts and that's got to be hard financially."

"Sounds like motive to me." Juliette mentally added Patrizia to her interview list.

"See," Alexa said with a wise nod. "Ninety percent of the time a murder victim knows their killer."

All three women glanced out the front window at the street, where several people walked by. The day was crisp and sunny, and if you didn't know a murder had recently taken place, it would look like any other small town. But there *was* a murderer walking around the streets of Labrador Falls.

And it could be anyone.

**BREWED AWAKENING ALWAYS** hit a bit of a lull around 4:30 p.m. Second to the quiet time before opening, it was Joel's favorite part of the day because he could slow down and enjoy the peaceful air of the near-empty café, where his "usuals" sparsely dotted the tables. The kind of people where the whole order could be little more than a series of grunts and nods, and both he and the customer left the exchange completely confident in what had been communicated. If not for them, he'd probably change the hours of the café to close earlier, since there wasn't much money to be made at this time of day in the colder weather. Summer was a different story, mind you. But once October hit, Labrador Falls definitely became a little sleepier . . . much to his liking.

He was wiping down the counter and loading a tray of cups and plates into the dishwasher, when the front door swung open. He'd half expected it to be Juliette, with the next stages of her Reddit-approved "how to solve a murder" plan.

Only it wasn't.

Detective Shane Dooley walked into Brewed Awakening wearing full uniform blues. Odd. Most detectives Joel had met wore business casual—usually slacks and a shirt, with a jacket over the top on the rare occasion it got cold in Southern California. But maybe things were different around here.

Or maybe Shane Dooley didn't want anyone mistaking him for a regular citizen.

With the uniform came respect. And assumptions. Joel knew that for a fact.

"Detective." Joel nodded as he approached. "What can I get for you?"

The detective was *not* a regular. In fact, Joel wasn't sure he'd ever been into the café before today.

"Triple shot no foam cappuccino," he replied. Guy liked his caffeine. He also didn't understand what a cappuccino was. "Extra hot, with a dash of milk. No more than 1.5 tablespoons."

Joel blinked.

"A quarter pump of vanilla syrup," he continued.

Joel opened his mouth to reply but the detective cut him off.

"—stirred clockwise three times, no more." He pulled out his wallet. "If you stir it counterclockwise it upsets my stomach."

Okay, Joel had to take it back. The frappuccino groupies with their extra syrup, extra whip and caramel drizzle were not the most ridiculous coffee drinkers. This guy was.

By a country mile and then some.

Joel punched in the cost for three espresso shots and charged the detective. "Why don't you take a seat and I'll bring it out?"

"Works for me." Detective Dooley found a table while Joel made his drink.

He did not measure the milk. He did not add any syrup. Instead, he added the smallest dash of regular sugar just so there was some sweetness. And, out of spite, he stirred the milk counterclockwise.

As he took the coffee to the detective's table, Joel noted that the café had suddenly become vacant. The three regulars who'd been sitting and either reading or working while they had their coffees, had all left. Usually at least one of them lingered until it was time for him to close up for the day. It was almost like a bad smell had wafted into Brewed Awakening, forcing everyone outside.

"Here you go." Joel placed the coffee cup in front of the detective, who held it up to his nose and sniffed before taking a sip.

"Ah, that's good stuff. Is your vanilla syrup organic?" he asked with a completely straight face. The guy had unnervingly pale blue eyes that lanced right through Joel.

"Yeah, I make it myself. It's not on the regular menu, so don't tell anyone," he lied. How could the guy have such a specific—*ridiculous*—coffee order and yet have no idea what he was drinking?

"So you make exceptions for a man of the law? I respect that." Detective Dooley nodded. "We protectors have to stick together, right?"

Joel froze. "Excuse me?"

"Protectors. Emergency workers. Keepers of peace and safety." The detective took another sip of his coffee. Joel stood rooted to the spot, a strange numb feeling filtering through him. "You were a firefighter, right? Wanted to work your way up to fire captain, maybe become a battalion chief one day."

How could he possibly know that? Joel hadn't told a *soul* where he'd really come from or what he'd been doing before he moved to Labrador Falls. He didn't want his past following him. Didn't want anyone knowing his secret shame, his pain or anything personal like that.

"Don't look so shocked—I check up on everyone who moves here," Detective Dooley said, interlacing his sausage fingers and placing his hands on the edge of the table. "This is my hometown and I take my responsibilities very seriously. We can't have bad folks poisoning the well. I wouldn't stand for it."

"Of course not," Joel replied stiffly. If Detective Dooley knew that he'd been a firefighter, then what *else* did he know?

*The smoke was a thick, shifting wall. Pressing in. Suffocating. Changing the landscape with every step. He breathed in and out through his mouthpiece, putting every ounce of his training to use. He must stay calm. Heat bored through his suit, trying to disintegrate him, and flames shimmered beyond the smoke. They grew brighter. Consuming. Hungry. An orange void of annihilation.*

"Seems you had a rough time before you moved, what with almost not making it out of that fire," he said.

*Joel surged forward, holding the line, stepping deliberately. Two people were trapped in the old home—the grandmother and one of the children. They were in the back room and the older woman had a mobility issue. He and his partner had one shot to get these people out alive. The child screamed for help, raw terror engulfed by the sound of shattering glass.*

"Guess you were the lucky one, in the end. Your poor squad-mate . . . not so much," the detective said. "No wonder you wanted to move all the way across the country."

*He burst into the room where the woman and child were supposed to be, but there was so much smoke he couldn't see them. Flames licked up the side of the wall, curling against the roof. There was a bed, the head of it scorched to cinders. Another scream. Yes! They were still alive. Joel searched, hands reaching. He found them. He grabbed the child, his partner took the grandmother. They were getting out. They were going to save them.*

*But then there was an almighty crack overhead.*

"Must have been hard to stay in the place where everybody knew what happened. I bet they looked at you differently after that," the detective continued, his pale blue eyes unwavering. The coffee sat half-consumed in front of him. "Must be why you haven't told anybody about it. Can't say I blame you. They did an investigation, right? To see if you were responsible for his death."

Joel's fists balled up by his sides. If the man sitting in front of him wasn't A, a police officer and B, the kind of guy who seemed like he'd do *anything*—no matter how unethical—to get what he wanted, Joel would have decked him. Any feelings he'd had of anonymity here in Labrador Falls were gone. Shattered. Burned to ash.

Someone knew who he was and what he'd done.

Clearly the detective had been sitting on this information for a while, since Joel had been living in Labrador Falls for just over a year. It seemed far too much of a coincidence that he was bringing it up now when Joel had agreed to look out for Juliette while she investigated Maurice's murder. A murder which, if she was right, he planned to use to further his career.

"Don't worry, I won't tell anyone." Detective Dooley winked. Then he grabbed his coffee cup and drained the remaining contents in one long gulp. "Not unless you give me reason to."

The real message was: not unless you get in my way.

"He wasn't just your colleague, though, was he?" Dooley stood and smoothed his hands over his uniform to ease the creases away. "He was more than that."

Joel didn't dare open his mouth. Instead, he ground his back teeth together, as if pulverizing everything he wanted to say into dust.

"Let's keep that between us, shall we?" Detective Dooley nodded, a cheery smile not even making it halfway to his emotionless pale blue eyes. "Oh, and I'm going to need to interview your staff. It's just April, right? I'll be back for her."

Then he left Joel standing there, his whole world rocked. Everything that he'd worked toward—finding a place to settle for a while where his past couldn't touch him—was gone.

## *Chapter Nine*

**JULIETTE WATCHED FROM** her position sitting on the edge of the fountain as Shane Dooley came out of Brewed Awakening, looking rather satisfied with himself. That wasn't an unusual occurrence. Shane almost always looked like that. But the real question was, *why* would he be looking like that after talking with Joel? Far as she was concerned, Shane had never set foot in the café before because he was doggedly loyal to Wandering Bean Co, the coffee truck at the dog park.

There must be a specific reason he went to Brewed Awakening.

Out of instinct, she raised her book to hide her face so he didn't catch her looking and gave it a good minute before she peered over the top again. A little thrill ran through her. As stressful as it was to be a murder suspect, this *was* the most excitement she'd had in a long time. Life had been kind of boring up until this point. She worked at the grooming salon, fostered dogs, hung out with Norah and Alexa, helped Bonnie around her house and . . .

Well, there was no "and." That was it.

*Not unless you count the fictional boyfriends.*

She was thirty-one years old, with no dating life to speak of, no real hobbies other than reading, and no exciting travel plans or anything else on the horizon. Even her dreams were filed down to be reasonable and moderate and not to risk failure.

*Dreams? What dreams?*

God, that was a sad state of affairs, wasn't it? After this whole murder thing was over, she would do something about it. Still, she had *a lot* to be grateful for! She was healthy, she had her twin sister and her best friend to keep her company, and she was doing good in the world by helping care for animals who had been abandoned. That counted for something, right?

Juliette waited until the detective disappeared out of sight, and then she hurried over to Brewed Awakening. After dropping Digger off with Norah and Marshmallow for a little playdate, she had plans to continue her sleuthing this evening . . . by taking a Pilates class. She wanted a chance to talk to Kacey Greenwood, the owner of the puppy training school, Right Paw Forward. Serenity had mentioned that Kacey took her classes on Wednesday nights, so that would be the perfect chance to "bump into her" and have a chat without it looking too suspicious.

And she fully intended for Joel to come with her. Partly for protection—because your chances of being murdered in a Pilates studio were low, but not zero. And partly because she really would not mind seeing Joel in a pair of workout shorts.

Strangely, the sign on Brewed Awakening's front door had been flipped to Closed even though Joel usually kept the place open another half hour. Sometimes longer. She tried the door and it was locked. Surely the Closed sign didn't apply to her! Juliette knocked several times, fast so he knew it was important. A second later, Joel appeared from the back area of the café, a strange, haunted look on his face just like the morning of the murder, when she'd come through the town square before dawn and seen him sitting here with that letter.

Something was going on with him.

Joel pulled the door open and Juliette stepped past him without waiting for an invitation.

"The sign isn't a suggestion," he grumbled. "We're closed."

"Brewed Awakening might be closed," she replied cheerfully. "But Joel's Sleuthing Adventures is not."

He closed the door again and flicked the lock, before scrubbing a hand over his face. He was wearing his usual uniform of faded 501s and either a soft cotton shirt or a chunky sweater—today in a dark forest green, which really suited him—and his hair was extra mussed. She fought the urge to reach out and smooth an errant hair back into place, but her fingers tingled with the need to touch him.

How did he make jeans and a sweater look so darn good?

"I regret ever agreeing to this," he said. "I should have let you get murdered."

"You know what they say, better to regret the things you've done than the things you haven't. Wise words." She smiled and that only made him frown further. "Now, you have a mission tonight, if you choose to accept it. And you will, because you previously agreed to accompany me and it would be bad karma to go back on a social contract."

"I don't care about karma."

"We're going to talk to Kacey Greenwood about how Maurice was telling everyone that her puppy training academy was a scam. No big deal." She lifted one shoulder in what she hoped was a nonchalant shrug.

Joel immediately narrowed his eyes at her. "Why did you add 'no big deal' to the end? What are you not telling me?"

"Nothing."

"Juliette."

The way he said her name, bristling with delicious grumpy Joel energy, took that tingly feeling in her fingertips and flooded it all through her body. It was like fairy dust. Magic. It made her suddenly alert and on edge in the best way possible. She hadn't felt like this in . . . had she ever felt like this? The sad few dates she'd had with men who could look past her family's reputation never made her feel like that. Probably because they were only looking for one thing anyway and were trying to rush through the date in the hopes she'd come home with them. She very rarely did.

Okay, like only one time.

But this man was different. He was . . . more.

"I thought the best approach would be to 'bump into' Kacey somewhere she'd already be, instead of cornering her at work. I'm hoping that will mean she's more relaxed, more likely to talk."

His eyes narrowed further. "Bump into her *where*?"

"Well, Serenity mentioned that Kacey takes her Wednesday night Pilates class—"

"No."

"But—"

"Absolutely not." He shook his head.

"Oh come *on*. You're not afraid of a few women in leggings and sticky socks, are you?" she cajoled. "It'll be fun."

"I think your idea of fun and my idea of fun might differ slightly." His tone was dry, but she would swear there was the slightest hint of amusement hiding underneath. Or was that just her ego begging not to be bruised?

"I thought all straight men liked the idea of a roomful of women bent in half."

"I'm more of a one-woman-bent-in-half kind of guy."

Oh *boy*. Juliette let out a surprised laugh, which was really a cover for the fact that her cheeks were now hot enough to sizzle an egg and her brain was currently showing a slideshow of every dirty fantasy she'd ever had, like her libido was glitching from the first drop of attention it had received in far too long.

Now she *really* wanted to see Joel in a pair of workout shorts.

"Cat got your tongue?" he asked, after a longer-than-usual pause from Juliette. "I don't think I've ever seen you be quiet for more than a whole second before. Should I call 911?"

Juliette smiled sweetly. "I was wondering if the reason you don't want to come to this class is because you're worried you won't be able to keep up?"

Joel bristled, and Juliette wanted to punch a fist into the air. Got him!

"I can keep up with a silly yoga class," he scoffed, folding two muscular arms over his chest. Oh yes, he could. But she wasn't going to acknowledge that.

"It's Pilates, not yoga. And it's quite challenging. I mean, you need good coordination, upper body strength, core strength. I wouldn't blame you if you were feeling a little self-conscious and—"

"I can do it, no problem," he said.

"Great! I'll see you there at 8 p.m.," Juliette said, barely able to contain her grin as she turned on her heel and walked out of Brewed Awakening before Joel had the chance to back out.

**UNDERESTIMATING JULIETTE WAS** a mistake.

She'd waltzed right into his café with a goal, and he'd fallen for her bait, hook, line and sunshine sinker. Now here he was, standing outside the ridiculously named wellness center—Live, Love, Labrador. The name was so on the nose he was sure there couldn't be an ounce of irony in it. They even had a chalkboard sign out front that said "You have to look through the rain to see the rainbow" drawn in colorful chalk, with a little rainbow capped by two clouds for good measure.

Joel *hated* this kind of shit. The type of meaningless, asinine quotes that drop shippers ripped off from someone's Instagram page and printed on cheap T-shirts, charging as if they were custom designed. The quotes offered little value to someone struggling—hollow sentiments that let someone tick a checkbox to say they'd offered a kind word.

He would bet money there were more useless quotes hanging on the walls inside.

*So go home. If Juliette thinks she can get information out of Kacey, then let her. She's not in any real danger here. You can go home and have dinner and . . . go to bed.*

Jeez. He'd really become a boring old asshole these past few years, hadn't he? At one point in his life, this kind of thing would have been fun. A chance to show off in front of someone he found attractive. A chance to stretch himself by trying something new. Old Joel never cared about making a fool of himself—he was the goofy guy, always ready to give it a go.

He'd turned into a stodgy old man *well* before his time.

"Joel! You came." It was Juliette.

She bounded up to him, long dark hair in the kind of ponytail that was so perky and swish-y it looked like it belonged on a cartoon character. Her body, however, was real, real, *real.* At work she dressed for practicality, but now she wore a pair of light blue leggings that showed off her long legs, a pink jacket with fuzzy sherpa lining and a thick knitted headband keeping her ears warm.

She looked fucking adorable and he hated it. Because now his "I'm more of a one-woman-bent-in-half kind of guy" comment was going to come back to haunt him when she was the one bent in half. He was going to end up with a mental image that would take a long damn time to disappear.

"I thought you were going to bail," she added.

"A promise is a promise."

The words stirred something inside him.

*A promise is a promise.* They were whispered beneath a bed sheet, lips grazing lips, hands and bodies entwined. *Take care of Chase, okay? For me. I don't want anything bad to happen to him.*

Joel slammed the memory right to the back of his mind where it belonged.

"I thought it was because I insulted your manhood by implying you couldn't keep up." She grinned. How had he never noticed how sparkly and perfect her teeth were? Maybe it was because he usually avoided eye contact, trying to look anywhere but at her when she came into his café.

"I'm very confident in my manhood." His gaze flicked over her face, catching all of the little details he'd tried so hard not to notice before. The tiny mole above her eyebrow, the dimple in her cheek when she smiled, the way her eyes weren't just dark brown, but had shades of burnished gold and red in them as well. "As you'll find out."

Now, why did he go and say that? "You'll find out" implied future time spent together, future interactions. Beyond making sure the damn woman didn't get herself murdered, there was no future anything between them. He didn't want to make friends with her. He didn't want them to be buddies or to say hello in the street or to "pop in" to see one another. This was an obligation made in a moment of weakness that Joel felt bound to uphold because . . .

Well, because maybe there was a hint of the old Joel still alive inside him.

But the second he was done and there was no longer a threat to her safety, he was out.

Juliette looked a little pink in the cheeks. Or maybe it was just the cold. She wrapped her arms around herself and said, "Let's go inside and see if we can find Kacey."

Live Love Labrador was exactly what Joel expected.

Almost everything was painted a soft white—probably one of those shades with a stupid name like Your Grandma's Old Lacy Doily or something like that. The back wall, however, was mint green with palm leaves curling up the sides. In the center, neon lights spelled out the words, *Love like you've never been hurt.*

What a stupid fucking phrase.

Because anyone who'd actually been hurt knew that wasn't possible, and someone who hadn't been hurt yet was still living in ignorant bliss.

Green velvet couches lined one wall, capped by two large white shelves that displayed some of the crap they were selling. He spotted water bottles with crystals in the bottom, jars of powder that probably claimed to have magical powers, and candles that had "no bad vibes" printed on the label.

If God judged Joel to be a bad person when he died, he'd probably end up here, sentenced to an eternity of listening to empty motivational quotes and people telling him he needed to heal his chakras.

"I hate it already," he muttered, taking off his shoes and placing them on one of the provided trays. Juliette didn't seem to hear him. She was busy looking around to see if their mark was here while she took off her own shoes.

He was distracted watching her long, vaguely hypnotizing ribbon of a ponytail, which was how he didn't notice that Serenity was almost upon him.

"Joel!" she squealed, grabbing his arm. "I'm so glad you're here."

Her blond pixie cut was slicked back, and she was wearing a matching workout set of leggings and a crop top in pastel yellow. She had the kind of tan that could only have come from a bottle at this time of year, and her eyelashes had a distinctly spidery appearance. He knew some women stuck those fringe things on their eyes to make their lashes look bigger but, frankly, he thought it made them look like those creepy dolls his sisters had found in the attic when they were kids.

"Come, come. Let's get your machine set up."

He didn't have the chance to call for help before she dragged him from the waiting area into the studio. The room was filled with machines that looked almost like small beds, except they were carriages that moved along the length of the frame. At one end a series of springs were hooked to the carriage and there was a bar at a slight angle. At the other end of the carriage were little stumps and some straps looped onto hooks.

"You sit right here." She pointed to one of the machines and Joel sat, because arguing seemed pointless. He tried to catch Juliette's attention, but he couldn't see her through the door. "Now, lay down. I'm going to adjust your bar."

A simple command like lying down should have been easy, but getting into the machine with his shoulders up against the little stumpy things felt like trying to climb into a box sized for a cat. Usually his long limbs were a plus—he could grab things off any shelf and he could stare over everyone's heads in a crowd—but here it felt like a hindrance. Serenity grabbed the bar at Joel's feet and lifted it so it made a *clank* before sliding it into a position that granted him a little extra room.

But it still felt like he was being squeezed into a sardine can.

"How's that?" She braced both hands on the bar and leaned over it, staring down at him and giving him an eyeful of her boobs.

"Fine." He struggled back up to a sitting position to get some distance from her. Out of the corner of his eye, he saw Juliette standing in the doorway, watching. She had a pinched expression on her face, though whether she was annoyed, distracted or amused it was hard to tell.

"You know, I offer *private* classes as well." Serenity sat on the machine's carriage next to him, her hip touching his. "You can have my full attention for the whole hour."

She was talking in a low, breathy voice that made it sound like she was auditioning for a phone sex hotline or one of those late-night ads promising to hook you up with horny singles in your area.

"It's great if you have any, like, *kinks* to work out," she added, staring up at him with creepy doll eyelashes. "I can help you with that. We can work on your alignment and mobility, too. Flexibility is my specialty. I'll have you in any position you want, no problem."

"I uh . . . I'm good. Thanks." He cleared his throat.

More people poured into the classroom, and Juliette came over to grab the machine next to him, her eyes studiously avoiding both him and Serenity as she slipped out of her jacket. Underneath she wore a T-shirt that said, "I'm Just Here for Feet in Straps."

"Cute T-shirt," Serenity said. "Feet in straps is my favorite, too. Nothing better than being on your back with your legs in the air, am I right?"

She gave Joel's thigh a squeeze and then stood, heading off to assist some other students with setting up their machines before the class started.

Juliette looked at him with a raised eyebrow. "Having fun already?"

"You dragged me here," he grumbled. "Not my fault that girl couldn't read the room if her life depended on it."

"Ah yes, you're so hot and sexually magnetic that everyone who comes near you has to hit on you. What a hard life it must be."

Despite his discomfort at being dragged to this hellhole of a workout studio, Joel found himself amused. "You think I'm hot and sexually magnetic?"

"No! I mean that's what *you* were thinking." She whirled around and pretended to fiddle with the straps on her machine. Unfortunately, that gave him a prime view of her backside, which she must have realized. Because she stood ramrod straight and folded her arms across her chest, unsure of what to do with herself. "Obviously."

"Ah yes, there's nothing better than a hot cup of coffee first thing in the morning while I watch the sun rise and think about how attractive I am," he replied drily. "It's a very satisfying life."

Juliette tried to conceal a laugh but it came out as a cute little snort. Joel couldn't help himself. The urge to grin was so strong this time *he* was the one to turn away and fiddle with the machine.

*Do you really think she'd be here wanting your help if she knew what you'd done? What you are?*

That was a sobering enough thought that it wiped the smile right off Joel's face.

"Anyway, it looks like Kacey isn't here," Juliette said as she plonked herself onto her machine, shoulders slumped.

"You're kidding." He'd come here for nothing. Was someone up there punishing him for dodging the lawyer's calls?

"You can go. I paid for your class, but you don't have to—" Her words stopped abruptly as a woman walked through the door, just as Serenity was clapping her hands to start the class. "That's her."

Kacey was short, but built like she'd spent her life hauling logs. Broad shoulders, strong legs. A tank top showed off biceps that made Joel nod his head in respect, and she had tattoos scattered across her arms and legs below the hem of her fitted shorts. What had Serenity said about her?

*I wouldn't mess with her . . . she's strong. Stronger than most men*

She definitely looked like she could take Maurice in a fight.

"Tonight wasn't a waste of time after all," Juliette whispered as Kacey took the last remaining Pilates machine. "We'll talk to her after class."

But first, he had to get through the next hour in one piece.

Joel looked around the room filled with women who seemed to know exactly what they were doing with all the straps, balls and contraptions provided for the class. He'd never felt more out of place in his life.

# *Chapter Ten*

**"OKAY, CLASS," SERENITY** said from the front of the room. "We're going to finish with everyone's favorite—feet in straps. Switch to two red springs, then lay down on your back and put your feet into the long loops. Float your feet up to the air like they're two butterflies, but please keep your tail bone touching the carriage."

Thank goodness. A light sheen of sweat slicked across Juliette's forehead as she pushed off the foot bar with her left foot while lifting her right one to hook a loop over it. Then she pressed into the loop to create tension while she lassoed her left foot. She could only hope there weren't any obvious or embarrassing dark patches on her light blue leggings—which she had stupidly chosen for maximum cuteness instead of sweat concealment.

Her only saving grace was that Joel appeared to be fully distracted by his own Pilates struggles.

She watched out of the corner of her eye as he attempted to hook the loops over his feet, looking rather like a bug that had been overturned against its will. Although the joke was on her, because her eyes went from noticing the funny "overturned bug" position, to how his arms and thighs flexed as he tried to get into said position. *Damn.* Juliette was suddenly sure she'd never seen him in a T-shirt before, because he often wore soft-looking plaid or denim shirts with the sleeves rolled up.

What a crime to hide those biceps away.

"Don't you dare laugh," he grumbled, as he tried to get his first foot into the loop. "I've got tight hamstrings."

"I'm not laughing," Juliette lied, stifling a giggle with her hand.

"You *are*. Why couldn't we have gone to see Kacey at her work?" He was keeping his voice low, almost like he was grouching to himself. "Stupid idea."

"Well, since you gave me a whole spiel about hating dogs, I thought you might find this preferable," she replied, feeling more than a little smug.

Joel's eyes flicked over to her and narrowed, but then he finally managed to get the loop on his foot. Now, unfortunately, he was at the mercy of the straps until he could get his second foot in.

"Float your legs up and down, keeping your thighs together like two lovers kissing," Serenity said, as she walked between the rows of reformer machines. Everyone in the class moved in perfect unison.

Everyone except for one person.

"Oh for fuck's sake," Joel muttered under his breath as he almost tipped onto his side, and Juliette clamped her lips shut to hold a laugh in.

"Your legs are strong but weightless. You are the ocean, undulating and tumultuous. Move like the ocean, class. But keep those thighs together!"

"What is she even saying?" Joel groused, still trying to get his second foot into the loop. Serenity must have noticed he was struggling because she came over to help him, taking far too long and touching his calves far too much.

"Up and down, up and down. Now we draw circles with the legs—take your feet up and then sweep them out to the sides. We want big circles. Paint with your feet. Your feet are the brushes of the universe!"

Joel was still figuring how to get his legs up and down, but that didn't stop him turning to look at Juliette with a murderous glance. She'd have to buy a lot of cinnamon rolls to pay him back for this.

And they didn't even know if Kacey would speak to them yet. She wasn't exactly known for having a friendly demeanor. In fact, she was a bit like a female version of Joel and didn't mince words when she had something to say. One of Juliette's grooming clients had left a puppy class in tears when Kacey had told her off for looking at her phone, saying she needed to work on her attention span if she wanted any chance of getting her dog to behave itself.

"Now reverse the direction, circle up and in. Caress the air with your feet like you want to seduce it. Make it yours."

Juliette rolled her eyes as she did her leg circles. Pilates was not a new activity for her, as she tried to come to the studio a couple times a month to work out the tightness in her muscles from long days in the grooming salon. But she'd never taken one of Serenity's classes before. And she likely never would again. All this talk about stroking and loving the air? Ick. Give her the instructor who was a former professional ballerina, who would make you cry when she lost count during the hundreds.

"Okay, everyone, let's finish with a stretch. Bring your feet up and put some tension on the ropes with your hands to deepen the pull on your hamstrings. Then open your legs wide and stretch out those inner thighs. Don't be shy! Let it all air out."

Joel was already trying to disentangle himself from the straps, looking like a fly desperately trying to escape a spider's web. His dirty blond hair was mussed, and when he finally freed himself, he raked it back away from his face. Juliette finished her stretch and carefully got her feet out of the loops and brought the carriage in slowly and safely to the stopper.

"What kind of fresh hell was that?" he asked as Serenity announced the class was over and that everyone should wipe down their machines with the disinfectant spray and microfiber cloths provided. "It's yoga meets bondage."

"I'm going to put that in the suggestion box," Juliette replied with a chuckle as she wiped her machine down. "Don't call it Pilates. Call it 'bondage yoga' instead. *Way* better marketing strategy."

After they finished cleaning the machines, they made a quick exit to the reception area so the next class could enter. As luck would have it, Kacey walked out and took a seat next to Joel.

"Hi, Kacey," Juliette said, balancing on one foot to peel off her grippy sock and replace it with a thicker, warmer one. "Tough class, huh?"

"Tough for some," she replied, looking toward Joel with a raised eyebrow and a slight tilt at the corner of her mouth. "First time?"

"Was it that obvious?" he drawled, leaning forward to change his own socks and wincing a little.

Kacey chuckled but it wasn't unkind. Up close, it was easy to see that her tattoos were a source of pride, as she had decorated a good part of her body with them. There was a butterfly with a torn wing, a broken chain wrapped around one forearm, and a blue ribbon with the name "Mary" written inside. Some seemed more expertly drawn than others.

She stuffed her feet into a pair of heavy-duty lace-up boots, the kind that might have steel toes. Apparently she'd turned a former warehouse into her puppy academy all by herself, which was pretty darn impressive since the closest Juliette had ever come to doing a renovation was putting up some peel-and-stick wallpaper in her bedroom.

"Don't sweat it," she said. "It's different than going to the gym. The first time someone suggested I try Pilates I told them I don't like girlie shit. Meanwhile, there are seventy-year-olds coming here that could hoist me overhead without breaking a sweat."

Well, knock her sideways with a feather. This was the most she'd ever heard Kacey speak in a nonwork setting. Although she didn't really speak at the puppy academy so much as bark orders.

*Ha, bark. I see what you did there.*

"You own the café right, Brewed Awakening?" Kacey asked, nodding toward Joel.

"That's right."

"It's a good spot. I try not to drink too much caffeine these days, but I appreciate having a place to go that's not diner dish-water or pumpkin spice bullshit." She nodded in appreciation. "I like your work."

Joel perked up and looked at Juliette, chest puffed out as if to say, *See? She agrees with me on the pumpkin spice bullshit.*

"Wild about Maurice Allsop, right?" Juliette interjected. Hopefully it sounded like a natural segue. But judging by the eye roll Joel gave, it probably didn't. Wouldn't be the first time she was accused of being subtle as a brick. Nor the last. "You know, with him getting murdered."

Kacey seemed to still and she didn't make eye contact with Juliette. "Yeah, wild."

Maybe they'd get more of a response if Joel asked the questions, since Kacey seemed to have taken a liking to him.

*Like every other woman in this town.*

Juliette looked at him, making a slight movement with her

head. Joel stared back blankly. Why were men always so terrible at nonverbal communication? Some of them couldn't take a cue if a butler served it to them on a silver platter.

"I heard he was hassling you about the puppy school." Juliette changed to her other foot to swap her sock before stuffing both feet into a pair of short rain boots. "Must be a relief not to have to deal with that anymore."

"I heard you had an argument with him the night before he was murdered," Kacey replied evenly. There was something guarded in her body language. "You know what gossip is like around here."

Shit.

When Kacey ducked her head to lace up her boots, Juliette looked at Joel again, nodding in Kacey's direction and making a talking motion with her hand for good measure. He frowned and didn't say anything. Not one to be deterred, Juliette nodded to Kacey again and he sighed silently.

"Lesser men make trouble with anyone they see as better than them," he said. "He was probably threatened by you."

It must have been the right thing to say, because Kacey's defensive demeanor immediately softened.

"He damn well should have been," she replied, yanking on the laces of her boots to tighten them. "I told him that if he got up in my face one more time, I'd make *his* face look like a pepperoni pizza."

An admission that Kacey had threatened bodily harm! Pepperoni pizza face didn't come from a single slap, now did it? She was talking about something worse than that. Far more than what Juliette had done to Maurice, anyway. She'd only threatened to call animal services on him. Were the police looking at Kacey as well?

"Lucky for me Maurice was a wimp. He had a hissy fit and threatened to call the cops if I came near him, so I told him to keep his distance and I would do the same." She stood and brushed her hands down the front of her leggings. "Shame such a nice dog ended up with an owner like him. Brigitte deserves better."

"Could not agree more," Juliette muttered to herself, but Kacey heard and nodded in respect. "Why was he getting up in your face?"

"I shot him down. He wanted to be business partners and turn my puppy academy into a franchise, but I'm in it to help local people not to become a millionaire." Kacey hauled her bag over one shoulder and shrugged. "Some assholes can't help but take rejection personally."

With that, she lifted one hand in a half-hearted wave and headed out of Live Love Labrador. Joel looked up suddenly, as if some internal siren had gone off, and Juliette followed his line of sight to where Serenity appeared to be walking straight toward them.

"Let's go," he said, standing up and heading straight for the exit with his head bowed. "Sleuthing time is over."

Unable to contain a chuckle, Juliette followed him into the crisp night air.

**"DID YOU *HEAR*** what she said? She was going to make his face look like a pepperoni pizza!" Juliette didn't even take a second to look around and see if Kacey was out of earshot.

*This* was why Joel had agreed to keep an eye on her—because she was as subtle as a cartoon sleuth dressed as a bush wearing a hat and a fake mustache. It was a miracle the woman hadn't gotten herself murdered already.

"You might want to wait until we're alone before you start your interview debrief." He glanced sidelong at her. Her dark ponytail fluttered out behind her like a gymnast's ribbon and her fair skin was dotted with pink where the cold touched her cheeks. But it was her eyes that got him—the hopeful, excited sparkle. She really thought she was going to beat the police at their own game. "Come on, let's go into the café."

They crossed the town square, which was shrouded in darkness now that the sun had set, every door shuttered for the day. There were a few lights illuminating the statue of the man and his dog atop the fountain—some important historical figure for the town—but Joel averted his eyes as he went past like always.

"I've always thought the square was quite romantic after dark," Juliette mused as they walked. There was a spring to her step. "I love the way the lights reflect off the water in the fountain. You could sit here and drink hot cocoa with your mittens on and it would look like a scene in a movie."

"Is your brain permanently wired to see the world through a Hallmark lens? Life isn't a movie."

"Oh I know. If it was, I'd be in my sequel era by now," she said, as though that made any sense at all. Joel must have looked suitably confused because she added, "You know, where I've already found the love of my life and we've got a home and a dog, and now we're facing the next plot twist together."

"Those movies don't have plot twists," he scoffed.

"Yes, they do." She frowned.

"Boy meets girl, boy does something dumb, boy grovels and girl makes the idiotic move of forgiving him. The end. There's not an ounce of surprise. Nor reality. Because if it were real, the happily ever after would last five minutes and the movie would end with boy and girl realizing that being alone is *way* easier and they would split their shit in half and go their separate ways."

Juliette gasped and pressed a hand to her chest like he'd told her that he liked to kick puppies in his spare time. "Your cynicism is borderline horrific."

"It's realism, not cynicism," he corrected. Okay, so maybe he was dialing it up a little. But it served a purpose—it ensured Juliette wouldn't see him as a project. A fixer-upper. Someone she could paint with a rose-colored brush and turn into the hero of her movie-worthy dreams.

Joel wasn't going to change. Not for anybody.

"Disagree. People live happily ever after all the time."

"Oh yeah, like who? Your parents?" He regretted the words the second they came out of his mouth, because the sparkle in her eyes dimmed. He knew nothing about her parents, but clearly happily ever after wasn't exactly the label she would apply.

"They've had a hard life." She folded her arms across her chest.

"Who do you know that has a movie-worthy happily ever after?"

She opened her mouth to answer, then closed it. Her eyes flicked to the side like she was thumbing through files in a filing cabinet. She opened her mouth again, then closed it once more. Open, close. Open, wrinkle nose, close.

He'd officially broken her.

"See?" he said, pulling his keys out of his pocket as they approached Brewed Awakening. "People like those movies because they idealize what most *don't* have. There's not much difference between happily ever afters and Middle Earth."

He pushed open the door and held it for her to go first. He might be a cynic, but he wasn't an asshole . . . most of the time.

She set her bag and jacket down on one of the chairs and turned to look at him. "Your parents weren't happy?"

The question hit him so much harder than her softly spoken words should have, and memories rushed up from the depths of his mind with stunning, dizzying clarity.

His mother dancing in their run-down pistachio-colored kitchen, coaxing a smile from his ever-serious father. Her brown hair a wild cloud of curls, skirt sweeping the floor, earrings jangling like chimes. And his father—hair close-cropped, haunted eyes softening just for her—stared with wonder, like he'd found a precious treasure and couldn't work out how he'd been so lucky. Joel could practically hear the music, something bohemian, blaring from the radio as she sang at the top of her lungs, charmingly and joyously out of tune. She'd turn his father's eyes smoky as she leaned in for a kiss and they held one another like they were clinging on for life.

His parents were the very definition of happy.

"My father died when I was young," he replied, swallowing against the lump in his throat. "He was a good man."

"Oh I'm so sorry." She bit down on her lower lip. "That must have been hard."

Watching his mother wither like a plant without water? Watching her stop listening to music, stop dancing, stop putting on her jangling jewelry? Watching her turn to stone with each day that passed? Yeah, it was pretty fucking hard. He'd become a pseudo father to his sisters, shielding them from their mother's ravenous grief, holding on to the idea that happily ever afters *were* possible. Trying to keep that dream alive for the girls.

Until experience showed him what a lie it was.

"That's life, isn't it?" There was something about her expression he didn't like—was it disappointment? Sadness? Pain? He shoved his hands into his pockets. "Death and taxes and stuff."

"Do you have siblings?" she asked.

"Two sisters, both trouble."

She smiled. "Older or younger?"

"Younger."

She nodded as though that was the answer she was expecting. "You've got big brother energy."

"Not the first time I've heard that."

"I'm a twin," she offered, lowering herself into one of the chairs and looking up at him, her face hopeful. She wanted him to sit with her. To keep talking. To connect. He could feel it. But he stood, awkward, not sure why he'd even suggested coming back here because the last thing he should do was open up to her. It was like his subconscious hadn't wanted the night to end.

*More like you don't want her last memory of tonight to be you making a fool of yourself in that Pilates class.*

"Are you the good twin or the evil twin?" he asked.

"The good one," she said, smiling proudly and pulling her shoulders back as though showing off a badge of honor. "And Norah would agree with me, so I don't feel too bad saying it."

Of course she was the good twin. He could imagine them—darkness and light, a bedroom split down the middle with unicorns and glitter on one side and heavy metal posters on the other. He'd seen her sister around town and she came into the café sometimes. It was freaky how similar they looked, though nobody would ever be able to mix them up. Juliette was Glinda the Good Witch, and Norah looked like the heroine of a Tim Burton film.

*What is this? A goddamn* Dr. Phil *episode? Enough with the sharing circle.*

He cleared his throat. "You can say whatever you want about Kacey now. Nobody around to hear us."

A smile tugged at the corner of her lips. "Message received. No more personal talk."

Only, he'd told her more in that moment than he'd told any other person in Labrador Falls in the whole year he'd been here. Not that she knew that. It might not seem like much to some. To many. But to him, who wanted to separate every aspect of who he was before the fire from who he was after it, it felt like he'd given her a secret key to his kingdom.

"What did you think about Kacey? Does she have the vibes of a killer?" she asked, planting her chin in her palms and sucking on her lower lip.

"Does she have the *vibes* of a killer? I don't know. Do you think the police solve murders based on someone's vibe?" he asked.

"I feel like you're mocking me." She narrowed her eyes. It was probably better not to incriminate himself, so he didn't reply. Instead, he decided to make them both a drink.

With the emptiness of the café, she could easily talk to him from where she sat, and he didn't need to ask her order—he knew it by heart. Double shot latte. Too bad there were no pastries left today. But since she always smiled when he did something fun with his latte art, he decided to make her a pretty design.

"She had an interesting collection of tattoos," Juliette mused, watching him work. "Did you notice?"

"Not really." He fitted a fresh basket into the double-shot portafilter and set it under the grinder, pulling on the tab to release the grinds. "Plenty of people have tattoos."

"Sure, but they seemed . . . sad."

He gently tapped the portafilter against the countertop to level the grounds and then tamped them down, pressing with the practiced perfect level of pressure. "How did they look sad?"

"She had this beautiful butterfly, but one of the wings was torn and then she had a chain wrapped around her arm with a broken link."

That caught Joel's attention. "Really?"

"Yeah. Why? Does it mean something?"

Joel fitted the portafilter to the espresso machine and started pulling the double shot for Juliette's latte. The machine hummed, and glossy, dark brown liquid began to pour slowly into the waiting cup below. He fetched the milk and frothing jug.

"A tattoo like that could mean anything, I guess. Symbolism is highly subjective. But I knew a guy with a tat like that years ago," Joel said, thinking back. He'd come across the man volunteering with the local youth center to help kids from troubled homes keep on the straight and narrow. Joel had coached a basketball team and this guy had been a counsellor. "He was an ex-con. Great guy, totally turned his life around after he got out. He told me the broken chain meant breaking the cycle of incarceration."

"You think Kacey might have spent time in prison?" Juliette blinked. Clearly the thought hadn't crossed her mind. Why would it? That wouldn't fit her Hallmark vision of Labrador Falls.

"Not necessarily. It just reminded me of someone I knew with a similar tattoo, but a broken chain could mean breaking *any* cycle. Might be drugs or booze. Maybe she was in an abusive relationship and she got out. It could be anything." He shrugged. "Hell, maybe she'd had a few drinks and it seemed like a good idea at the time. Tattoos don't *always* mean something."

"True." She bobbed her head.

Joel finished making the coffees and brought them over to the table. He lowered hers, eagerly waiting for her reaction as she saw the design on top. It was a double-winged swan with the head shaped like a small heart. Her eyes lit up and her mouth popped open.

"Wow! That's really good."

"I was just messing around."

*More like you've been practicing that one for weeks.*

Practicing for *her*.

“You need fuel if you’re going to catch a killer,” he said. “And one potential suspect with a possible prison tattoo does not a solution make.”

She nodded and sat back in her chair, cradling the cup in both hands. Was it his imagination or was she fighting a smile as she looked down at the swan?

Because he was fighting one, too.

# *Chapter Eleven*

**THE FOLLOWING DAY** Juliette closed What The Fluff earlier than usual. Appointments continued dwindling with rumors running high about her involvement in Maurice's murder. First, she was a professional dognapper. Then she was having an affair with Maurice. Then she was a killer for hire! Ridiculous . . . especially the last one. What kind of killer for hire would strangle a guy with a leash from her own workplace?

She wasn't a killer. And she wasn't an idiot.

Then Shane Dooley turned up at lunch time to poke around the grooming salon and ask more questions. More like make a show of embarrassing her.

He had nothing new to pin on her, but he was sniffing around all the same, almost foaming at the mouth for a fight. No way was she going to take the bait. Instead, she was polite, cooperative and let him look at everything he wanted to, even if it meant making one of her clients' appointments run late, all the while keeping a *very* close eye on the detective to ensure he didn't plant any evidence. Thankfully he hadn't come with a search warrant, so he couldn't ask her to step outside.

He found nothing, of course.

Thoroughly rattled, Juliette went to visit Norah and Marshmallow rather than heading home alone to her empty apartment. She was due to look after Marshmallow that evening when Norah went off to her cleaning job, so she had to pick up the little dictator, anyway. Digger was happy, as always, to tag along.

After letting herself into Bonnie's apartment with her own key, she found her sister and the dog in a standoff in the kitchen. Marshmallow had something in her mouth and was growling as Norah attempted to retrieve it.

"This bitch stole my damn credit card!" Norah said, throwing her hands in the air.

Indeed, the fluffy little dog had a thin plastic rectangle in her mouth and was hanging on with all her needle-toothed might.

"That's not very nice," Juliette said. "You shouldn't call her . . . Well, I guess technically she *is* a female dog and all. But still."

"Hang on, she stole my credit card and you're annoyed at *me*?" Norah folded her arms across her uniform from job number one, a pale yellow polo top with Petal Pusher's logo embroidered at the chest pocket, underscored by a trailing vine of flowers. The pastel shade made Norah's skin look even paler than usual which, by contrast, made her heavy black eyeliner verge into Ozzy Osbourne territory. RIP. "That doesn't seem fair."

"What's she going to do with it? Put you into debt ordering knickknacks on Amazon?" Juliette shot her sister a look. "How did she even get it?"

"She knocked over my purse, which was sitting on the dining table, and when everything clattered to the floor, she grabbed it."

Norah had a habit of throwing things into her purse without rhyme or reason rather than, say, putting her cards back into her wallet where they belonged.

"Don't you dare say anything about me not putting my cards away properly," Norah said, glaring in her sister's direction as if she could read Juliette's mind. "I don't want to hear it."

Digger watched with fascination. Juliette had unclipped him from his harness as they entered the house, and when he took a step toward Marshmallow, the growling resumed.

"Can't you just take it from her?" Juliette asked.

Norah gestured to Marshmallow. "If you can do it while retaining ownership of all your fingers, be my guest."

Juliette crouched and held a hand out, but Marshmallow's growling intensified. With a lot of dogs, their bark—or growl—was worse than their bite, but she knew that wasn't the case for the sassy white Pomeranian. Marshmallow wouldn't hesitate to chomp off a digit if someone got in her personal space. In fact, she'd seen the dog lunge at people's ankles on several occasions when they'd done nothing more than dare to stand where Marshmallow wanted to be.

She'd asked Bonnie one time how she could put up with Marshmallow's antics on a daily basis.

*Difficult animals deserve love, too, Juliette. Love isn't just for the nice and the polite, it's for everyone. People and animals. It's for the grumpy ones and the reluctant ones and the reclusive ones. And folks who snap usually do so because they've been hurt before. Pushing people away isn't a natural instinct, it's a learned one. Remember that.*

Those wise words were as true now as when Bonnie said them. Look at Norah—she absolutely deserved love, but she pushed people away because too many times she'd been betrayed. Look at Joel. Juliette was *certain* something bad had happened to make him so eagerly misanthropic.

"Come on, give up the credit card." Juliette waggled her fingers. "I'll give you a treat."

Marshmallow hunkered down, not even mildly stirred by the offer. Unfortunately, this canine was not particularly food motivated . . . at least, not when she had something she wanted more.

"You know it's a crime to steal people's credit cards, right? I could have you locked up."

The dog was unmoved.

Juliette would just have to snatch it from her mouth, come hell or broken fingers. But before she had the chance, Digger decided he wanted in on the action. The little dog lunged forward like a furry assassin, snatched the card right from Marshmallow's mouth and darted off, skidding around a corner like he was an extra in *The Fast and the Furious: Tokyo Drift*.

*More like* The Fast and the Furriest.

Marshmallow looked stunned. Then she tipped her face up to Norah with utter defiance and trotted away in the opposite direction from where Digger had gone.

"She doesn't even want it. She only does it to mess with me," Norah said, shaking her head. "That dog knows my weak points and she exploits them like a first-rate sociopath."

"Better than a second-rate sociopath, I guess," Juliette joked. "If you're going to do something, at least do it properly."

The twins followed Digger in the direction of the bedrooms. Bonnie's apartment was decorated in wild shades of pink and green and with every wall and surface cluttered with photos and tchotchkes from her rich and vibrant life. There were carved giraffes from an African safari, photos of her holding a Koala in Australia and a python in the Amazon, a painting of the northern lights from an Icelandic artist. There were several statues of Pomeranians, including a miniature bobblehead. One of the dogs wore a glittering crown.

Her home would never be featured in an interior design magazine, and plenty of people would find it tacky as hell—minimalists might even call it borderline hoarding—but Juliette loved that Bonnie filled her life with things that made her happy.

"Digger!" she called out. "Come here, boy!"

There was rustling further in the house and a thump.

"Oh God. What's he gotten into now?" She turned the corner and saw the door to the spare room—aka Norah's temporary bedroom—was open. But Digger was not inside. Down the hallway, the door at the end was ajar.

"He's gotten into Bonnie's room." Norah tutted.

The twins reached the door and pushed it open, finding Digger on Bonnie's bed, the credit card abandoned on a pink crochet throw while he engaged in a fistfight with a sparkly velvet pillow. A pile of debris was on the floor—a notebook, a spine-cracked paperback with the bookmark jettisoned a foot away, a pair of reading glasses, a folder with some papers that had spewed out, which looked as though it had been knocked off the bedside table.

Norah snatched up her credit card, inspected it for damage and then tucked it into her bra. Meanwhile, Juliette scooped the terrier up before he could rip a hole into the pillow.

"Enough with that," she said. "Bonnie will be so sad if you ruin her pillow."

He looked up at her, brow crinkled as if to say, *You can't call me Digger and not expect me to dig. Like, duh. That's asking for trouble.*

"Hey, look at this," Norah said, holding out a piece of paper.

Juliette gave the squirming dog a kiss on the head before releasing him to the ground, where he zoomed off, presumably to terrorize Marshmallow. She'd keep an ear out for trouble.

"This brochure is for the cruise Bonnie is on but . . . the dates don't match." The glossy folded paper featured pictures of crystalline blue waters and a majestic-looking cruise liner. "It says the cruise doesn't leave until next week."

"Maybe she received that brochure but ended up booking a different cruise," Juliette said. While it didn't seem wildly suspicious, it *did* stir something uncomfortable in her gut. Clearly it had done the same to Norah. She could feel her twin's concern as if it were her own.

"And there's this." Norah held out an open notebook. The page was filled with Bonnie's curly cursive, where one word always seemed to flow into the next. "Flight DAL499 7:35 a.m. for the day she was leaving to fly to Miami."

"And?"

"I had a weird feeling so I looked up the flight number." Norah held up her phone screen. "It goes to Denver, not Miami."

"Maybe she wrote it down wrong?" As soon as she said the words, she knew she didn't believe them. "Or maybe it's for a different cruise out of Colorado."

"Jules, Colorado is landlocked."

She scanned the rest of the page. Most of it was difficult to decipher, which wasn't unusual as Juliette often had to ask Bonnie what the heck she'd written in the communications book they kept at the salon. As she'd gotten older, Bonnie had developed arthritis and a bit of a tremor in her hands, and her handwriting had gotten even more unwieldy. All Juliette could make out was:

DAL499 7:35 a.m. - 4hrs 37m

Meet Michael in lobby. Reservation at Firefly.

Juliette snapped a photo of the page with her phone. "I'll see if I can figure out where Firefly is and confirm if Bonnie was there."

Norah nodded. "I know I brushed off your concerns when Bonnie didn't respond to texts that first day. But I'm worried now, too."

That was *not* a good sign. Usually Norah was the one to keep Juliette's helium balloon worries tethered to the ground.

"I'm sure it's just a miscommunication," Juliette said, though she absolutely did *not* think that.

They walked back through the house, leaving Bonnie's bedroom tidy and closed up like it had been before Tornado Digger went through. As they made their way out to the main room, Juliette told Norah about Shane Dooley's visit to What The Fluff.

"Ugh! I would have smacked him right in his smarmy mouth," Norah declared, jamming her hands into her pockets. "I *hate* that guy. Seriously, most punchable face ever."

Juliette knew not to take Norah's comments entirely at face value. Unlike Marshmallow, her bark was absolutely worse than her bite. And no one in their family condoned physical violence, obviously. But when it came to Norah and the police . . . well, the more distance between them the better.

"And of course the murder happened while I was at home by myself," Juliette said with a sigh. "He was harping on about me not having an alibi."

"I'm not going to say this is karma for leaving me to deal with Marshmallow, but . . ." Juliette shot her a dirty look, and Norah shrugged and held up her hands to indicate she was joking. "It wouldn't have mattered anyway. Even if I wasn't sleeping here, I would have been out working my regular shift regardless."

Thank goodness for that. There was nothing Shane Dooley could do to drag Norah into this issue, because the particular office she was cleaning the night of the murder had security cameras. So her whereabouts weren't in question.

"I heard he's bringing *everyone* in for questioning," Norah said. "One of the ladies at the flower shop said today that everyone who owns a business or works at one in the town square is getting interviewed."

Juliette's eyes widened. "That's a lot of people."

"Reina had to provide a list of employees. She said they *all* got called in. That's like, all fifteen people who work at Live Love Labrador. Same goes for the bakery. Chief Dooley must have put the whole team on interviews."

"Not Shane. He was too busy getting up in my face." She sighed.

"Probably means Joel and April are going to get called in at some point, too."

Shit.

"I need to figure this out quickly. I'm scared Bonnie is going to come back and find her business in shambles."

Norah's eyes suddenly brightened. "Why don't you come to work with me and we can chat to Patrizia? She's always in early before her shift. If we leave now, we can catch her before she sets off."

"Great idea." Juliette reached for her bag. "Let's go."

**THE CLEAN SWEEP** Cleaning Co. offices were in an old warehouse with a dusty gravel parking lot and an unassuming front entrance. Anyone new to town would have no idea one of the most lucrative businesses around lived inside. Norah had been doing night cleaning shifts ever since she dropped out of high school one week into the twin's senior year. Back then the only shifts she could get were cleaning offices, because folks didn't want someone like her in their homes. But her boss, Dragomir Bibic, had taken Norah under his wing and made sure she earned enough to get by.

People who didn't know the man might be foolish enough to take him at face value. But Juliette had long suspected he'd supplemented Norah's pay on more than one occasion when she was going through a hard time, not that he would ever want anyone to know that.

"You're late," he barked at Norah as she walked through the front door, Juliette and the two dogs trailing behind. Clean Sweep allowed people to bring their pets into the office, but not on site. Dragomir's daughter watched over the dogs while their owners came and went from their scheduled jobs, and Dragomir himself was often found playing with the dogs when he thought no one was looking. "And what are you wearing? You look like a teenage boy."

"One, I'm not late. I'm *early*, for once. Check your roster," Norah retorted. "And two, thank you. That's exactly what I was going for."

"*Pojdi se solit*," Dragomir muttered as he came ambling toward them. This roughly translated to "go salt yourself" which was one of his favorite Slovenian sayings, kind of like telling someone to get lost. "How will your father ever marry you off when you look like that? If you were my daughter, I would buy you some appropriate clothing."

Dragomir towered over the girls at almost six feet four, though an old back injury made him stoop slightly. Either that, or he'd bumped his head on the doorway to his office so many times he now walked with a hunch. His hairline was in a race to find the back of his head and he wore a shirt tucked into black pants with dated chunky black leather dress shoes, though they were polished to a high-shine finish, and a heavy gold watch poked out at his sleeve cuff. Juliette had often mused that he looked like an Eastern European mobster hiding a heart of gold.

"Can't you take your sister shopping?" Dragomir asked Juliette. In his defense, Norah was wearing a sweatshirt that said "I came. I saw. There were people, so I left," which was probably not the most appropriate way to represent the company, but Dragomir didn't enforce a uniform. "You always dress so nice. Like you care about the world."

Juliette blossomed under his praise. "Thank you. I've always believed the way we dress expresses something important about who we are."

Norah gestured to her sweatshirt. "This *precisely* expresses who I am."

Dragomir tutted. "How do you kids say . . . I can't even?"

Juliette snorted. Dragomir always managed to repeat their colloquialisms in the most dad-like way.

"And what the hell is this?" He gestured to Marshmallow with a sniff of disdain. The dog stared back at him with equal contempt.

"A dog," Norah replied.

"Bullshit. That is something my cat coughed up." He looked over to Digger. "This one is also too small, but at least it looks like a dog and not a hairball."

Norah hooked her arm through Juliette's. "We wanted to chat to Patrizia before she heads out. Is she in?"

"Yes, her and the rat dogs are by the payroll desk." He wrinkled his nose. "I swear, I remember a time when people had real dogs. Like Alsatians or Dobermans. Not this . . . fucking joke fluff."

Norah let out a hearty laugh. "I'm officially renaming her Joke Fluff."

Marshmallow sharply swung her head toward Norah and narrowed her eyes. Juliette was starting to wonder if maybe she'd had too much stress, because she was sure she saw Marshmallow drag a paw across her throat.

*I'm watching you, peasant. One wrong move and it's lights out for you.*

"Come on," Norah said. "Let's catch Patrizia."

"Don't take too long. I don't want you distracting people," Dragomir grumbled as he retreated toward his office. "All everybody wants to do is talk, talk, talk."

"Meanwhile he's the chattiest one of all," Norah whispered to Juliette as she guided her and the dogs into the main office area. "He's always asking me a million questions. Norah, are you eating your vegetables? Norah, why are your pants touching the floor? Norah, you should get some sun, you look pale. Take a multivitamin."

Juliette thought it was adorable how her boss looked out for her, even if he did it in his own unique way. She'd come home more than once with a bag of lemons or squash or zucchini from Dragomir's personal veggie garden, or even a couple of jars of delicious roasted red pepper spread that his wife made from scratch.

The office space wasn't huge—four desks in total. There were two customer service officers who answered the company emails, managed the booking system and took calls to the business's main phoneline. They wore headsets and tapped away at their keyboards with a pleasing, mechanical clacking sound. There was also an accounts and administration manager, who had a serious Diet Coke addiction if the cans piled up under her desk were anything to go on, and a payroll officer who worked part-time.

The bulk of the team was the cleaners themselves.

The twins spotted Patrizia immediately. It wasn't difficult, since she was dressed head-to-toe in animal print. But not one type of animal print. Oh no, she had a whole damn safari. A zebra print top, leopard print pants, a cow hide belt and snakeskin boots. The "rat dogs" were Chihuahuas, each with tiny bodies, soulful brown eyes and satellite dish ears. Juliette only knew the Chihuahua with the long hair, since short-haired Chihuahuas were easily groomed at home and so Patrizia had only ever brought one of her dogs into What The Fluff.

"Norah, dahling. How *are* you?" Patrizia came over to the twins, having concluded her business at the payroll desk. She wore two of the dogs in slings crossing over her body and held the third one on her forearm, like a server balancing a dinner plate at a restaurant. Its little legs dangled on either side and it appeared perfectly content. "I was about to leave these three with Drago so I could head off to Mrs. Carver's house."

"They're so cute." Juliette leaned forward, but the tricolor dog in one of the slings suddenly bared its teeth and made a strange growling sound like a tiny chainsaw.

"Don't get them wet," Norah whispered, leaning in. "I heard they turn into monsters if you get water on them."

"Don't mind Nacho, he's not a big people person. Take Cashew instead." Patrizia thrust forward the little chocolate-colored dog on her arm.

"Uhh . . . okay." Juliette took the dog in her free arm, while hanging on to Digger's and Marshmallow's leashes with her other.

The Chihuahua felt as though it barely weighed two pounds, and it stared up at her with glossy eyes. Juliette almost felt like it was trying to hypnotize her.

*Look into my eyes. You are feeling very . . . much like you want to give me a treat.*

There was something almost alien-like and yet strangely adorable about the tiny breed. The little dog clambered up her chest, resting its head under her chin, and Juliette's heart melted. An indignant huff came from her feet, where Digger looked on, tail not—for once—wagging.

*Are you* holding *another dog? What about me?*

"We wanted to have a chat about Maurice," Norah said as the trio and all the dogs headed to the office's "doggy day care" area.

"What about him?" Patrizia snorted. "I'd be happy never to hear that asshole's name again."

"I was curious about the item he claimed you stole from him," Juliette said.

Patrizia's eyes narrowed and it caused deep lines to form in her leathery forehead. The woman looked like she'd never heard of SPF and had a skin tone the approximate color of a copper penny.

"I didn't steal anything," she said. "Especially not some stupid Bob Dylan album! Don't even like that kind of music. But Maurice was always blaming me for things I didn't do. Like leaving the iron on—when he didn't even pay me to do his ironing. Or knocking over a photo. I swear, he either was losing his marbles or there was a ghost in that house doing all the things he blamed on me."

"That's weird." Juliette cocked her head. "Did Corinne still have a key?"

"I don't know. I would have assumed he got the keys off her when she moved out, but . . . who knows. That guy was all over the place when it came to women. Loved them one minute, hated them the next." Patrizia made a scoffing sound. "That's a lot to keep track of, and I've been divorced three times!"

"I heard he cheated on all of his wives," Norah added.

"It's true." Patrizia nodded. "Couldn't keep it in his pants. Apparently he knocked up his secretary while he was still married to his first wife! Bastard."

Good old Labrador Falls gossip—it never failed to deliver.

"Do his kids have a key to the house?" Juliette asked.

"They do," Patrizia said, jostling the grumpy Chihuahua in her sling as someone walked past and the animal growled. "But the boys both live in Boston. Jack and . . . Jonas. The younger one is at Harvard."

Juliette vaguely knew them, but they'd been several grades lower than her and Norah so they'd never run in the same circles. Far as she knew, the boys' mother—Maurice's first wife—also lived in Boston.

"You don't think they could have stolen the vinyl when they came to visit?" Juliette asked.

"It's possible. But what twentysomething wants a Bob Dylan album? Kids these days have no taste in music. All this Taylor Swift and Angry Bunny stuff makes my ears bleed."

"You mean *Bad* Bunny?" Juliette asked.

"Bad Bunny, Angry Bunny, whatever. All I know is that Maurice was spitting mad about someone stealing his Bob Dylan album because it had his favorite song on there: rocks something. Or maybe it was gravel? I don't know." She shrugged. "I'm more of an Elvis gal, myself."

"I wonder if one of the boys had a fight with their dad and they stole it out of spite?" Norah speculated.

"Family drama could absolutely be the answer." Lord knew that had always been the root of Juliette's problems.

"Well, whatever it is, I maintain I didn't steal a goddamn thing. I'm an honest woman and an honest cleaner. I work my ass off with two jobs *and* a side hustle to look after my family, and I never stole a cent in all my life no matter how tight things got."

"Oh, what's your side hustle?" Juliette asked. She always respected people who started something on their own—she'd never had the guts to do it herself.

"Patrizia has an awesome eBay shop. She finds cool things in thrift stores and resells them online," Norah chimed in. "One time she found me a vintage Rammstein band tee from the nineties."

"Somehow I knew you would be into that," Patrizia replied with a raspy chuckle.

"What's your shop called?" Juliette asked.

"Patty's Pretty Treasures," she replied. "Anyway, why are you two poking around in this mess? I heard the cops were talking to you about it."

"I found Maurice's body so that's standard procedure," Juliette replied, but Patrizia didn't seem convinced. "And I was curious if you thought the theft of the vinyl and his murder might be linked."

"How would I know?" She shrugged. "I'm just a cleaner."

But for some reason, Patrizia's nonchalance didn't seem to reach her kohl-rimmed eyes, and Juliette wondered if the woman knew more than she was letting on.

# *Chapter Twelve*

**AFTER LEAVING NORAH** to her office-cleaning duties, Juliette took the dogs back to her place, gave them dinner and tried to settle in for a relaxing evening. Only, she couldn't relax. Not even a little bit.

Admittedly, it wasn't one of her strengths even on a good day. Writing to-do lists and organizing drawers and working hard, those were her strengths. All those people who sang the praises of naps and weekend sleep ins, or who thought that going to a spa sounded appealing? Blech, no thanks. She'd rather be going out for a walk or *doing* something. Which was how she ended up outside again, Digger and Marshmallow on their leashes, taking the dogs for a stroll.

Totally nothing to do with how she was now paranoid about being home on her own, lest another murder occur for which she had no alibi.

*You're safe in the presence of CCTV.*

Besides, this was the *best* time of year for an evening walk. The air was cool but not cold, and the streets were brimming with seasonal decorations—pumpkins on porches, wreaths made of maple leaves, harvest baskets filled with apples, garlands and lanterns galore. The world seemed tinted in gold. Hopeful. Peaceful. Thankful.

It was almost too easy to believe for a few moments that she wasn't a murder suspect.

Digger charged ahead and Marshmallow lagged behind, the former turning around to bark impatiently at the latter, while Juliette played monkey in the middle. After a while, she found herself walking right past Joel's house. How did she know where Joel lived, exactly? Well, that was the thing about small towns—someone always lived next door to the new guy. In this case, it was a client at What The Fluff.

*I heard he moved here from California*, she'd said, frowning. *You know what those people are like. They all smoke the marijuana.*

That was another thing about living in a small town, even the simplest of things—like not smiling or being from California—could raise suspicions.

Joel's house was simple and sparse, not a single decoration to be seen. Not even a miniature pumpkin, which seemed the least someone could do at this time of year. Marshmallow sniffed derisively in the direction of the house, while Digger wagged his tail eagerly and tugged toward the front door like he knew fun times lay ahead.

Juliette's phone buzzed with a text message.

**JOEL:** Are you standing in front of my house?

Juliette smiled and warmth suffused her belly as she wrote back.

**JULIETTE:** The polite thing to do would be to come to the door.

**JOEL:** The polite thing to do would be to knock.

That was all the invitation she needed! She strode up the driveway, Digger almost having a conniption from excitement and Marshmallow sighing with resignation, barely allowing herself to be dragged along.

At that moment, Juliette looked down at her leggings—the comfy, patterned kind she wore at home, not the cute kind she wore to Pilates—and her faded Donald Duck sweatshirt that she wore under a denim jacket she'd "borrowed" from her dad once and had never returned. Not exactly a "come hither" outfit. More like "chick with a Peter Pan complex."

*You're here to discuss the case, not to look cute.*

Sounded logical. Was still a total lie.

Juliette wanted to see Joel in his own habitat. Really, she just wanted to see Joel. Period.

Her knuckles had barely grazed the front door when it swung open to reveal the man currently occupying her thoughts. Only this version of him had wet hair and wore a fitted long-sleeved T-shirt that had a small logo of a bear and a maple leaf at the chest and WPFG 2023 down one arm. His grey sweatpants hung low and drew her eyes leisurely down his body.

*Since when is ogling someone in their own home a respectable thing to do?*

It was hardly her fault. The man was made for ogling.

Flushing, she snapped her head back up as she scrambled for something to say before he passed comment on the lusty once-over she'd just given him. "Uhh . . . which side did you play for?"

"Huh?" His brow wrinkled.

"WPFG is the World Police Fire Games. Were you police or fire?"

"Fire." Joel looked taken aback as though he hadn't expected her to know what it meant. "Triathlon."

"Wow." She nodded. "Impressive."

Joel stepped back to allow her and the dogs inside, though he raised an eyebrow at Marshmallow. "You know dogs aren't Pokémon, right? You don't have to catch them all."

"This one's a loaner. My sister is dog-sitting for my boss while she's on her cruise, but Norah is at work tonight so I said I'd look after her."

Marshmallow eyed Joel and then . . . the strangest thing happened. Her tail wagged.

"Are you freaking kidding me? Norah and I have been trying everything to make you happy, and still you plot our murders. But one glance at this man and suddenly you're a tail wagger?" Juliette shook her head. "Unbelievable."

Even Marshmallow liked Joel. What kind of black magic did this guy have up his sleeve? And how could she get some?

Digger bumped his head against her leg as if to say, *I wag for you* all *the time!*

Joel's eyes crinkled in amusement, although he didn't quite allow himself to smile. "So, what brings you around? I'm not even going to ask why you were standing creepily outside my house before I texted. Or how you know where I live."

"I was in the neighborhood." Technically true, although it glossed over the fact that she had no reason aside from him to be here.

"And?"

"I thought you might want company." She straightened her shoulders. "Besides, I had a chat with another suspect today and I figured you might want to hear about it."

Marshmallow trotted over and sniffed his foot, her tail giving another tentative wag. To Juliette's surprise he crouched and gave her small furry head a scratch and the wagging intensified.

"You must be magic, seriously," she said with wonder. "She doesn't let *anyone* near her."

"I've got the touch," he quipped. "You can let those two monsters loose if they're not going to destroy my house."

"They'll be good."

Crouching to release the dogs from their leashes, she took a moment to absorb Joel's environment. The house was semidetached, with a staircase on one side and a living room stretched out next to it. It was cozy, but . . . generic. A brown leather couch, flat-screen TV, plain coffee table with a paperback and a MacBook sitting atop it along with an abandoned espresso cup, rings of coffee like the age lines of a tree inside the white porcelain. A faded rug sprawled across the floorboards and there was a small wood fire heater glowing brightly in the corner. No art on the walls, no quirky personal touches.

Nothing that showed who Joel was.

It looked like a nicely appointed rental space for someone who'd just moved in. Not so much a home as a temporary landing space.

Joel motioned for her to take a seat and suddenly it felt quite intimate. She'd turned up at his house with two random dogs and expected that he would be free to see her. What if he'd had friends over?

*Or a woman?*

For some reason, an image of Serenity in her teeny tiny workout top flashed into her mind.

"Oh uh . . . Do you want a drink?" he asked suddenly, just as she'd taken a seat on the couch. "I can make you a coffee or get you a glass of water or juice."

"It's okay, I'm fine."

"Sorry. It's been a while." He cringed slightly and dropped onto the other side of the leather couch, leaving a good amount of space between them. "I'm a little rusty on the whole hosting etiquette thing."

"Since when do you care about etiquette?" she teased. "Besides, I dropped in unannounced. I'm not expecting you to wait on me."

Marshmallow and Digger were scoping the place out, wandering around and sniffing every little thing. Eventually Digger decided the best spot was right in front of the heater, where he curled up into a small kidney bean shape, front paws tucked against his body, and Marshmallow trotted right over to Joel, sitting at his feet and looking up as if wanting permission to climb aboard. When Joel didn't say anything, she got impatient and jumped up, scrambling into his lap and lying down without an invitation. Joel patted her awkwardly and Juliette stared on, utterly bemused.

*Norah is never going to believe this.*

"Your dad was a cop, right? That's how you know what WPFG stands for," he said, out of the blue as if he'd clicked a puzzle piece into place. "Did he compete?"

"Yeah, table tennis. He was pretty good."

"But he's not on the force anymore?" Joel raised an eyebrow and looked on with genuine interest.

"No, he's not." Juliette's finger found a small hole in her leggings. She worried it with her nail until it grew, revealing a small circle of pale skin. Was Joel probing because he'd heard rumors? Or was it an innocent question?

If he was helping her on this investigation, she *should* tell him why everyone was so ready to believe a Macintyre could commit such a crime. It was only fair.

"My dad was fired," she said. "He um . . . He got caught destroying evidence. That's why everyone is suspicious of me, because my family has a history of covering up crimes."

Joel's face revealed nothing.

*In for a penny, in for a pound. Might as well tell him the whole story.*

"Dad's brother—my uncle—had a gambling problem, and he got into debt with some dangerous people," she continued, working at the hole in her leggings until it stretched. "To pay off the debt he started breaking into people's homes and stealing stuff to pawn. When Dad found out what was going on, he destroyed fingerprint evidence that tied his brother to the crime. So when people found out who was behind the robberies *and* the fact that my dad tried to cover it up, people labeled him a 'dirty cop' and from then on, our family name was mud. My uncle stole from *a lot* of people here, and I understand why they're angry. I would be, too. After that, nobody wanted us around. Dad was fired and we were shunned."

Joel nodded slowly, digesting the story.

"I probably should have told you this sooner, since it might impact how people view you for being friends with me," she said, not able to meet his eye. "I'm sorry."

"Did *you* cover up a crime?" he asked.

"I wouldn't do that." She shook her head vehemently, still staring at the hole as if it might give her a hiding place to crawl into.

She loved her dad, of course, but she didn't agree with what he'd done. Theft was a serious crime and her uncle should have faced consequences. All those years of her father teaching her to tell the truth and do the right thing and be a good person had stuck, even if he hadn't lived by that code himself in the end.

It had taken years to forgive him. Sadly, the same could not be said for Norah. And even now, all these years later, there was still a giant crack running through their family.

"Then I'm not worried," he replied.

Juliette looked up. "Really?"

"Absolutely. It's not fair that people hold your father's indiscretions against you and your sister." His look was filled with burning intensity. He'd never looked at her like this before—like he knew her. Knew her pain. Her scars. Hell, *no man* had ever looked at her like this before. "You didn't do anything wrong. You were just a kid."

She could still remember the day the news started to spread—Juliette hadn't even known the truth herself until that moment.

Shane Dooley had marched down the corridor right toward her and Norah.

*"Your dad is a dirty cop," he said, eyes glittering with malice. He'd always been the sadistic type, taking pleasure in watching people squirm like they were a worm on the end of his fishing hook. "Dirty, filthy lying piece of shit who doesn't deserve to wear a badge. And you're just like him. I bet you knew this whole time your uncle was stealing from people. I bet you were covering for him. Fucking liars."*

But they hadn't been—neither her nor Norah. They'd been in the dark like everybody else. That day they came home from school to find their dad on the couch, an empty whiskey bottle on the floor, phone off the hook so no one could ring through. Norah had stomped off to her bedroom, slamming the door so hard the family photo on the wall next to it had swung and fallen off its hook, the glass smashing on the ground.

*"Did you really do it, Dad? Did you really try to cover up for Uncle Pete?" Her lower lip had wobbled, hoping against all hope that he'd tell her it was all a big misunderstanding. A mistake. A bad dream.*

*"I failed you, Jules," he'd slurred. "I fucked up big-time."*

"I'm sorry everyone took it out on you," he said. He was so close that if she reached out, her fingers would be able to touch him. Pinpricks of stubble dotted his jaw, outlining full lips. She could almost imagine them parting, the warmth of his breath on her cheek, the pillowy softness of his kiss. "You were a victim in all that, like the people who'd been robbed. Only you were robbed of something more valuable—respect."

To her horror, tears welled in her eyes. This was the first time anyone aside from Bonnie had ever said that to her. All these years she'd been made to feel like a crook and a cheat for something that was fully outside her control, and knowing Joel didn't tar her with that brush was like . . . God, it was everything. Feeling one fat teardrop plop right onto her cheek, she tried to cover it by faking a cough.

Which turned into a real cough.

"Let me grab you a water." Joel placed Marshmallow on the empty cushion between them, and she glared at Juliette for interrupting her lap time.

*I was just getting comfortable there! Do you know how hard it is to find another misanthrope to bond with in this godforsaken town?*

Still coughing, Juliette got up and followed him through an archway into a small kitchen. The cabinets were painted a soft yellow and there were blue-and-white tiles making a pretty checkerboard on the floor. The backsplash behind the oven featured a row of tiles with a daisy chain running through them.

"Don't judge me based on the kitchen okay. Martha Stewart is not my usual vibe," he grumbled, fetching a glass and running the tap until it filled.

On the fridge, Juliette noticed something—two photos. One with a young Joel and two tween girls, matching crooked smiles and Christmas sweaters. But it was the other photo that had her attention, pinned with a magnet in the shape of the sun with the words *the golden state* written underneath. The picture showed five men, all in blue firefighter T-shirts and beige turnout pants with high-vis stripes at the bottom. Joel was in the center, clutching a young dog—a chocolate Lab who appeared just out of puppyhood. He cradled the dog to his chest as it tried to lick his face, the full laugh transforming his expression into something of pure joy.

"Here." Joel handed her a glass and gently steered her away from the photo, as if she'd peeked into his bedroom without permission. "Tell me about what you found out today."

Juliette swallowed the water, trying not to feel a little sting at the fact that she'd opened up to Joel, while he still had his past under total lock and key.

**JOEL'S HEART HAMMERED** as he led Juliette back out to his living room. The second he'd noticed her looking at the picture on his fridge, it was almost like something had seized his body. A cold sweat had broken out across his skin, the edges of his vision warping as he tried to keep control over the situation. He'd experienced this before—blind panic, as if he was back there.

*Joel stumbled outside the house, a young girl in his arms. The change in temperature was sheer primal relief, like someone had shut the door on a blazing oven.*

*"Where's Chase?" someone screamed. He didn't know who. The child he was carrying was covered in soot and coughing, the hacking sound shaking her entire body. Paramedics swarmed and collected the girl, whisking her away. "Where's the grandmother?"*

*"Joel?" It was his fire captain. "What happened?"*

*Joel couldn't speak. All he could hear was the sound of the beam cracking overhead and the scream of the little girl as it came crashing down. He'd glanced behind and seen nothing but a wall of flames. There were two choices; save the girl, or get them both killed trying to rescue Chase and the grandmother.*

*His priority had to be the little girl.*

*"Joel?" the captain barked. "Fuck. Someone get him to the ambulance. I think he's in shock."*

*"Cap?" Another voice, wire-tight with worry. "What do we do? Where's Chase?"*

*"Inside," Joel said, his whole body starting to shake. "Inside. Inside. Inside."*

"So anyway, I asked her what she thought had been stolen and she said it was a Bob Dylan vinyl. Weird, right?" Juliette's voice cut right through Joel's flashback. Thankfully she'd been so busy chattering that she appeared not to have noticed that Joel was about to be in the midst of a full-blown panic attack.

Despite all the therapy it still happened sometimes, out of the blue. The past rushed up and gripped him at the base of the throat, choking him harder than the smoke.

"You have to go," he said suddenly, the warping at the edges of his vision getting even more unstable. It felt like the world was twisting, forcing the walls of his home to wrap around him. Everything was blurring. "Now."

"Huh?" Juliette whirled around, blinking in surprise. "But—"

"Just go, please."

"Is it because I mentioned Bob Dylan? I'm sorry if I—"

"Juliette. Go."

The hurt that splashed across her face was like a knife to his gut. It wasn't that she'd done anything wrong, but he couldn't let her see him like this. He couldn't let anyone see him like this. It was too raw. Would raise too many questions. Would take a blade to his barely healed wounds.

"Digger," she called. "Marshmallow."

She bundled the dogs up and scurried out of his house, while Joel stood stock-still, eyes unfocused, hanging on with every ounce of internal fortitude until she was gone.

And when she was, he sagged against the door, flicking the lock closed, before the memories completely dissolved him.

# *Chapter Thirteen*

**"I HEARD YOU** went to Pilates the other night," April said.

Joel was subsisting on espresso and almond croissants after a shattered night of sleep, where he'd woken up in a cold sweat around 3 a.m., and spent the next hour and a half trying to get back to sleep before eventually giving up and abandoning his bed.

He'd attempted to text Juliette no less than five times already to apologize for unceremoniously shoving her out of his house yesterday. But what was he supposed to say? It wasn't just a can of worms. It was a whole case. A whole worm canning factory.

"I wouldn't have believed you'd set foot in Live Love Labrador if it wasn't for my friend Amy saying she saw you there," April continued. She'd finished cleaning the countertops of Brewed Awakening and was now hanging around like a bad smell while Joel was unpacking some stock from a local dairy farm. "What were you *doing* there?"

"Shouldn't that be obvious."

She laughed. "I guess."

"Is *this* what constitutes gossip? Must be a slow news day," he grunted.

"Well, it was more that you went to the class with Juliette Macintyre." She leaned against the counter as Joel stood. "That's an interesting choice for a first date."

"It wasn't a first date." He stacked the empty delivery boxes so he could flatten them later and put them out for recycling.

"Second? Third?" April's hair was still Fanta orange but she'd added a purple streak to the front.

"Zero. It wasn't a date at all."

"Somehow that's even weirder." She wrinkled her nose and the gemstone winked at him. "You didn't strike me as the Pilates type."

"I'm not." And he would never be going back to that hellhole—one, because he'd embarrassed himself quite enough with his lack of flexibility, and two, because he wanted to avoid Serenity's helping hands.

"Then what's going on? I mean, she clearly has a crush on you. Even *you* can't be too oblivious to notice it," she said. Joel opened his mouth to warn her that she was about to get her ass fired, but April barreled on unperturbed. "What are you? Friends? I mean, you don't really *have* friends here. Oh, maybe it's a friends-with-benefits arrangement? A situationship? Something like that?"

A situationship? What did that even mean?

At that moment a customer walked through the front door. Saved by the bell.

"You take this. I'm going to clean up outside," Joel said gruffly, and headed off before April could ask any more asinine questions.

"You got it, boss!" she replied cheerily, like she hadn't been poking and prodding at his personal life.

One day he would fire her. One day.

Outside, it was crisp and sunny, and the pet garden had been bustling all day. Now that it was getting later, only a few people remained. One of them was Corinne Mursell, Maurice's almost-ex-wife, and her gorgeous Afghan hound, Brigitte. The champagne-colored dog lay quietly at her owner's feet, head resting on her front paws. As Joel approached, he saw the barest little wag of her tail and he swallowed the urge to smile. Corinne was tucked away in the corner and she had large sunglasses covering half her face, the kind you'd see on a paparazzi photo of a celebrity trying to disguise a hangover.

Joel collected discarded plates and mugs and other items that had been left behind by customers, and it was only when he got closer to Corinne that he heard sniffling. His first instinct was to see if she was okay, which was swiftly replaced by his second instinct to pretend he hadn't heard anything and to not get involved. It was a constant push-pull in his head—old Joel vs new Joel.

But he hesitated a moment too long, clearly, because Corinne waved at him.

"Can I get you anything?" he asked. Her red lipstick had left a perfect impression on the empty white cup in front of her. "Another latte?"

She sniffed. "No, thank you."

Brigitte looked up as if concerned about her owner and made a soft whine. Corinne immediately patted the dog's head reassuringly, stroking her fingers through the silky fur.

"Are you . . . okay?" Score one for old Joel. "It must have been a hard few days."

"It's been something," she said. "I spent all morning at the police station while the detective picked apart my personal life for his own amusement."

Sounded on brand for Dooley.

She lowered her sunglasses. Her green eyes were bloodshot and red-rimmed, and a large diamond glinted on her finger as her hand moved.

"It might seem ridiculous to have my ring back on, since Maurice and I were supposed to be getting divorced," she said with a sigh. "But his funeral is tomorrow and I miss him a lot. I still had it in my heart that we might get back together."

That surprised him. No one had been shocked by the news they'd split up. More gossip he'd heard against his will.

"It's all so messy," she sighed. "Death, I mean. It drags up a lot of feelings that don't make sense, and there's guilt, knowing you said things you can never take back."

Boy, did Joel know *that* feeling. Death was so permanent. A knot that could never be untangled.

"I should've tried harder to bond with his sons, but they hated me from day one," she continued, clearly looking for an ear to bend. Joel felt sorry for her. She mustn't have anyone to talk to. "It's hard with adult children, you know. They're so protective of the family unit. And they'd been scarred before. Maurice had . . . proclivities."

Wasn't jealousy one of the classic motives for murder?

"His eldest told me Maurice wouldn't think twice about cheating on me. That he'd done it to both his previous wives multiples times and that he had a couple of illegitimate children scattered all over the country. I think they wanted to be cruel by saying I was nothing but another notch on his bedpost." She sighed. "I tried asking him about it once and he blew up at me. So I became paranoid—checking his phone, suspicious when he wasn't home on time."

Sounded like a whole lot of drama to him. Some people seemed to thrive on having chaos in their lives, but he couldn't think of anything worse. Give him a boring, stable existence with one person to love and he'd be happy.

*That's not what you want anymore, remember?*

"I thought he was seeing someone behind my back, and I was furious—so I fabricated an affair of my own. It was *so* stupid." A tear rolled out of the corner of her eye and dropped onto her heavily made-up face, streaking through her foundation like a fingertip trailing through dust. "Of course Maurice was hurt. It turned out he'd been planning a big surprise for my birthday, and *that's* why he was sneaking around. I let his kids get to me. They thought I wanted to take their inheritance away from them, but I loved him. Truly."

"I'm sure you did," Joel said. And he believed it. He believed *her*.

"I don't want much from the estate," she continued. "Just a sentimental item. A record he used to play for me when we first started dating."

"Oh?"

"Bob Dylan *Rocks and Gravel*," she said with a dreamy sigh, looking off into the distance. "That was the soundtrack of our romance."

Joel's ears pricked up. Hadn't Juliette mentioned last night that it was a Bob Dylan album Maurice claimed was stolen from his house? What a strange coincidence. The *one* thing Corinne wanted from the divorce was the very item that had gone missing under dubious circumstances.

Maybe this was the best way to apologize to Juliette—to bring her another clue for her mystery.

**ALL AFTERNOON, JOEL** couldn't wait for the workday to end. It was a new and unfamiliar feeling. Not even a feeling from Old Joel. Work had *always* been an integral part of his life, previously because being a firefighter was his passion and the way he kept his dad's memory alive. And now, because work was the anchor that kept his days from floating away. It was his purpose. His distraction. His numbing agent.

But today, all he wanted was to close the café and see Juliette.

That feeling was only made stronger by the fact that Detective Dooley stopped in for a visit, ordering the same coffee—triple shot no foam cappuccino, extra hot with a dash of milk, a quarter pump of vanilla syrup stirred three times clockwise—that he did previously. Joel served him a regular cappuccino with normal sugar . . . stirred anticlockwise because he couldn't help himself.

At least this time Detective Dooley didn't give Joel any thinly veiled threats. Didn't need to. His mere presence was enough to remind Joel of what was at stake.

What would he do if everyone found out about his past?

*You know the answer to that. You'd leave.*

He looked around Brewed Awakening and, maybe for the first time, thought about the community that gathered here. They weren't *his* community, necessarily, because he kept himself separate from all their goings-on. But they came here to his space. They drank his coffee. They smiled at him and tried to talk to him and attempted to include him, even if he always declined.

And today, he hadn't minded the smiles quite so much.

Maybe he was spending too much time around Juliette and her sunshine ways.

As if on cue, his cell phone started to ring. It wasn't a number in his contact list but he recognized it from the text messages he'd gotten recently—Marissa.

At one time there wasn't anything he wouldn't have given to hear her voice again. But now, as time had slowly crusted ice over his heart, the thought of talking to her made him want to throw something. Or throw up. Now she wanted him to sign some papers so she could move on and marry someone else? She could wait until he was good and ready.

He sent the call to voicemail.

A second later, when the little notification popped up that he had one new voice message, he pressed play and held the phone up to his ear while he loaded dirty mugs and cups into the café's dishwasher.

*"You couldn't even let it ring out so I could fool myself into thinking you were busy instead of actively avoiding me?"* Her voice sounded so damn familiar and yet . . . changed. Harder. Older. *"Why am I not surprised? Look Joel, I know this is probably the last thing you care about. But I want to move on with my life. I don't want anything from you. I don't want money or half your stuff. Hell, I don't even want some of the stuff that legally should be mine. I want peace, okay?"* He could hear the tears in her eyes and his need to throw something—break something—intensified. *"Hanging on to the past isn't going to do anything. It won't bring Chase back. You know my brother would want me to be happy, Joel. If you can't do it for me, then do it for him. Please."*

The phone clicked off.

He stood over the dishwasher, staring blankly at the coffee-streaked mugs and cups, plates smeared with cinnamon dust and sugar crystals, evidence his life was not what it used to be. The life he'd shared with Marissa . . . well, it was as dead as Chase.

He swallowed against the boulder in his throat, anger and grief and regrets a tightening fist in his stomach.

*"How can he be gone?" She'd cried so much her throat had turned raw, the words rasping out of her like a zombie clawing itself from a grave with dirt-caked fingernails. "He was my whole life after Mom and Dad died. It was just me and him and now he's gone. My whole family is gone."*

*He sat on the bed, head cradled in his hands, pounding so hard he almost winced with each beat of his heart. Tiredness dragged his body down. It was like quicksand, the court-mandated therapist had said. The harder you struggled against it, the quicker it swallowed you.*

*He ground the heels of his palms into his eyes, trying to shut out Marissa's crying.*

*Chase's funeral had been earlier that day, and he'd somehow managed to hold it together, so he could hold her. In front of everyone, they were husband and wife. But behind closed doors they were being torn apart. He was the well for her to pour her shock into, the sponge of her endless grief.*

*"He always looked up to you, like you were the big brother he never had," she sobbed. "What happened in there, Joel? You have to tell me why he didn't come out. Did he suffer? Oh God, did he suffer a lot?"*

*Joel pushed up from the bed and whirled around to face his wife, her tearstained cheeks red from exertion. He couldn't be the man she needed him to be. He hadn't been able to save her brother. He wasn't able to soothe her pain. He couldn't do anything anymore. Between the nightmares and the migraines and panic attacks . . . he was completely useless.*

*So he left her there, stalking outside even though it was after midnight.*

*"Joel, where are you going?" she cried from the door. "We have to talk about this. One day you have to talk about this."*

Joel pressed his fingertips to his temple in the hopes a migraine wasn't coming. Then he noticed something. Detective Dooley was now standing over a woman at one of his tables, coffee cup in hand. As he shifted his position, Joel noticed it was Kacey from the puppy school. The conversation looked tense.

"Hey." He nudged April, who was pouring a bag of fresh coffee beans into the hopper, the *shh* sound of them tumbling into the waiting cavity drowning out any chance he had of overhearing what the detective wanted with Kacey. "I need you to go and clean up the tables out there . . . and if you happen to hear what the detective is saying to her, I would appreciate you passing it on."

April put the bag of beans down and looked at him, incredulous. "You want me to eavesdrop?"

"Like you don't *already* eavesdrop." He nudged her again. "Quick, before they finish."

Shaking her head, April made her way out from behind the serving counter with a rag and some disinfectant in hand. She made a show of cleaning the tables, slowly making her way toward them.

However, it wasn't long before Kacey got out of her chair and stalked out of the café, throwing the detective a dirty look over one shoulder. Shane Dooley put his coffee down and left not long after. April continued to clean for a minute, so it wasn't obvious she had only been there to listen in, and then returned to Joel.

"Firstly, I do *not* usually eavesdrop on our customers," she said, tossing her cleaning towel into the washing basket and hanging the spray on its designated hook behind the counter. "I'm shocked you would insult my professional integrity like that."

Joel raised an eyebrow, not buying her outrage even for a second. April was as nosy as they came and she'd told him on *many* occasions what she'd overheard the customers talking about.

"Second, what's in it for me?"

"What happened to professional integrity," he muttered. "And immediately trying to profit off what you heard is kind of hypocritical."

"I'm just trying to make my way in the world." She adjusted the lime-green bandanna currently trying—and failing—to hold her Fanta-orange-and-Barney-purple hair away from her face. All three colors clashed wildly with the pastel blue-and-pink-striped shirt she was wearing. Not that Joel was an expert on fashion, but the woman dressed like a finger painting session gone wrong.

"How about I offer you continued employment?" he said wryly. "Now, what did you hear?"

Realizing she wasn't going to get anything out of him, she

huffed. "They were talking about something that went missing from Maurice Allsop's home. A CD or album or something."

The vinyl!

"Okay," he said eagerly. "Go on."

"It sounded like he thought Kacey broke into Maurice's house. Or at least, that she was capable of breaking into someone's house if she wanted to. She went white as a sheet when he said that."

Interesting. Was it possible that Kacey's tattoos *were* related to a prison stint, and that maybe she'd done time for robbery? If anyone would know that, it would be Detective Dooley. What had he said to Joel a few days before?

*I check up on everyone who moves here. This is my hometown and I take my responsibilities very seriously. We can't have bad folks poisoning the well.*

"But then he said that it was some Bob Dylan album that had been stolen and she said . . . who's Bob Dylan?" April chuckled. "I thought everyone knew of him! Great musician. Anyway, Detective Dooley looked like he wanted to throw his damn coffee cup at the wall. He's got a head full of scorpions, that one."

"You're not wrong." Joel nodded.

"Then Kacey told him to quit harassing her and she stormed out." April shrugged. "They mustn't have anything on her, or else he would have dragged her into the station to talk instead of accosting her here."

"Maybe it was a coincidence she happened to be here," Joel replied. He was sure the detective had popped in to make a point to Joel, that he was keeping a close eye. But maybe that was paranoia.

"Could be." April cocked her head. "Why are you taking an interest in things all of a sudden? That's not like you."

There was something about her tone that went beyond casual curiosity. Was she worried for him? That he was getting mixed up in something he shouldn't?

"If it's going on in my café, I need to know about it."

April narrowed her eyes at him. "I don't buy it."

"I'm not selling it. It's the truth."

"Look Joel, I'm not going to tell you what to do. But I'd be careful about messing around with the Dooleys' business," she said. "If that family decides they don't like you, life becomes harder around here."

"Yeah, I get that impression."

"You should stay out of it," she pressed. "Seriously. Just do what you normally do and mind your own business."

At that moment, almost like the universe was reminding him precisely *why* he wasn't going to follow April's advice, the front door to Brewed Awakening swung open and in walked Juliette. A tentative smile blossomed on her lips and she raised one hand in a small wave. Joel's return smile was already there before he could stop himself, and April caught the whole damn thing.

# *Chapter Fourteen*

**JULIETTE HAD ANTICIPATED** Joel being a little frosty since she'd clearly stepped over some invisible line at his house the previous evening. But rather than pushing her away, he'd asked her to come back an hour after the café was closed because he'd found out some interesting information. What a nice surprise! Both him seeming pleased to see her *and* that he'd been clue hunting himself.

Did he care, or was he eager for the killer to be caught so he could divest himself of his commitment to keep an eye on her? Only time would tell.

Now they were walking to Vinyl Destination, a funky shop that sold records during the day and turned into a bar on Friday and Saturday nights. The evening carried a damp chill, the air heavy with the scent of rain to come and distant fireplace smoke. Juliette sucked it in, wondering whether she should say anything about what happened last night.

Joel hadn't mentioned it. In fact, he was unusually chatty, as though determined to make sure the conversation didn't stray *anywhere* close to last night. Juliette stole a glance at him as they walked. He was wrapped up in a chunky navy sweater that looked as though it could have been handmade. Pale blue snowflakes stretched across his broad chest, and over the top was a worn brown leather jacket and knitted scarf.

She wasn't sure how he made such cozy clothing look as hot as if he were wearing a skintight white T-shirt, but he did. Then there was the stubble dusting his jaw and the way the crisp fall air ruffled the thick, dirty blond strands of his hair and—

*Can you knock it off? You're trying to catch a killer, dammit! If you're too busy fawning over him then you might miss something important.*

"Where's Digger?" he asked suddenly.

"At the apartment. He ran a marathon at the dog park today and so I left him to have a nap."

"Not worried he's going to tear your place apart?" he asked with a raised brow.

"He wouldn't . . . would he?" She'd convinced herself Digger would be fine, but the first words out of Joel's mouth suggested otherwise. "Now I'm worried."

"It's okay, we've got our eye on the prize. This shouldn't take long."

Vinyl Destination was situated one street back from the town square, in a quiet spot where some of the less touristy businesses lived, sandwiched between a dry cleaner and a bicycle shop. A bluesy rock ballad came wafting out of the store, and Juliette found her head bobbing to the beat as they approached. Outside were several neon plastic crates sitting on a table, each one filled with vinyl sleeves. They appeared to be secondhand—some of the sleeves were beat up and even had names written in marker and old price stickers on them. Juliette idly flipped through the one labeled A-B-C to see if there were any Bob Dylan records. She found two, but neither had the track "Rocks and Gravel" that Corinne had mentioned to Joel.

By the door was an A-frame sign decorated with chalk that said: *I hate when I'm singing a song and the artist gets the lyrics wrong.*

A funny memory immediately popped into Juliette's head.

"My mom was a big Elton John fan and we used to sing all his songs in the car on the way home from school," she said. "For *years* I thought the lyrics were 'hold me closer Tony Danza' and Mom never corrected me! I thought it was so nice Mr. Elton wrote a song about his friend hugging him, too. I only found out I was wrong years later because I watched a rerun of *Friends*, and Phoebe made the same mistake!"

Joel burst out laughing and the sound was delicious and warm and heartfelt, like a big mug of cinnamon-spiced cider with extra sugar. It might have been the first time she'd seen him laugh. *Really* laugh.

"You thought 'tiny dancer' was 'Tony Danza'?" He scrubbed a hand over his face. "How did you even know who Tony Danza was? Isn't he a bit before your time?"

"My mom was low-key obsessed with him," she replied. "Norah and I grew up watching reruns of Who's The Boss with her *all* the time. She used to tell my dad if Tony Danza ever proposed to her, she'd divorce him immediately. I knew at six years old that Tony Danza was my mom's hall pass."

Joel chuckled. "I don't know if that's adorable or messed up."

"Welcome to my childhood," she replied with a wry smile. "Now, let's see if we can find anything out about a stolen Bob Dylan record."

Stepping inside Vinyl Destination was like being transported to a cool underground club in a big city. It was dark and yet bright, with dim overhead lighting and funky vintage neon signs throwing glowing shades of pink, green and violet. The bar was currently shuttered with antique collapsible iron doors, which looked as though they might have been salvaged from an elevator or old city apartment building. But the shop floor was bustling with people picking through the rows of vinyls, both new and secondhand. There was a record player set up, with the album currently being played proudly on display.

On one side of the shop, a set of well-lit glass cabinets held music memorabilia, including a signed electric guitar from some band Juliette had never heard of, a few framed gold and platinum LPs, signed records and sleeves, a signed concert T-shirt from a band she *did* recognize—the Red Hot Chili Peppers—and even a Britney Spears version of Monopoly, though it wasn't signed. The bright pink text on the box matched a pink Post-it note stuck to the corner that read "I'll always visit you in jail."

*Must be some kind of inside joke.*

"Look, they have a whole lot of rare vinyls here," Joel said, moving past the memorabilia cabinet to one that featured items for sale behind its locked doors.

"Five hundred bucks!" Juliette gaped at a KISS vinyl from a live concert that was still sealed in what looked like original shrink wrap. "People really pay that?"

"It's a piece of music history." A voice came from behind Juliette and Joel, and they both whirled around.

The owner of the store, Beau Gerrard, was standing there, wearing a leather vest that exposed his muscular tattooed arms and a pair of ripped blue jeans with heavy black combat boots. His thick blond hair was almost to his shoulders and he had the kind of lean, wiry physique befitting someone who spent their nights running around on a stage and doing other energetic rock star things. He was a local guy, grew up right around the corner from the Macintyre family in fact, but had spent his twenties touring the world with his band. Beau Gerrard had been on the path to global superstardom when his best friend and bandmate died unexpectedly. After that he came home and opened Vinyl Destination.

Rumor had it that he hadn't written a single lyric since.

"This is a KISS Alive Millenium Concert album, perfectly sealed straight from the factory, pressed on 180-gram vinyl. It features a live recording of their performance from the BC

Place stadium, which is in Canada, from December 1999. Fantastic concert and the perfect gift for any rock enthusiast." Beau grinned. "Absolutely worth every one of the five hundred dollars I'm charging."

Juliette found herself looking at his intricate tattoos, the music notes woven into words and through images of dragons and angels that curled across the exposed slice of his chest where the edges of the vest didn't quite meet. Each piece looked as though it could hang in a museum. Out of her peripherals she caught Joel watching her, and she straightened up. He probably thought she was checking Beau out!

To her amusement, Joel frowned.

"Do you remember that much information about *every* vinyl in this place?" Juliette asked.

"I have a brain for music facts," he replied. "Some call me a music nerd. I call it a special talent."

"That's cool," Juliette said. "You've got music Wikipedia in your head."

"This is quite a store you've got here." Joel nodded in appreciation. "I've got a few old boxes of my dad's vinyls at home and I've been meaning to get myself a player so I can listen to them. He was a big-time Pink Floyd fan."

"I can help you with that," Beau mentioned, gesturing to a small display of turntables.

"Actually," Juliette interjected. "The main reason we're here is about a specific album we're trying to track down."

"Oh? I've got a great selection here, but if I don't have what you're looking for, then I can always reach out to my contacts and see if I can find it for you." Beau cringed as two teenage girls went past, not-so-subtly holding a rhinestone-encrusted cell phone to take a photo of him. He didn't ask them to stop, however.

"That happen a lot?" Joel asked with a raised eyebrow.

"Only a hundred times a day." Beau ran a hand through his hair in a way that made him look like a model in a shampoo commercial, though he clearly wasn't *trying* to look like that judging by the slight stoop in his shoulders. "But I don't fight it. That only encourages them."

"Must be hard being famous in a place like this," Juliette mused.

"The locals are great, actually. Folks have let me settle back in and mostly mind their own business. It's the out-of-towners who take the photos and want autographs and my life story." He shook his head. "Anyway, about that vinyl you're looking for?"

"Yeah, it's a Bob Dylan album featuring the track 'Rocks and Gravel,'" she replied. "Have you heard of it?"

Beau's eyes, which had the natural crinkle at their corners of someone who'd spent many years smiling before tragedy struck, suddenly turned cold. "'Rocks and Gravel,' you say."

"Yeah." Juliette glanced at Joel, who'd shoved his hands into his pockets. He looked a little on edge, almost like he'd noticed the change in Beau's demeanor as well.

"You know *which* album that's from, do you?" He was looking at her very intently, like he was trying to figure something out.

"Uhh . . ." Juliette wrinkled her nose. Why did it feel like she'd walked into a trap?

"Let me help you out," Beau said, crossing his tattooed arms over his chest. "It's from the *Freewheelin'* album, released in 1963 by Columbia Records. 'Rocks and Gravel' was one of four songs that Dylan was pressured into dropping from the final album, though not before 300 copies were pressed. They were supposedly destroyed by Columbia, but some clearly weren't, because they ended up in circulation and are considered highly sought-after collectibles that often sell for between twenty and thirty thousand dollars."

Juliette gaped at him. "I'm sorry, *what*?"

"The vinyl you're asking about is a *highly* valuable rare find. So no, I don't have it here because if it were in my possession I would have that thing locked up in a safe somewhere off-site. And I wouldn't be selling it." He cocked his head. "But my guess is that you're not an interested customer, because if you were then you would know its history."

Shit.

"There's also the fact that this is the second time I've been asked about it this week," he added.

Juliette and Joel exchanged a look.

"Who else was asking about it?" Joel looked around, as if wanting to make sure no one was listening to their conversation.

But the only people in the store were the small gaggle of teenage girls, two older men energetically debating the art on an album one of them was holding, and a twentysomething guy with too much eyeliner who was listening to something with a pair of headphones.

"I don't know," he said. "I got an email from an address I didn't recognize and the person said they had a copy of this rare version of *Freewheelin'* that they wanted to sell. They were asking for twenty-five thousand and for the sale to remain anonymous. Obviously, that's suspicious as hell, so I thought it was a scam."

"Do you still have the email?" Juliette asked. "Could we take a look at it?"

"What's this all about?" Beau didn't seem like he would hand out any further information without some context.

Juliette sighed. "You know Maurice Allsop?"

"Of course. He was a great customer of mine." Beau looked genuinely sad. "He used to come in all the time and we'd talk music and the industry. He had an incredible personal music collection. I've been to his place a few times for a drink and to listen to his latest buy."

"Well, we have reason to believe that he owned this special version of *Freewheelin'* and that maybe the person who contacted you stole it from him before he died. They may or may not also be responsible for his death."

Beau visibly paled and he dropped his arms to his sides as he stared at them slack-jawed. "You're kidding."

"Afraid not," Joel said.

"Then why aren't the police here asking about it? Surely they would want to know about this possible connection."

Juliette had that feeling of stepping too close to a trap again. Because Beau was right—the police *should* be here asking about the vinyl. They obviously knew it had been stolen, since Detective Dooley had been questioning Kacey about it at Brewed Awakening earlier. But did they know about the rarity and resale value of the album? Maybe. Maybe not. Perhaps they thought the theft was personally motivated and hadn't even looked into how much it was worth.

"Detective Shane Dooley is on the case," Joel said, cutting into Juliette's thoughts.

"Oh. Right." Beau's expression soured. "Say no more."

"Someone might have broken into his house and taken it, and now they're trying to sell it. Staying anonymous makes sense, if they're tied to the murder," Juliette said.

"I don't know about anyone breaking into his house, though," Beau said, frowning. "Maurice was *obsessed* with home security. He had the most intense system I've ever seen, and I've spent time with some pretty famous people over the years. Every door and window on the whole house was protected with laser sensors, and it all had remote access and control so he could check things on his phone. There were security cameras *all* around the outside of the property, too."

"That's probably why whoever murdered him didn't do it

in his house," Joel mused. "There would have been a record of them coming and going."

"Your average thief was *not* getting into that place, I would put my last ten bucks on it," Beau said resolutely. "If someone stole that record, they were either a professional jewel-heist level thief—"

"Or they had a reason to be there," Juliette finished.

"Exactly." Beau nodded. "But I still don't understand why you two are involved."

Juliette sucked in a breath. Beau had been away from Labrador Falls long enough that he might not know the history between her father and the police, nor what had become of her reputation since. He also seemed like a guy who had a history weighing on his shoulders, so he might understand her plight. If she wanted access to the email address of the person who was trying to sell the record, then she had to give him something.

"Let's just say I've found myself on the wrong side of Detective Dooley's esteem, and he'd be more than happy to kill two birds with one stone—have someone to pin this murder on *and* find a way to make my life miserable." She knotted her fingers together, fighting the urge to gloss over her situation to save face. She didn't want Beau to think poorly of her. But hopefully his genuine friendship with Maurice would encourage him to help her. "And I think Maurice deserves the truth to be told, don't you? If the detective is chasing after the wrong person, then the real murderer is out there potentially profiting off Maurice's death."

Beau looked at her for a long, intense minute before turning to Joel. "And what are you? The muscle?"

Joel let out a small grunt that sounded like half laugh and half disbelief that he was still in this ridiculous situation. "Something like that."

Beau chewed on the inside of his cheek, gaze flicking between them as though he was weighing up his options. Eventually he let out a sigh. "Maurice was more than a customer to me. He was my friend. I want him to have justice."

With that he pulled out his phone and brought up the store's email inbox, showing the email to Joel and Juliette.

"I'll send you a screen cap," Beau said. "But this is what they sent me."

To: contact@vinyl-destination.com

From: NotSoGoodGirl02@secretmail.com

Subject: extremely rare record for sale

Hi Beau,

I have an extremely rare edition of Freewheelin' by Bob Dylan to sell that includes the tracks "John Birch", "Let Me Die in My Footsteps", "Rambling Gambling Willie", and "Rocks and Gravel." I want $25,000. Non-negotiable. This is a fair price because a Bob Dylan stan would definitely buy it from you for more. If we go ahead with this sale, it must be anonymous.

Thx.

Were these the words of a killer? Juliette certainly thought so.

# *Chapter Fifteen*

**WHEN THEY LEFT** Vinyl Destination, Juliette was buzzing with excitement. Her cheeks were flushed pink and it made her big, brown eyes sparkle.

"I can't believe that!" She grabbed his arm and gave him a little shake, although it felt a bit like a mouse trying to shake a tiger. "We have the email address of the person who might have killed Maurice! At the very least, it's the person who stole the album from him."

"Technically we don't know either of those things, but I have to assume, given how rare the album is, that there's unlikely to be *two* in Labrador Falls," Joel conceded. "So what now? What's the next step in the How to Solve a Murder plan?"

Juliette immediately pulled her notebook from her bag and Joel laughed. Of *course* she had the details of the plan on hand. "I guess we've finished interviewing witnesses, right? At least, for the first round of questions. It also says we need to establish a timeline and analyze the evidence . . . which is a bit hard since we can't do things like DNA and fingerprints and stuff."

Further down the street, they came across a set of stalls outside the old pub, Stumble Inn. Joel had always claimed the name was corny, though he secretly chuckled every time he walked past the old building with its leadlight doors and charmingly cracked paintwork. There were three stalls sitting out front, strung with fairy lights and surrounded by a small crowd of people as the scent of mulled cider wafted into the air. Cinnamon, clove and star anise called to him, rousing memories of cool mornings around a campfire, the thickness of his father's wool sweater swamping his small frame and the slightly metallic taste of a thermos as he drank the spiced beverage his mother always prepared.

"Do you want some?" he asked, before he even had a second to think about whether it was a good idea.

*What's the harm in stopping for a drink? Surely, you're not in a rush to get home to your cold bed and your lonely couch and your empty life.*

The thought came out of nowhere. Or rather, the tone of it. Since when did Joel equate his home here with being empty and lonely? It wasn't empty, it was peaceful. And it wasn't lonely, it was safe. He liked his solitude. Needed it, even.

"Yes, I do." Juliette's face lit up like the lights dancing across the awnings of the stalls. "Great idea."

She tugged him toward the line where the cider was being dispensed. One stall was managing the orders and the other two stalls were making the different fall-themed beverages and food items, including the mulled cider as well as a pumpkin ale and chocolate stout beers, and cinnamon twists which looked doughy and delicious. People milled about, paper cups in gloved hands, scarves around their necks, as the evening chill began to settle in. While they waited in line, Joel noticed that Juliette was underdressed. The delicate curve of her neck was exposed and when she shivered, he slid the knitted scarf from his own neck and passed it to her.

"Won't you be cold?" she asked, frowning.

"My dad would smite me from heaven if I let a woman go cold on a damp night like this," he replied gruffly.

She smiled and wrapped the scarf around her neck. It was

checked with red, green and navy blue, and she buried her chin into the warm bundle. "He was a real gentleman type, was he?"

"Absolutely. Didn't say much, but he was a stickler for manners."

"Sound like anyone you know?" she teased, her face tilted up to his. The flickering lights reflected in her eyes and flashed across her cheekbones. The line inched forward and he gave her a little nudge to step ahead. "I noticed that about you. Even though you pretend to hate people, you're actually very considerate."

"Oh yeah? How so?" he asked.

"One time, I saw Mrs. Faulkner in the café, and she sloshed a load of her coffee into the saucer because her hands are so shaky these days. You went over with a new cup of coffee without her even asking and cleaned up the old one without saying a word."

He remembered that day. Mrs. Faulkner had looked so sick and frail, and it had reminded him of how his mom had gotten after his dad had died—shaky, unsure of herself, embarrassed that she couldn't do simple things.

It hurt to watch someone struggle like that.

"Doesn't cost much to be a decent human being," he mumbled. "I don't want a prize for it."

Juliette opened her mouth to reply, but they were suddenly at the head of the line. They ordered two ciders and two cinnamon twists, and split up to collect the items from the respective stalls. Once their spoils were acquired, they came back together.

"Shall we walk and eat?" Joel suggested.

"Aren't we going in different directions?" she asked.

"I'll walk you home."

"Ah, there's those manners again." She tipped her face up to the sky. "Thanks, Mr. Cunningham. You did good."

Joel blew on the steam coiling up from his cider. He'd hiked his cinnamon twist up, so half of it poked out of the white paper bag, ready for him to take a bite. When he did, the soft dough yielded, sending sugar crystals scattering and the flavor of spices warming his tongue.

"Damn, that's good," he mumbled through his mouthful.

Juliette copied him, taking a hearty bite out of her twist. Sugar crystals got stuck to her lips and cheeks and one even ended up on the tip of her nose. She groaned, eyes rolling momentarily in pure pleasure. A woman who ate like that—so unreserved, so joyful—well, it was damn near the hottest thing he could think of.

Drawing his eyes away for his own good, he said, "Okay, so where are we at, Miss Murder Investigator? We have one dead man, one stolen highly valuable vinyl and one murder weapon tied to you."

"I was thinking about the comment Beau made about Maurice's obsession with security and his home system. I think he's right—the person who stole the record must have had a *reason* to be at the house, rather than having to break in. Because if they did break in, there would be proof. The alarm system would have been disabled or triggered or *something*. And if that was the case, then Detective Dooley wouldn't be asking questions at the café. He'd be taking someone to the station for questioning."

The sugar crystal was still clinging to the end of her nose, winking at him like it knew how much he wanted to lean forward and kiss it right from her skin.

"You uh . . ." He was feeling flustered all of a sudden. She looked so damn pretty with his scarf around her neck, and her lips all sugary sweet. "You have . . ."

He reached out and brushed the sugar crystal from her nose and her eyes widened in surprise.

"Sorry." He shook his head. What the hell was wrong with

him? Why was he being so weird all of a sudden? "And yes, I agree. I think it was an inside job."

She smirked. "Who sounds like a murder investigator now, huh?"

"Just trying to be helpful." He took another bite of the cinnamon twist. "Who has access to the house?"

"It's possible Corinne does, especially since she and Maurice weren't separated *that* long ago. And maybe he was fine with her keeping her key so she could drop Brigitte off as part of their custody arrangement."

"That all makes sense, but when I spoke to Corinne, she mentioned that the vinyl was the only thing she wanted from the estate because it had sentimental value," Joel pointed out. "Which implies she doesn't currently have it."

"She could be lying."

"True. But she really did seem sad that he's gone—and I feel like my bullshit detector is pretty active."

"Overactive, some might say." Juliette snorted.

"What motive would Corinne have to mention it to me—unprompted, no less—if she was the one who stole it? Especially if she was trying to get Vinyl Destination to agree to an anonymous sale. That doesn't make sense. She would be drawing attention to herself for no reason," Joel argued, ignoring her teasing. "I don't think she did it."

Juliette thought about it for a moment and then nodded. "Yeah, you're right. She has no reason at all to mention it if she was behind the theft."

Joel took a sip of his cider, finding himself unexpectedly and wholly invested in solving this mystery with Juliette. And not just to keep her out of harm's way. It reminded him of the days he supported the arson investigators back in California. He'd even thought about specializing, at one time. Moving into investigation full-time.

But his career had been cut short before he ever got to that point.

"I think we can also strike Kacey off the list," she said. "Even if she *was* a thief in the past, the chances of her breaking into a home that has a high-tech security system without the police finding out are pretty low. She's also the only suspect who has no reason to be at his house."

"That's if we're convinced the vinyl had something to do with his death," Joel countered.

"A guy is murdered in a town where nothing ever happens and a rare vintage item worth thirty-ish thousand dollars is stolen shortly before? Seems like way too much of a coincidence to me." Juliette blew on her cider before taking a tentative sip. "They have to be linked."

"But why murder him *after* stealing the vinyl?"

"What if he found out who did it and threatened to go to the cops?" she suggested. "Maybe they had a confrontation at the dog park. Or maybe the murderer followed him there? It's dark at night, easier to get away without being seen."

"I buy that." Joel nodded. "Okay, so who are we left with?"

"Just Patrizia." Juliette stuffed the last of her sugary snack into her mouth and crushed the white paper bag in her fist before shoving it into her pocket. *"Mph mphmph pam phignph."*

"Sorry, I don't speak cinnamon twist," he said, laughing.

She brought her hand up to cover her mouth, cheeks reddening as she chewed and swallowed. "I said, she cleans his house."

"Okay, so she has reason to be there. Check."

Juliette stopped dead in her tracks, her mouth falling open.

"Oh my gosh! How did I not think of this sooner? She has an eBay store where she sells secondhand things. Like trash and treasure stuff. Norah told me about it because Patrizia found her a vintage band T-shirt she'd been wanting."

Joel's ears pricked up. "You think she might have stolen the record to sell it herself?"

"Could be. If she's in that line of work, then maybe she knew it was worth a bunch!" Juliette brought up her phone and searched for Patrizia's eBay store—Patty's Pretty Treasures. "Look! There are several listings here. She has vinyls from Fleetwood Mac, Led Zeppelin and The Beatles. There's music memorabilia too—a *Rolling Stone* magazine signed by Steve Tyler and a bobblehead of Elton John. You're telling me she didn't know the album was worth something? Come on."

"That's pretty damning," Joel agreed. "Although why go to Beau if she could sell it herself on eBay?"

"She wants anonymity. Selling it in her store wouldn't give her that." Juliette frowned. "It's weird, though. Something about the wording of the email made me think it was written by someone younger."

"Why do you say that?" Joel asked.

Juliette brought up the screen cap Beau had sent her. "See here, look at this line . . . *This is a fair price because a Bob Dylan stan would definitely buy it from you for more.* I don't know anyone over forty who would say 'stan' in this context."

"I'm nowhere close to forty yet and I don't know what that means," he admitted.

"A stan is a really enthusiastic fan. Like, someone who's *obsessed* with an artist or celebrity beyond a regular amount of fandom," she replied. "But it's not something I could imagine Patrizia saying."

"Maybe the person is purposefully trying to conceal their age? Especially since they said they want to remain anonymous."

"Could be," Juliette said. "There are still too many things that we don't know."

"And could Patrizia have gotten access to the leash at What The Fluff?" he asked.

"Yeah, I groom her long-haired Chihuahua. They were in the salon recently."

The streets grew quieter further from the town square, glowing shops transitioning into the cozy windows of family homes, reflections in the glass from flickering TV screens and fireplaces. Some yards already had their Halloween decorations out, ghosts ooo-ing and skeletons cackling and cobwebs shuddering in the chilled fall breeze. Instead of being scary, it made Joel want to pull Juliette close to him, to tuck her under the crook of his arm as they pointed out funny things to one another—like the house who had their skeletons spelling out YMCA on the front lawn, complete with iconic Village People costumes.

For the first time in years, he felt at ease with another person. He felt festive and engaged and . . . alive.

"How cute is that?" Juliette pointed to a set of three jack-o-lanterns that looked like tiny homes for small woodland creatures. They had bits of moss stuck to the front, a small swing set made out of twigs and twine, and a stone pathway to the front door. "They've put so much care into it. I wonder if little mice go in there to take a nap!"

The Disney princess vibes were at an all-time high.

"Why? Are you looking to recruit some creatures to do your housework?" he asked.

"Very funny." She went to sip her drink and frowned. "Aww, I thought I had another sip left. Don't you hate that?"

Joel gave his cider a shake and there was still some left. "Here."

She hesitated a moment but accepted his offering. "Thanks."

They were stopped in front of a building that at one point would have been a grand family home. Now it was divided up, a brick letterbox with several slots and numbers written in gold. A furry little face pressed against the glass of one of the windows. Digger was clearly eager for her to be home.

"Someone is waiting up for you," he said.

He could already imagine the scene when she walked inside—the tail wagging, toenails skittering across the floor, the textured swipe of a tongue across her hand. He remembered those days, how good it felt to walk into a home that wasn't silent.

*You don't want that anymore.*

"Thanks for the cider," she said, her tongue darting out to moisten her lips. She tossed the empty cup into a trash can that was out for collection and he did the same. "And thanks for coming with me tonight,"

"I made a promise, didn't I?"

She nodded, her eyes drifting down. "You always stick to your word."

"That a question or a comment?" he asked. Behind them, Digger jumped up and slapped his paws against the window. It looked like he let out a bark, though Joel couldn't hear it.

"I guess I don't really know here," she said, touching a fingertip to her temple. "But I feel like I know it here."

She touched that same fingertip to her chest.

He didn't want her to see him like that—as the good guy. The right guy for her. Because he wasn't right for her. He wasn't right for anyone.

"I don't know why you pretend to hate people, Joel. Why you act so gruff and so disinterested when it's clear you're a good person underneath." Her dark chocolate eyes searched his face, moonlight gleaming down across her skin, giving it an ethereal glow. "You're kind and helpful and you care. I can tell you care."

He should deny it. He *wanted* to deny it.

"Caring is dangerous." The words were off his tongue before he could think about why they were too much. Too vulnerable.

Joel didn't *do* vulnerable. Not anymore. Not after the fire. No after losing Chase and losing his wife and having his whole life crumble down around him. Not after having everyone scrutinize his every action and word, looking to place blame or see the cracks or watch with popcorn in their hands.

"Anything worth chasing is dangerous," she whispered. "Trust me, I know."

"You don't know what I've been through," he said, the words tight as cutting wire.

Juliette looked up at him, lips parted and glossy eyes so full of sincerity it cracked something open inside him. A black box of emotion he'd tried so hard to keep locked and hidden, but it had been splitting at the seams for some time now. Begging to be opened.

"So tell me," she said.

But he couldn't tell her. If she looked at him like he was a monster—or worse, a failure—then he didn't know how he would face her every day.

"Joel, you can trust me," she said. "I . . . I want to know. I want to know *you*."

And with that—with those silky, whispered words and her wide, honest eyes—she knocked a nail out from the cage walling off his heart. Just one nail. Just one tiny thing. But it was enough to push him into action. To push him to do the one damn thing he'd been trying so hard *not* to think about ever since he'd met her.

He touched the length of his scarf wrapped around her neck, curled his fingers around it, and pulled her close. She gasped, eyes flaring and pupils turning to black holes. She came, willingly. Without hesitation. Her hands landed on his chest, fingers splayed and her body bowing toward his. His hand moved to her face, thumb brushing the edge of her lips.

*You're breaking your rules.*

He was. Greedily. Gloriously.

He lowered his head, nose hovering in front of hers as her

hands curled into his jacket. The scents of cinnamon and apple and spices tempted his nose, and they hovered for a moment. There was time to back out. Time to stop what was about to happen. But neither of them did. Soft lips met his, gentle and sweet at first. Then eager. Harder.

Juliette snaked her arms around his neck and rocked up onto her tiptoes. The heat from her body was like standing in front of an open fire—he felt thawed. Returned to life.

"Juliette," he whispered against her lips. "You taste like fall."

"So do you."

He cradled her head with one hand, feeling her silky hair slide through his fingers, and his other hand traveled down her back, finding the perky curve of her ass and filling his palm with it. They were fused together, a melting and meeting of lips and teeth and tongues and palms. Her fingertips danced across his jaw, tracing the outline of him, cupping his face with sweet tenderness. Her body, however, was anything but sweet.

She rocked against him, tilting her pelvis so that her heat brushed against the hard length of him. What happened to the sunshine Disney princess? She was fire. All-consuming. There was no hesitation in her kiss. Her lips demanded his response. Demanded that he give in to her. Joel wrapped both arms around her and held her tight, lips moving against her skin. Trailing a path down her neck to the edge of the scarf.

But the moment was shattered when a phone pealed out into the quiet night, shocking them both. She took a step back, shaking her head and reaching for her phone. He caught "sis" scrolling across the screen.

"It's Norah." She canceled the call, liquid eyes turned back to his. "She can wait."

He laughed and raked a hand through his hair. Reality was bleeding in, the chill of the night, the light flicking on in an apartment behind them as a neighbor spied on their moment. But Juliette's gaze was still full of fire.

"Do you . . . Well, would you . . . maybe . . ." She broke off in a self-conscious laugh.

*Yes.*

But her phone started ringing again. Juliette frowned. "Sorry, Norah doesn't usually call twice unless something is wrong."

"Take it."

She swiped her thumb across the screen. "Hey, Norah. What's up?"

A second later, the blood drained from her face and all of that sizzling heat was extinguished by a look of pure shock. Her hand dropped to her side, the phone call suspended.

"It's my boss, Bonnie," she said. "She's dead."

# *Chapter Sixteen*

**JOEL STOOD IN** the middle of Juliette's apartment, a small white terrier looking up at him with his head cocked and a tail wagging tentatively.

*Hello, stranger. What are* you *doing here?*

"Trust me, bud. I'm asking myself the same question," he said.

One minute he and Juliette had been kissing and she'd awkwardly—adorably—been trying to ask him to come up. For what? He didn't know. A drink. Another kiss. More. The next minute she'd been frantic, needing to go to her sister, who'd found out that Juliette's boss had passed away unexpectedly.

Without thinking, Joel had offered to help. *You go*, he'd said. *I'll look after Digger and feed him his dinner.*

"What are you *doing*?" he asked himself as he stood there. Digger circled him slowly, as if sizing up the situation.

*Beats me, dude. I was expecting a pretty brunette tonight. But I guess you'll do!*

Juliette's apartment was filled to the brim with cozy, personal objects. Everywhere he looked there were signs of the things she cherished, stuff that interested her and little moments of her history. By contrast, there were splashes of black and moodier accents, which he assumed belonged to her sister. It was a strange mélange of the two women's personalities—from the faded pink couch with the floral handsewn patch and rainbow grandma-style crochet blanket strewn over the back, to the vintage horror movie posters and the glossy black statue of a raven perched on a side table, a small skull clutched in its claw. There was a paperback sitting on the coffee table, the spine cracked as though it had been read many times, and on the cover a man with a suit jacket and shirt open to reveal a muscular chest and abs. The title, *Hard Deal*, glowed in yellow font.

"He took the time to put a belt on, but not to button up his shirt? Okay, then." He picked up the book and fanned the pages with his thumb until the bookmark showed him where Juliette was up to. "This is what you like, huh?"

His eyes glanced over the words, widening with each sentence.

Joel let out a surprised cough and dropped the book onto the table, sending the bookmark flying across the slick wood surface and onto the floor. "Shit."

Digger immediately took this as a game and darted around to pick it up.

"No! Digger, stop." He tried to beat the little dog to it, but instead he cracked his shin on the corner of the coffee table and yelped. Digger easily got to the bookmark before him and picked it up in his mouth, darting off into the apartment. "Give that back!"

Now Juliette was going to know he'd been snooping in her things.

*Hot damn, Disney princess likes the dirty stuff!*

How was he *not* going to think about that next time he saw her?

"Where did you go?" He had to get that bookmark back and make sure it looked like he hadn't even noticed the steamy romance novel on the coffee table.

Joel rounded a corner into a small corridor off which there were three rooms—he assumed, two bedrooms and a bathroom. The first door was closed tight. No way the dog went in there. The second door was ajar and he poked his head in. This must be Norah's room, judging by concert posters on the wall for Mastodon and something called Fleshgod Apocalypse. The bedspread was black-and-white check, and there were clothes strewn everywhere, as though she had been looking for something and then left in a rush.

But there was no sign of Digger.

He closed the door and continued on to the last room, Juliette's bedroom. By comparison, it was light and cheerful—with white bedding and two pink velvet pillows propped up against a pale wood bedhead, pink floral wallpaper behind it. There wasn't an item out of place, not even an errant sock under the bed. A tufted stool sat at the end of the bed with a pair of bunny slippers set neatly underneath.

"Of *course* she has bunny slippers."

Digger poked his head out from the other side of the bed, the tassel dangling out of his mouth.

"Come," he said. But the dog darted back behind the bed. "This isn't a game, okay? I'm about to out myself as a giant snoop. I can't have that, because then Juliette will think I'm the biggest hypocrite of all time."

But Digger showed no mercy.

He let out a playful growl, and Joel found him backed up against Juliette's bedside table. His tail was wagging and he jumped from side to side, paws dancing across the large floral rug that covered most of the cramped yet cozy room.

"Give it." He held a hand out. Digger continued to weave like a boxer ready to dodge a punch. "Come on, man. Help a brother out."

Digger stilled, as though he might be ready to concede defeat, but just as Joel relaxed, the dog took off, darting between his legs. Joel turned to chase him, but the space was tight and he clipped a dressing table, making several perfume bottles rattle. One impractically designed bottle with a long neck and small base wobbled and then dropped over the edge.

"No!"

Joel dove like a pro baseball player, arm outstretched toward the bottle as it hurtled toward the ground. It would be bad enough for Juliette to know he'd been looking in her steamy romance novel, but even worse for her to know he'd been in her bedroom without permission.

His fingers brushed cold glass and he wrapped a hand around the bottle, landing with an inelegant thump on the ground, the bottle safe and protected inside his fist. But Digger saw this as the next most exciting game they could play, and he abandoned the tasseled bookmark to jump up on Joel's chest, assaulting his face with a frantic pink tongue and stomping all over him with eager little paws.

"Stop." He laughed, seizing the dog with two hands and trying to pry him off. But Digger took this as an invitation for playtime, and he wriggled like a worm on a fishing hook and managed to get one long swipe of his tongue across Joel's cheek. "That's gross."

He'd been here before—rolling on the ground with a furry friend, laughing so hard his eyes watered while the puppy threw her chaotic energy all over the place.

*"I rescue you from a burning building and this is what I get? Pure violence." He laughed, hoisting the small chocolate brown Labrador off his chest. She was soft as a teddy bear, with paws that looked four times too big for her small body, and she always seemed to be careening around, like she only knew two speeds—100 mph or fast asleep in your lap.*

*"You gotta give that dog a name," the chief said. "Can't have a station dog with no name."*

*He looked at the puppy, who was scrambling back into his lap before he'd even had the chance to press up onto his feet. She was a cuddle-bug, for sure.*

*"How about Myla?" he said. "Because she goes a mile-a-minute."*

Digger leaped easily off Joel's lap and then head-butted his leg as if to say, *can you finish that walk down memory lane, already? It was dinnertime like an hour ago.*

Joel gave himself a shake and stood, swiping the bookmark from the ground before the dog could steal it again. "You hungry, little guy? Want some dinner?"

At the *d*-word, Digger immediately started turning in circles like he was chasing his own tail, then he took off out of the room like a rocket. Joel chuckled. If only he had *half* the energy of that dog, then he'd get way more done in his day.

He found Digger waiting by a blue ceramic bowl with yellow paw prints all over it, tail wagging and one paw raised like he was ready to shake, beg or do any trick required to get food in his belly as quickly as possible. Juliette hadn't given Joel many instructions—she was far too shell-shocked for that—but he could figure it out. Can opener, tin of dog food and a little sprinkle of dry kibble for good measure. He picked the bowl up to serve everything, figuring the little guy might try to stick his head in before he was done, and when he placed it on the ground, Digger practically dove in headfirst, wolfing everything down.

"Hey, slow down there," he chided gently. "You'll give yourself a stomachache."

He made a mental note to suggest Juliette get one of those "gulp bowls" that were designed to slow down the eating process. He'd bought one of those for Myla, because she was the most food-motivated dog he'd ever met, and she'd thrown up a few times after eating too quickly. The special bowl had been a game changer.

*Oh Myla. What are you doing now?*

He could imagine her big, warm eyes and the silky chocolate brown of her fur, and the way she lay her heavy head on his knees and let out a long sigh, content to be touching him. A pain grabbed at his chest and he pressed a palm there to soothe it. The day he'd come home to find Marissa and Myla gone . . . that pain didn't compare to anything he'd experienced except the death of his father and his best friend.

But that was Joel's life in a nutshell: loss came hard and frequent. Anytime he got attached, it felt like the universe ripped him away to teach him some lesson that he still hadn't figured out. So it was easier not to get involved. Not to get attached. And stupid as it might sound, it was why he moved to the other side of the country, away from his sisters. Maybe then Fate wouldn't lay her dirty hands on them.

*Not invested, huh? Sure seems like you're invested—helping a woman solve a murder and kissing her and feeding her dog and caring about what happens to her.*

It was a conundrum, but one Joel didn't have the mental energy to untangle tonight. Instead, he noticed there was a washing basket full of towels and microfiber cleaning cloths and socks sitting on the couch. Wanting to keep busy so he could avoid thinking about whether he really *did* care about Juliette—on more than just a "being a good person" level—he decided to take one thing off her to-do list.

As he was folding, Digger finished his dinner and came over to join him on the couch. The little dog leaped up, snuggled right up against his thigh and promptly fell asleep, his little pink belly sticking out. Joel couldn't help himself—he ran his fingers through the dog's wiry white fur, chuckling as Digger sighed contentedly in his sleep.

And in that moment, it was really damn hard for Joel not to wonder what life *might* be like with a woman to come home to and a dog to cuddle.

# *Chapter Seventeen*

*Three days later . . .*

**THE LAST THING** Juliette expected to see at a wake was an army of inflatable flamingos. Not to mention the soundtrack for the funeral itself had been less than somber—there couldn't be too many people who'd had their caskets loaded into the back of a hearse to the upbeat tune of the Bee Gee's "Stayin' Alive." And the funeral invitation had declared everyone *must* wear pink.

This was no average send-off for the dearly departed.

"I still can't believe she's dead." Juliette's eyes welled up and she attempted to blink the tears away, partially because Bonnie wouldn't want her to cry and partially because she knew Bonnie abhorred smudged mascara.

It had all happened so suddenly. She had set off for her cruise and that was the last any of them had heard from her. Though it turned out Bonnie's death wasn't a surprise to Bonnie herself, and she was never really going on a cruise. Instead, she went to a specialized cancer clinic in Colorado for a trial of some new, experimental treatment. She'd been fighting a battle, quietly, without wanting to worry anyone.

But she hadn't made it.

"She's not dead. She's . . ." Alexa paused for a second, her expression turning thoughtful as she twirled a long strand of strawberry blond hair around one finger. "Evolved to another plane of being. *Dead* sounds far too pedestrian for someone like Bonnie."

Norah nodded. "That's *exactly* something she would say."

The conversation paused as a topless waiter with rock-hard abs, wearing a pair of highlighter pink trousers and a matching bow tie, offered them more margaritas. The women replaced their empty glasses with fresh, full ones.

Alexa grinned. "This has got Bonnie written *all* over it."

It was beyond Juliette's comprehension how Alexa couldn't understand basic social conventions like telling a white lie to save someone's feelings, but totally jived with a hot pink funeral featuring knock-off Chippendale waiters. But even Juliette had to agree it *was* a perfect send-off for a woman whose life had been dedicated to spreading happiness and laughter to those around her.

God, Juliette would miss her. She'd loved working for Bonnie all these years, listening to her wild and crazy stories—half of which she was sure were embellished to the precipice of fiction—and learning all she could about running a pet grooming business. What would she do now, without her? What would happen to What The Fluff?

"This dress code certainly has Bonnie written all over it," Norah said with a sigh. Her style—which had once been described as "funeral chic" by a salty ex-boyfriend—didn't work for this all-pink occasion. Juliette had insisted Norah borrow something to adhere to the theme, because she couldn't handle the stress of her sister dishonoring a dead woman's wishes in front of the whole town! Besides, it was the least they could do for the woman who'd given them so much love over the years.

Close by, a group of older women wearing pink feather boas cheered, raising their glasses together and making whooping sounds. The cheers died down and were lost to the disco music pumping through the speakers.

"I'm still shocked she lied about going on that cruise." Juliette sipped her margarita and blinked at the tears that had started to spring anew. She and Alexa had both had a good cry during the funeral, and Norah had sat between them, dry-eyed but holding their hands. She never easily displayed her emotions—not the vulnerable ones anyway—but Juliette knew her twin was grieving deeply on the inside. "Why didn't she tell us what was going on so we could support her?"

Norah slung an arm around Juliette's shoulders and squeezed. "She knew we loved her and she wanted to spare us the worry. You know what she was like—always putting on a smile, even if things were hard. That was just her way."

"I guess," Juliette murmured. "But I wish we'd had the chance to say goodbye."

Bonnie must've had faith there wouldn't be a need for goodbyes if she'd put her hopes in an experimental treatment. Juliette was *sure* she would have come home to see them one last time if she'd had any inkling the end was near. Her heart squeezed. All she could wish for now was that Bonnie had died with hope still in her heart.

"Let's say goodbye now." Alexa raised her margarita glass. "To Bonnie, who lived fiercely and didn't take shit from anyone. Who advised us to always be ourselves and never let a man speak over us and to always carry a condom, just in case."

"To Bonnie," Juliette said with a watery smile. "For always listening to our dating woes, for wearing rhinestones to breakfast and for never letting anyone dull her shine."

"To Bonnie." Norah raised her glass. "If we're half as kickass as her when we're in our seventies, then our lives will have been a success. May she rest in peace."

"Hear, hear!" Glasses were clinked and eyes were wiped and each took a hearty sip as they soaked in the retina-searing splendor of the wake.

Inflatable flamingos bobbed against the ceiling and a giant candy buffet lined one side of the room, above which hung a picture of Bonnie. The portrait they'd chosen was perfect. It showed her in the midst of a full laugh, a touch of pink lipstick on her teeth, and her snow-white hair streaked with pink and purple, making her look like the love child of Betty White and a particularly fabulous unicorn. She was wearing one of her famously quirky T-shirts with "Have you seen my wiener . . . dog?" written across the front.

"What will happen to What The Fluff?" Juliette asked, worry edging into her voice. "Bonnie had been talking about me taking over for a while, but I refused to listen because I didn't even want to think about her not being there anymore."

"She made you sign on as a business partner, right? So you could run the show while she was away," Norah pointed out. "I told you at the time I thought that was overkill. But now it all makes sense."

"It was her backup plan," Juliette said, shaking her head. "In case she didn't come home."

Right at that moment, a man caught her gaze and crossed the room toward them. He wore a light gray suit with a pale pink tie and a matching pocket square, his silvery hair neatly styled. He looked like he should be on the cover of Distinguished Older Gentleman monthly. Perhaps he was a friend of Bonnie's. Or a relative.

Maybe he was a lover.

"Would you happen to be Ms. Alexa Anderson, Ms. Juliette Macintyre and Ms. Norah Macintyre?" the man asked.

The three women nodded. How strange that he knew their names. After all, it wasn't like they'd signed into the wake. Plenty of people here seemed to be from out of town, too. Bonnie had friends scattered everywhere, it seemed. She'd lived a whole other life before moving to Labrador Falls almost twenty years ago.

"I'm Arthur Harrington, Ms. Knight's attorney." He stuck his hand out, and each of the women shook it in turn. "I was hoping that you three would be here today. You've saved me a lot of work in tracking you down."

Norah raised a brow. "Tracking us down?"

"Unfortunately Ms. Knight was great with ideas but not so great with . . . well, details." He bobbed his head. "That's why I took care of her funeral arrangements. It's quite unconventional, but she said she wanted a pink funeral and to have "Stayin' Alive" played very loudly, bless her. Anyway, since I'm not from around here, I was worried I'd have my investigative work cut out for me. Ms. Knight spoke very highly of you three."

Juliette found it curious that Bonnie had spoken about them with her lawyer, but perhaps he was also a friend. Bonnie liked to collect people. They'd met a few members of her eclectic social circle today—a clairvoyant, a professional chef, a seventy-year-old burlesque dancer named Wanda, who was possibly the sexiest woman Juliette had ever seen. But there were lots of local folks, too, like Corinne Mursell and Patrizia Pisano and Reina Brown from Live Love Labrador. Even April from Brewed Awakening was here.

"I know this is short notice," Arthur continued. "But I'm hoping you might be free to meet with me tomorrow morning at Bonnie's place of business. I believe it's called . . . What The Fluff."

If she hadn't been so sad, Juliette would have cracked up at the well-spoken older gentleman saying What The Fluff in such a formal manner. "Of course. I can let us in. I worked with Bonnie."

"What's this meeting for?" Alexa asked.

"As beneficiaries of Ms. Knight's estate—"

"Beneficiaries?" Norah blinked.

Juliette shook her head. "What on earth are you talking about?"

"You three are named in Ms. Knight's will. Normally we would provide a copy of the document to any beneficiaries and heirs in the mail, but since I did not have your addresses, I was unable to do that." Arthur clicked his tongue as he pulled a business card and an envelope from the inside of his jacket. "She's also left a letter for you, which I was instructed to deliver."

Juliette took the envelope and inspected the business card, which had heavy cream paper with elegant gold embossing. While she wasn't particularly acquainted with the intricacies of business card production, it was clear this guy was no strip mall lawyer.

"See you tomorrow," he said. "I'll come past around 2:30 p.m."

With that, he melted back into the crowd.

"We're in her will?" Norah asked, shaking her head. "Since when? She never mentioned that."

Bonnie didn't have family, that much Juliette knew. It was why the three women tried to look out for her. Juliette would take her to appointments because Bonnie didn't drive anymore, and Norah often visited to clean her kitchen and bring groceries over. Alexa was 24/7 tech support for everything from restoring the internet to getting Bonnie logged back into Netflix and keeping her antivirus software up to date.

But did any of that really warrant an inheritance? Juliette didn't think so. Being a decent person was the bare minimum, wasn't it?

She used the edge of her nail to break the envelope's seal and inside was a single sheet of letter paper with Bonnie's old-fashioned cursive flowing across it. It looked like she'd tried to write as clearly as possible.

*My darling girls.*

*If you're reading this letter then something wonderful has happened. I am dead. That means, since I most certainly am going to heaven, that I will be partying with Elvis Presley, David Bowie and Dean Martin on cotton candy clouds. I'm pretty sure heaven gives you your best body back, too. Now I won't have to tuck my boobs into my trousers anymore! It's all I've ever wanted.*

*I'm sorry I didn't tell you what was going on. I loathe goodbyes and much prefer an Irish exit, but the times you three girls came to visit me were truly some of the highlights of my life. You dears are the daughters God refused to give me. I love you all and I want you to do great things with what I leave behind.*

*To my precious Juliette I leave my animal grooming business, What The Fluff. Make the business your own and stop being afraid of what everyone thinks of you.*

*To my quirky spirit-in-kind, Alexa, I leave my collection of vintage clothing and jewelry, and the contents of my safety deposit box. I know you will appreciate the treasure hunt that lies ahead.*

*To my independent and rebellious Norah, I leave my apartment. You're the only person I trust not to renovate it into an appalling minimalist nightmare. This also means you're now the custodian of my darling Pomeranian, Marshmallow. I know you will take good care of her.*

*Live fiercely, love harder and, most important of all, don't let the fuckers get you down.*

*Bonnie.*

Juliette leaned her head on Norah's shoulder and Alexa came in close from the other side. None of them said a word. An inheritance like this was life-changing. The business Juliette had always dreamed of but hadn't had the money (or confidence) to invest in, a permanent place for unsettled Norah to call her own and a collection of special items for Alexa, who'd always felt that she was overlooked by those who were supposed to love her.

Trust Bonnie to know exactly what each of them needed.

"I need a moment." Juliette thrust the letter into Alexa's hands and scurried off toward the woman's bathrooms, tears filling her eyes.

It was all too much. Bonnie was gone, Juliette now owned What The Fluff and nothing seemed right with the world anymore. How could she fill Bonnie's shoes? It was an impossible task. Bonnie *was* What The Fluff, through and through. There was no way Juliette could do her memory justice, not when she was already running the business into the ground with everyone thinking she killed a man while trying to kidnap someone's dog.

Her breath started to come quicker, panic clogging her throat.

What if she failed Bonnie? What if she turned What The Fluff from a thriving business into a sad empty storefront?

She turned into a hallway, her eyes filled with tears and the world a blurry mess in front of her. Each breath felt as though it was being dragged through a straw. Unsteady on her feet, the toe of the ridiculously high pink heels she'd worn—because they were Bonnie's favorite—caught on a ridge in the carpet and she stumbled, almost plowing right into someone coming the other way.

"Sorry!" She turned in time to see a figure dressed in a long pink coat and matching knitted wool cap disappearing around a corner. Weird. Why would they be wearing such heavy clothes inside? It felt like it was a hundred degrees in here, but that could simply be the grief and margaritas talking.

Holding back a sob, Juliette planted her palms against the swinging door marked with a small golden woman, and stumbled inside. Thankfully it was quiet in here. She needed a moment alone to think. To cry without people watching her.

"Oh Bonnie, I wish you'd told me what was going on," she said, looking tearfully at her reflection. "I wish you hadn't gone through it alone."

She hung her head, overwhelmed with emotion. But when she looked back up a moment later, something caught her attention. Several hot pink feathers dusted the countertop, and when she followed the trail of them downward, Juliette noticed several more on the floor. But there was something else—a crumpled heap of fabric sticking out from one of the toilet stalls.

"What the . . . ?"

A sickly sense of déjà vu flooded her. It wasn't a crumpled heap of fabric. It was a body, with two feet sticking out from under the stall door. Dropping to the ground, Juliette peered under the door and when she did, she let out a bloodcurdling scream.

It was Patrizia Pisano, and she had been strangled with a pink feather boa.

# *Chapter Eighteen*

**"OKAY, SO YOUR** foster mom is going to be really sad today, and it's your job to cheer her up." Joel looked down at the little white fluff ball in front of him, whose warm, treat-motivated gaze was locked firmly onto the piece of dried meat in his hand.

Digger cocked his head.

"Remember what I taught you?" Joel stepped backward, keeping his free hand up in a Stay position. "Digger, where's Juliette's present?"

Digger's ears pricked up at the familiar command and he immediately set off, nose to the ground, sniffing his way around Joel's living room, until he found what he was looking for. Snapping his jaw around a single plastic rose, he came trotting back, tail in the air, looking proud as punch.

"Now give it to me." The dog released the rose at his feet. "Bow."

Digger lowered his front half and lay his chin on both paws, looking like he was bowing to a queen.

"Good job! High five." He held his hand out and Digger jumped up, smacking one paw against his palm. "You've earned this."

He held the treat out and Digger hoovered it up from his hand, running away to go enjoy his spoils in peace. Joel shook his head, laughing. The dog was super smart! He'd learned all that in one single afternoon, only needing a few repeats to understand his role. Color Joel completely impressed.

"You catch on way quicker than my Myla ever did," Joel said. "But that's still too many treats for one day. You're going to be like a toddler wired on sugar and red food coloring if we don't get some of that energy out of your system."

He picked up the rose and stashed it in his leather satchel with a few of Digger's things, like the poop bags Juliette had given him and some hypoallergenic wipes for his paws, since it had been rainy and muddy overnight.

He couldn't believe he'd volunteered to look after the dog *again*. But when Juliette had come home that night, eyes red and puffy, saying there was already a funeral planned for her boss and she didn't know what she was going to do with Digger since her sister would be at the funeral, too, Joel put his hand up to help without thinking twice. It'd been years since he'd hung out with a furry friend and he'd forgotten how much fun it could be. And what good company.

Dogs didn't judge. They didn't poke at you or demand answers or want more than you had to give. They were simply happy to hang out.

Joel checked his watch, frowning. The wake should have been over by now, but Juliette hadn't texted him yet. Maybe the life celebration had run longer than planned. Weirdly, he didn't mind. A few more hours with Digger would be a good time . . . even if he'd never admit it out loud. The little guy had charmed him. And after April had asked for a day off to attend the funeral, he'd decided to close the café for the day. To his surprise, he was actually enjoying having time off.

After helping Digger into a red-and-blue-check doggy jacket—which made him look like a tiny lumberjack—they set off. Outside, the air was blanketed in gloom and the footpath was splattered with mud and filthy, leaf-drenched puddles. But tiny bits of sun peeked through between silvery clouds, almost like it was trying to stay positive no matter how much the cold persisted.

He'd been thinking about Juliette all day. She was really close to her boss and was totally blindsided by her passing. Joel understood that feeling better than anyone, the way fate could rip a person from your life like they'd never even existed. Maybe he should pick her up some pastries from the bakery. It wouldn't cure her grief, but he knew how easy it was to go off one's food when you were sad like that.

"Quick detour," he said to Digger. "We're going to pick up a snack for Juliette."

Digger looked back over his shoulder, *Roger that, boss.*

They turned off the road and headed toward the town square so Joel and Digger could swing by the bakery for treats. But just as he was about to tie Digger up to wait outside, Serenity McFarlane approached, dressed in her signature colorful workout gear. She must be heading to work, since she was wearing a pink hoodie that said Live. Love. Labrador across the front with the wellness center's logo embroidered beneath it.

"Hi, Joel." Serenity's face lit up and one of her hands immediately landed on his arm. The woman had no sense of personal space.

*You wouldn't mind if it was Juliette touching your arm.*

"I'm *so* sorry to hear about your business neighbor passing away," she said, looking in the direction of What The Fluff and frowning. But her compassion seemed like an excuse to get closer to him and press her boobs into his arm. "Are you okay? You must be devastated! I heard the funeral was today. Did you go?"

One of his regulars exited the bakery and looked on with a raised eyebrow. Joel attempted to pull his arm away, because the last thing he wanted was anything getting back to Juliette about him being cozy with someone else. And the way rumors started here, that information would fly around town like a 747. But Serenity held on tight.

*Why would it matter? You're not dating Juliette. You didn't make any promises.*

He was also categorically *not* interested in Serenity—she was too young for him and, worse, too pushy.

"No, I didn't know her that well. But yes, it's very sad."

"You feel so tense." She squeezed his bicep. "I can help you with that. Why don't you come by the studio at eight? I've had a cancellation. I could give you a private lesson."

He disentangled his arm, but not before two more people had come out of the bakery and made note of her touching him.

"I'm afraid I have . . . uh . . ." He looked around, scrambling for an excuse. Digger shuffled by his feet, *Bro, sub me in. I can help!* "Dog sitting duties."

"You can bring this little cutie." She smiled, but then cocked her head. "This is Juliette's dog, right?"

"She's fostering him." He carefully squeezed past Serenity to get to the bakery door. "I have to get going. Errands and . . . stuff."

"Come see me anytime." She waggled her fingers and headed off in the direction of the wellness center.

Jeez, that one laid it on *thick*.

After acquiring the pastries and untying Digger's leash, something caught his attention across the town square. Shadows moved in the front window of What The Fluff. It was Juliette. Why hadn't she called him to pick up Digger if she was done with the funeral? He walked over to the front door and tried the handle. Locked. A handwritten sign said: We Are Closed Unexpectedly, Apologies.

Juliette glanced up from the front desk and came over to unlock the door. She was wearing a pink pantsuit that looked like a costume from the *Barbie* movie, with fitted pants that showed off her legs and a pair of pointed stilettos in an equally obnoxious shade of pink. But despite the cheery outfit, her skin was pale, her eyes looked hollowed out and the corners of her mouth pulled downward. The overwhelming urge to cradle her surged through his body.

"Hey, sorry I didn't call. I . . ." Tears filled her eyes and her lower lip wobbled. "Oh Joel, something terrible has happened."

"What?" He came into the salon, Digger trotting ahead of him, and she locked the door behind them.

"Come out the back, I don't want anyone to see me," she said. He followed her out to the grooming room, where she bent to unclip Digger's harness and help him out of his jacket. Her hands were shaking.

"What's going on?"

"At the funeral, I . . ." She sucked in a breath. "Someone killed Patrizia!"

"Someone killed Patrizia at your boss's funeral?"

"And I found the body."

"Oh." He nodded slowly. "That's probably not good."

"No, it's not. Detective Dooley came after we called 911, and they took me back to the station again to question me. He said . . ." She sniffled. "He said it was 'highly unlikely' that I would find two bodies without being involved in the murders. That he was close to having something to pin on me. That he knows I did it. But I didn't! I swear."

She was spiraling.

"And now that Bonnie's dead, she's left her business with me. I have to meet with her lawyer tomorrow and I'm scared. Everything is going wrong." She was talking quickly, her breath coming in shallow puffs. "People will stop coming here because they hate me and the legacy Bonnie built is all going to be ruined because of me."

"Slow down." He placed his satchel and the bag of pastries on the silver table next to them. Then he grasped her shoulders and squeezed gently. "Take a breath."

She sucked in a tiny breath that wouldn't do anything to calm her nervous system.

"Bigger than that," he said. "Follow me."

He sucked in a long, slow breath, held it for a second and then released it. Juliette did the same and he immediately saw a little more clarity come into her dark brown eyes.

"And again." They breathed together and her shoulders dropped a little more. "Whatever happens with all this, we'll figure it out."

"We?" she asked, smiling even though she still looked stressed out of her mind.

"I made a promise, didn't I? And we're not done, yet. This murder hasn't been solved."

"*Murders*, now. Plural." She sighed. "I guess we were wrong about Patrizia. Whoever killed Maurice more than likely killed her, too. Unless there's a second murderer . . . but I don't believe it. This is all connected."

"I agree. Maybe Patrizia knew who took the Bob Dylan record and someone killed her to keep it quiet," Joel mused.

"It's possible. I don't know what I'm going to do. Detective Dooley is hunting me and he's getting close. You should have seen him, Joel." She looked up at him, worry creasing her forehead and knitting her brows together. "He looks at me like I'm nothing. Less than nothing."

"You're *not* nothing," he said fiercely, the words slipping out before he even had a chance to think about what they meant.

Shit. He was getting in *way* over his head.

"I brought you pastries." He gestured to the bag. It felt like a stupid thing to do, but food was safer than words. Because his words were betraying him. His words showed he cared.

"Why?" She looked confused.

"I know I forget to eat when I'm stressed and I didn't want you going around without something in your stomach." He swallowed. Damn. The words were betraying him again. "And I taught Digger a trick as well."

Her eyes brightened. "You did?"

"Let me show you." He turned around and stealthily grabbed the plastic rose from his satchel, hiding it behind his back so she couldn't see what he was doing. "Digger, where's Juliette's present?"

Digger trotted over from where he'd been sniffing around the floor, tail pointed in the air and furry ears perked straight up. He looked around, searching for his target. Behind his back, Joel let the rose hang down so it was low enough for Digger to reach it. The little dog grabbed it in his mouth and came trotting back around, trying to give it back to Joel.

"No, it's not for me." To be fair, this was *exactly* how they'd practiced it. Digger got tired of waiting for Joel to take it and released the rose onto the ground. "It's for your foster mom."

Digger tilted his head as if to say, *you're supposed to say bow next, dummy.*

"Bow," Joel said. Digger performed the final part of his trick, just to the wrong person. "Ah, sorry. That didn't quite work out the way I'd hoped. He was supposed to do all that for you."

Joel bent to pick up the rose and handed it to Juliette, whose eyes were still red-rimmed but now had a slight sparkle to them. And her mouth wasn't turned down so much anymore. It warmed him in some deep, dark place that hadn't felt a glow in a *very* long time.

"You taught him to do that *today*? In one afternoon?" she asked, accepting the rose.

"He's a quick learner."

"Sounds like you might be a good teacher."

Digger pawed at his leg, looking for a treat. "You've had enough treats today, bud. You'll be pinging off the walls tonight if we keep going."

"You're pretty good with him for someone who claims not to like dogs." She bent and ruffled Digger's fur, so at least he got something for his efforts. He nuzzled up into Juliette's hand, eyes squeezing shut in happiness.

"I may have exaggerated my feelings a bit," he admitted. "I . . . had a dog, once. I rescued her from a warehouse that caught fire. She had been chained up by some asshole—might not have made it out alive if we hadn't found her so quickly."

Juliette gasped. "Oh my gosh, that's awful. Thank goodness you found her!"

"She was a chocolate Lab. We called her Myla because she raced around the fire house a mile-a-minute." He raked a hand through his hair, feeling unsure of why he was saying any of this. Juliette didn't need to know about his past. About his wounds. "She was a good girl."

*She was the best girl.*

Juliette opened her mouth as if to ask a question but then snapped it shut like she thought better of it. She probably wanted to know what happened to Myla.

*You and me, both.*

All he knew was that Marissa loved that dog as much as he did and, truthfully, Myla had chosen Marissa to be her number one human, despite it being Joel who'd found her. And yes, there was part of him that would never forgive Marissa for taking her away without giving him the chance to say goodbye. A *big* part of him. Most of him, even. But at least Myla was safe and loved. He clung to that thought in the moments where he missed her like crazy.

It felt like he should say something else, but he didn't know what. Juliette had been through a lot today, and he wasn't sure if pastries and dog tricks were enough to help. It felt like he needed words, too. But his mind was all gummed up.

Just as he was fishing around, trying to think of the right thing to say, the sound of glass shattering had them both running to the front of What The Fluff.

Juliette almost tripped over Digger in her haste, but Joel was hot on her heels, scooping the little dog up to keep him out of harm's reach. The salon's black-and-white-tiled floor was covered in glittering shards from the front window, which now had a big hole through it. Among the glass debris lay a heavy orange brick, a note taped to it.

"Careful," Joel warned as Juliette stepped gingerly toward the brick, avoiding the larger pieces of glass. Smaller pieces crunched underfoot as she crouched, tearing the note away from the packing tape that had kept it stuck to the brick.

"You'll regret what you did," Juliette read out loud. She turned to Joel. "What if this is from the killer?"

"This is some Scooby-Doo shit." He frowned, trying to hang on to the squirming Digger. "No way. I am not putting you down, little friend. Not until we get this place cleaned up."

"I'll get a broom," Juliette said, but Joel blocked her path.

"You can sweep up *after* you call the police."

Her face hardened. "I'm not calling the police."

"Juliette—"

"They will be *no* help to me, Joel. They've already made that very clear." She shook her head. "You have no idea what it's been like since my dad left the force. Every single one of them has been waiting for Norah or me to screw up for years, so they can get back at my dad for what he did."

"But you *haven't* screwed up. Someone defaced your place of work and made a direct threat to you."

"Too bad they didn't sign it," she said, looking at the piece of paper.

"Yes, but this is proof you're not the killer," he insisted. "If you clean up now and tell them about this later, they won't believe it happened. You've got proof in every piece of glass here. They could dust the brick for prints . . ."

She let out a long sigh. Joel got the feeling she wouldn't admit that he was right, so the sigh was probably as close as it would get.

"Do you want me to call them?" he offered. "Maybe they'll take it more seriously if it comes from someone else?"

She stood among the glass, an expression of being utterly lost marring her beautiful face. It was the haunted look of a woman staring into some dark abyss, unsure whether she could avoid being sucked in.

"Sure," she relented. "If you think it will help."

"I do." He passed Digger over to her and she turned to take him back into the grooming room, away from the broken glass.

For some reason, the sight of her walking away felt like a bad omen.

# *Chapter Nineteen*

**DETECTIVE DOOLEY HAD** been through What The Fluff's front doors for less than three seconds before Juliette regretted calling the police. She should *not* have let Joel convince her. The detective surveyed the area with his hands behind his back, thick chest puffed out in a way that obscured the view of his neck, making it look like someone had rested a particularly unattractive cantaloupe atop a beer barrel.

"And you touched the note, you say?" Shane Dooley asked.

"Yes, I did." Juliette's arms were folded defensively across her chest, and Joel shot her a look from behind the detective's back. She uncrossed them but felt naked. So she folded them again and Joel rolled his eyes. "A brick came through my window with something attached to it. I wanted to see what it was."

"That creates quite the pickle, you see." The detective sniffed, his ice blue zombie eyes roaming almost listlessly over the salon like he was doing his utmost to show how little he cared. "Because you've tampered with evidence."

"I didn't tamper with it. That implies this place was a crime scene I wasn't supposed to be at," she replied through gritted teeth. "And I *am* supposed to be here."

"It also conveniently puts your fingerprints all over the note. I suppose you touched the brick as well?" His tone made it sound like he was talking to a particularly small, particularly unintelligent child, and Juliette's blood boiled hot enough to flash fry an egg.

"I removed the note from the brick, so it's possible I touched it in the process," she replied. "But I didn't move it. Where you see it now is where it landed when someone threw it through the window."

"Someone," he murmured.

"The murderer, I assume." She glared at him.

"And they think you regret something, do they? What do you regret, Juliette?" He turned to her and she instinctively took a step backward, her shoe crunching over a piece of glass. Shane Dooley had always made her feel that way—backed into a corner, targeted. "Have you done something that might interest the police?"

She hesitated. In truth, she didn't actually know *what* the note was referring to.

Maybe they thought she would regret poking around in the investigation.

Or maybe the killer thought she'd seen their identity as they ran from the bathroom where Patrizia was killed—which, sadly, she hadn't—and told police.

Or it could be something else entirely. Maybe they simply wanted to rattle her cage.

*Good job then. Consider me rattled.*

"All I know is that you're looking at the wrong person," she said stubbornly. "I didn't do it."

"I think what Juliette means to say," Joel added in a weirdly smooth, soothing voice Juliette had never heard come out of his mouth before. "Is that this should provide proof that she's not the person who killed Maurice or Patrizia."

Detective Dooley looked at Joel, a strange expression on his face. It was almost . . . amusement. But why?

"I'm afraid it provides no proof at all," he replied.

Joel frowned. "But someone threw a brick through the window with a threatening note. That means Juliette isn't the killer."

"The note says that Juliette should regret what she did," the detective pointed out. He scrubbed a hand over his jaw, where pinpricks of ginger hair pushed through his fish belly pale skin. "How do we know it isn't simply a concerned citizen saying she should regret murdering Maurice Allsop?"

Oh shit. What if the killer was trying to set her up by making it look like someone knew she'd killed Maurice? And she'd walked right into the trap without even realizing by calling the cops and drawing their attention to it.

"A concerned citizen throwing a brick through someone's window is ridiculous," Joel scoffed. "There's a million other ways they could express their concern before doing that."

"It's also the kind of suitably vague note someone might write to throw suspicion off themselves," the detective added.

Juliette gasped. "You think *I* threw the brick through my own window? That's . . . outrageous."

"Do you have security footage for the front of the shop?" the detective asked.

"No," she admitted. "Bonnie didn't believe in surveillance, and besides, Labrador Falls is a safe town. Lots of businesses here don't have security cameras."

The detective made a *hmm* noise. "That's convenient."

"I don't have security cameras outside my café, either," Joel pointed out. "It's hardly a sign of anything. And I was here with Juliette when the brick came through the window, so there's no way she could have done it herself."

"I have your word for it and no concrete proof. So I'm afraid, it doesn't count for much." The detective shrugged. "Especially given you're not exactly known for telling the truth."

Joel paled.

Juliette looked at him, her brows coming together. "What's *that* supposed to mean?"

"Joel isn't exactly here in Labrador Falls simply for a change of scenery, like he enjoys telling people." The detective was almost glowing with enjoyment at Joel's discomfort. It was as if he grew a foot taller, puffing up like some tropical bird in a mating ritual, shaking his feathers for everyone to see. "He's keeping his past hidden."

"You're a bastard," Joel growled.

"Did you know he's married?" the detective said, smiling gleefully at Juliette. "What's her name? Marissa, isn't it?"

Joel looked like he was ready to take a swing at the detective.

But all Juliette could think about was the kiss they shared. That warm, passionate, cozy, delicious cider-tinged kiss. The memory was in vivid technicolor—the Halloween decorations glinting off his dirty blond hair, the warm golden tones in his eyes, the touch of pink in his cheeks. The way everything went dark when his lips descended on hers, allowing her to focus only on the feel and taste of him.

"I'm *separated*," Joel gritted out. "And I have divorce paperwork on my desk."

"Ah, but have you signed it? I know for a fact that letter came in well over a week ago. Maybe longer." The detective was almost levitating with how much he loved having power over the situation.

"That's *not* what we're here to discuss."

"To be honest, I thought you'd move on to that hot little piece, Serenity. I saw you two talking earlier," the detective added.

Joel took a step toward the detective, but the other man didn't budge.

"Don't threaten me, Joel. It would be easy for more people to know about this . . . about how you left your brother-in-law to die in a burning building."

Juliette's mouth dropped open in shock. "What?"

It felt like blow after blow.

"It's none of anyone's business," Joel snapped.

Juliette's heart sank like a stone plummeting to the bottom of the ocean. The whole time Joel had been opening up—telling her about Myla, taking care of Digger, helping her with the investigation, *kissing* her—he'd been married and keeping it a secret. Not to mention the thing about leaving his brother-in-law in a burning building. What the hell was that even about?

Oh, and talking with Serenity? What could they possibly have to talk about? Maybe he was more interested in her than he was letting on.

"Both of you get out," she said, drawing in a ragged breath. "I need to clean up this mess."

Joel looked crestfallen. "Juliette—"

"Please, Joel. It's been a very long day and I need to be alone right now." In the background, there was a scratching that sounded a whole lot like a little white dog pawing to be let out of the grooming room.

"Should I take that as a sign you don't want to file an official report?" Detective Dooley asked smugly.

"No, I don't." Juliette turned her back on both men and went to get the broom from the cleaning supply closet.

The detective's leather shoes crunched loudly over the glass as he left, almost as if he was trying to make more work for her on the way out. A few seconds later a second set of footsteps followed, softer and without the crunching.

Only then did Juliette let her head fall.

**AFTER JULIETTE SWEPT** up the glass so she could release Digger from his temporary imprisonment, she called a glazier about fixing the window. Then she taped cardboard across the hole so no critters could get in during the night because the last thing she needed was to find a family of raccoons squatting here. Frankly, she wasn't sure she would back herself in a fight against a raccoon. They might have cute faces and tiny hands, but they were scrappy creatures who didn't back down.

"Ugh, *why* are you thinking about raccoons?"

Digger looked over and sniffed. *Okay, now she's talking to herself. Should I be worried? Or only if she starts answering herself.*

"Maybe I am losing it," she muttered. "I'm thinking about raccoons and giving a dog an inner monologue."

Digger backed away slowly. *She's answering herself. I'm officially worried.*

"Can you believe that Joel is *married*?" She flopped down into one of the chairs usually reserved for her waiting customers. Digger trotted warily over, his toenails clicking against the black-and-white-tiled floor. "He *did* say he was separated, so I guess that's not as bad as if he was, like, actually with his wife. Is it cheating? Probably not, right? Unless she thinks they're getting back together. And what was that comment about Serenity? He doesn't like her, does he? He should have told me he was married before he kissed me."

She was totally discombobulated.

On one hand, it wasn't like Joel had promised her anything besides keeping an eye out for her as she investigated Maurice's death. On the other hand . . . she thought the kiss meant something. If it wasn't for the news of Bonnie's death, who knows where it might have led.

"Just a few weeks ago my life was ticking along fine! Bonnie was running the show here, and I was happy being a simple worker bee, flirting with Joel on my lunch break and *not* being a murder suspect." She dropped her head into her hands. "Now I've got all the responsibility and . . . I don't know if I can manage it."

She felt a light pressure at her shin. When she parted her palms to peer through the gap, Digger was sitting in front of her, one paw gently pressed to her leg like he was trying to say, *hey, everything is going to be okay, human friend.* She leaned down and picked him up, placing him on her lap, where he immediately nuzzled into the crook of her elbow. Jack Russells weren't always the cuddliest breed, despite their small size, due to their strong independent streak. And while you couldn't fault a JR's loyalty, it didn't always translate into snuggles.

But Digger seemed to know what she needed right now.

This little guy was the only thing she didn't need to worry about—so long as she walked him and fed him, he was happy. And that made her happy. There were no mind games, no secrets, no hidden agendas. The warmth of his small body was such a comfort that her heart rate immediately began to settle.

"Maybe I should get a cottage in the woods and keep an army of dogs," she said, her voice muffled into the top of his head. "I'll be like a nicer version of a hag or something."

But running away didn't solve problems.

Look at her parents, for instance. After her dad was fired from the police force and shunned by the locals, he and her mother had retreated to their property on the outskirts of town, where they'd become as self-sustaining as possible, growing their own vegetables and using solar panels for electricity and only venturing close to the center of Labrador Falls on rare occasions. But what had it done? It had left the townsfolk to direct their ire toward Norah and Juliette, since the person they were truly angry at wasn't around. And it had let people speak on their behalf, stoking the flames of his indiscretions so that they continued to burn brightly while he hid away from the world.

It hadn't blown over. It never would.

So she couldn't run away like her parents had; she had to stay and fight. It's what Bonnie would want.

"That's enough wallowing for one day," she said, giving herself a shake. Since the glazier wasn't coming until the morning, there was no point sitting around. "Let's get some fresh air. That will make everything feel better."

Outside, the weather had turned, almost as if soured by the afternoon's events. Thick black clouds clustered overhead and the wind whipped, but the sky over the dog park still looked blue enough. It wouldn't be a long play at the park—but she owed Digger at least a *little* romp around. He'd been such a good boy, learning that trick Joel had taught him and comforting her when she needed it.

However, by the time she reached the dog park Juliette was starting to wonder if she'd been overly optimistic about the patch of blue sky. It was rapidly darkening, and dots of water speckled her pink suit jacket. She shivered. Since she hadn't planned on going anywhere after the funeral, she was underdressed with only a scarf knotted around her neck to keep the chill off. But the wind cut right through her clothes.

"I probably should have bought some other shoes, huh?" She looked down at her high heels, which were totally impractical for the grass. But Digger was tugging hard on his leash, beelining straight for the enclosed small dog area. "Might have to be a quick visit today."

There wasn't a soul around, because everyone else was doing the smart thing and getting the hell inside to hunker down before the heavens opened up. It seemed to turn black within minutes, the wind pushing the clouds across the sky until they blotted out every last bit of light. As they made it to the gate, a prickling sense of intuition halted her.

"I think this is a bad idea," she said. "Sorry, Digger. We need to turn back."

If she hurried, she might make it back to What The Fluff before all hell broke loose, and then she could call Norah or

Alexa to come get her. The sound of something crunching behind her made Juliette whip around—a sense of déjà vu sliding down her spine like a raindrop streaking across a car windshield. The morning she'd found Maurice's body, she had been *sure* someone was watching her. But it had just been a raccoon, hadn't it? Or was someone there? The wind stole a strand of hair free from her bun, slashing it across her face. Shadows crept along the path that led back to the parking lot. Trees juddered in the wind. She heard another sound, this time to the left. Louder. Like someone was getting closer.

Juliette's heartbeat kicked up a notch and she clutched Digger's leash so tight her knuckles were paper white. "Who's there?"

The only response was the whistle of wind and a distant howl—a wild animal? Or someone's dog? The raindrops grew fatter, leaving darkened polka dots on her suit jacket. They needed to go. Now.

"Come on." She tugged Digger away from the park, but he resisted, throwing every single one of his fifteen pounds into standing his ground. His little body tilted away from her at such an angle that he would go tumbling over if she let go of the leash. *Pleeeeeease! You promised park time!* "Digger, come on. We have to go. It's—"

Her words were cut short when a flash in her peripheral vision wrenched a scream from her throat, just as a gloved hand clamped over her mouth. A wiry, strong arm snaked around her waist, pinning her arms to her side.

Juliette struggled against the assailant, but she was held firm like a fly in a spider's trap. She felt the leash slip from her fingertips and she tried to call out, to tell Digger to run, but the sound was muffled against the gloved hand. What was she supposed to do? Juliette had always begged her mom to get her out of the self-defense classes they tried to foist on the girls at school. She should have attended!

*I'm not going to die today, dammit. My funeral would never be as cool as Bonnie's!*

Throwing her head back, she tried to make connection with the person behind her, but they were quick, leaning out of the way. Digger let out a frantic bark. He raced around them, sharp cries piercing the howling air. Juliette felt the person's weight shift behind her as a leg shot out to try to kick Digger.

"You should have been arrested by now." The words were hissed into her ear, but the low tone and raging wind made it hard to recognize the voice. It could have been anyone. Juliette struggled to turn her head, trying to get a look at the person who'd grabbed her. "Then I could have everything I wanted."

Out of the corner of her eye, Juliette saw a flash of fabric as something was brought up over her face, replacing the area where the gloved hand had been a moment ago. Digger's barking intensified. There was an oddly sweet smell, almost lemony like a cleaning product, but it was followed swiftly by an acrid nail polish remover scent. The world suddenly tilted and Juliette swayed, her eyes fluttering as nausea roiled through her.

Her knees buckled and the strength went out of her body.

Digger panicked, his high-pitched yips cutting through the building storm. The rain was coming down harder now and Juliette's heels slid across the grass, her body sluggish and struggling to keep balance. All of a sudden there was a blur of white and a scream from behind Juliette, which was so loud in her ear that she winced, clamping her eyes shut against the flash of blinding pain in her skull. Her stomach protested violently but she managed to keep control. Barely. The arms loosened around her body and Juliette slumped to the ground, landing hard on her hands and knees, rainwater soaking through her suit pants. She heaved. Dammit. Why did she have that second margarita at the wake?

But then there were footsteps. Running. The person who attacked her was gone. Juliette tried to lift her head, but it felt like a bowling ball. Digger was all up in her face, swiping his tongue across her cheek and dancing from paw to paw.

"Did you save me?" she said, her voice sounding strangely muffled. "Good boy."

The cold air and even colder rain streaked across her skin, the fuzziness that had gripped her starting to clear. She had to get out of here in case her attacker came back. On the ground, next to where Digger was fussing over her, was a torn piece of fabric with what looked like small brown hairs stuck to it. She stuffed it into her pocket and grabbed her phone, clumsily dialing Norah. She tried to push up to sitting but the nausea rolled in ferociously, forcing her to close her eyes and take a few slow, deep breaths.

Whatever the person had used to try to knock her out had gotten damn close.

*"Hi, this is Norah's voicemail. Leave a message if you want, I probably won't check it—"*

She hung up before the beep. Alexa was next, but her number went to voicemail as well. Juliette was soaked and shivering, and Digger huddled beside her. She needed to get out of here fast.

And there was only one other person she knew she could count on.

# *Chapter Twenty*

**JOEL BARELY SAID** a word the whole drive to Juliette's place, but his gaze continually flicked over to where she sat in the passenger's seat, Digger cradled on her lap. Knowing he was keeping watch over her was a small comfort. But she was still shaken, vulnerable and unsure what the hell to do next. How did one bounce back from almost possibly maybe being murdered? If not for Digger, then . . .

She shivered.

*You should have been arrested by now. Then I could have everything I wanted.*

What did that even mean? Perhaps Detective Dooley's insistence on Juliette being the number one suspect wasn't *only* due to his family's beef with her father. Was someone setting her up? But why? How was Juliette the barrier to the killer getting what they wanted?

Rain streaked across the glass, the windshield wipers furiously trying to bat the water away. It was almost like being in a car wash. There was something private about it, the way it blocked out the rest of the world. For a few moments, Juliette was happy to pretend there was nothing but the inside of this car . . . even if it did smell like wet dog.

"Thanks for coming to get me," she said softly as they pulled up outside her place. The lights were off, because Norah was still staying at Bonnie's with Marshmallow. It might be like that permanently now, once the will was sorted. "I uh . . . I'm sorry I told you to get out before."

Joel killed the engine and pulled the handbrake up, then twisted in the seat to face her. The headlights of a passing car glimmered on the streaks of rain coating the window, lighting up his face for a moment, before sending them back into near darkness.

"I'm just glad you're safe," he said, and he seemed to mean it. His warm eyes searched her face, his lips pinched slightly. "And I regret convincing you to call the police about the brick through your window. You were right, they're no help at all."

She bit down on her lower lip and nodded. There was so much to say and yet . . . did she want to say anything? Did she want to *know* anything more about Joel, the married-but-separated man who now felt like a complete mystery to her. A complete stranger.

He swallowed. "I should have told you I was married."

"You don't—"

"I kissed you. So yes, I should have said something if only to assure you I'm not the kind of man who cheats on his wife." He blew out a long breath and ran a hand through his hair. The longish strands parted but sprang back into place. Even the hair on his head had a stubborn streak. "Marissa and I haven't seen each other for years. Our marriage has been over a long time. It's simply that I haven't done the paperwork to make it formal. That's all."

The rain pattered down on the car, drumming across the metal roof and hood like a tiny marching band, but without any pizzazz. She stroked Digger's head and the little dog squirmed, agitated that he still hadn't gotten to race any of his energy out.

"You don't owe me anything," she replied. "We're not dating."

"Right. I don't want the cow, just the milk for free, remember?" he said, quoting Ruth.

In spite of herself, Juliette let out a little snort. "Thanks for defending me by saying I'm not a cow."

"No way you could be, farm animals aren't really my thing." The second he said those words, a frown crossed his face. "Not that I'm saying . . ."

"So I'm not *your thing*." She wished it didn't sting quite so much, but even after all this, there was a little part of her—okay, more than a little part—that still wanted to invite Joel inside and see if a second kiss might be even better than the cider-flavored first.

"Juliette, you are about as far from 'my thing' as one could possibly get, and I'm not sure I could pay you a bigger compliment," he replied, scrubbing a hand along his jaw. "Because 'my thing' is running away from my problems and burying myself in my work as a way of numbing out and telling myself that I don't need anybody, ever."

She tilted her head.

"And you," he continued, "run headlong into things with wide eyes. You're always looking to make a friend, even with the person most likely to avoid friendship, and you're still hopeful and caring and kind even after years of the folks in this town blaming you for something you didn't do. So no, you're not 'my thing.' You're far better than that."

"Do you regret kissing me?" she asked, deciding to take the bull by the horns. It was terrifying to put things on the line, but maybe now was the time to stop worrying about people rejecting her and find out where she stood.

"I probably should, but I don't."

"Would you like to come inside?" she asked, holding her breath as she waited for his answer. "It's been a hell of a day and that apartment is very empty right now, and I don't want to be alone."

Joel's gaze roamed over her. She must look a sight—hair drenched, suit plastered to her, and she was pretty sure she had something fluffy stuck to the corner of her lip. Probably lint from her scarf. Thank goodness she'd had the forethought to wear waterproof mascara to the funeral, or else she'd be panda-eyed on top of it all.

"Yeah." He nodded. "I'll come inside."

She pushed the door open before he had a chance to change his mind and held Digger as she bumped the car door closed with her hip. Then she dragged her soggy self up the stairs to the front door and hoped Joel was following her inside.

**TEN MINUTES LATER** Juliette was freshly showered, her face washed, and she'd changed into a pair of soft pants and a cozy buttoned-up cardigan. Joel had offered to give Digger his dinner and make them a coffee while she was warming herself up.

It was a good thing he was here—both the man and the dog. If Juliette had needed to come home alone after today, she would have been checking every window and lock, jumping at her own shadow and feeling utterly miserable.

She padded down the hallway in sock-covered feet and hovered at the open archway, watching Joel and Digger playing in the living room. Joel was crouched, holding on to a toy that Digger had firmly in his mouth, and a fierce game of tug-of-war was going on. Even at this distance, she could see the crinkle at the edge of Joel's eyes. She didn't say a word, not wanting to interrupt the moment between them.

But Joel clearly felt like he was being watched and suddenly looked up at her, releasing the toy and standing. He cleared his throat. "He needed to burn some energy off, otherwise he'd be keeping you up all night."

Digger's tail wagged and he jutted his head forward, thrusting the toy in Joel's direction. *Come on, man, playtime can't be over yet! We just got started.*

"Also, he was trying to dig a hole in your couch so I distracted him."

Digger looked up at Joel, his tail stilling. *I thought we were bros. And you rat on me like that?*

"It's okay, the couch is old." Juliette wrapped her arms around herself, feeling some of that "take the bull by the horns" energy dissipate as self-doubt crept in.

"I made coffee." He pointed to the small kitchen table and she made her way over, dropping into a seat. Joel followed.

Why had she even invited him here? What was she doing to herself?

*You know exactly why you invited him here, and it wasn't* only *because you were scared to be alone.*

"You're really good with him," she said. "Digger, I mean. I can tell you had a dog before."

"My ex, she . . . when she left, she took Myla with her. I haven't seen her since." The words seemed to tumble out of him like water running over the edge of a waterfall. "I miss her a lot."

*Oh.* That was why he pretended to hate dogs—because he was mourning the loss of his own pet. Not because she'd died, but because she'd been taken from him.

"I didn't say anything about my life before, not because I wanted to lie or misrepresent myself but . . . my life has been pretty fucking hard these past few years and I don't like talking about it."

Juliette looked down into her coffee and breathed in the steam, letting the soothing scent work on her tense muscles and brittle fingers. "I get it."

They were both quiet for a moment and Juliette decided that she wasn't going to press Joel to talk. If he wasn't comfortable, then that was okay. She wanted to know him more. She wanted to slowly unpeel the layers of him and help him see that she could be trusted with his secrets. With his pain.

But she couldn't impose on him. *He* had to make the call to open up.

"Her brother was my best friend," he said, looking down at his hands. "He was like the little brother I never had."

Digger had trotted up beside him, and Joel reached out to absently scratch his head, causing the little dog's tail to thump softly against the chair leg.

"We were firefighters—I helped him through his training. We got put into the same squadron and always had each other's back. But . . . one day we were at a call. There was a grandmother and a little girl trapped inside a family home. We went in to rescue them and put out the fire."

Juliette's stomach sank. She knew the ending already, since Detective Dooley had said as much. But she wanted to hear Joel's version.

"The house was really old and not up to code. An electrical fault started the fire, and it chewed through everything so quickly. I had the little girl and . . . Chase, he had the grandmother. A beam came down while we were doing the extraction." Joel squeezed his eyes shut.

Juliette watched on, her heart almost splitting in two at the pain in his voice. Even Digger sat still, a paw resting on Joel's shin like he was trying to comfort him. To let him know he was safe.

"I had a choice—turn back and see if I could get to them, or ensure I got the girl out." He hung his head. "I left him behind."

"That's not much of a choice, is it?" Juliette said. "Save one life for certain, or risk everyone dying. Yourself included."

"Some days I wish I had. Chief made me see a therapist and it helped some, but when I returned to work . . . the way everybody looked at me, I was either a broken hero or a failure.

I couldn't take it." He sipped his coffee and grimaced, putting the mug down and pushing it away. "Marissa was inconsolable. She and her brother were extremely close because their parents died in a car accident when they were young, and I think she blamed me for what happened to Chase."

"You didn't deserve that," she whispered. "It wasn't your fault."

Joel pushed up out of his chair and paced in front of the couch. Juliette followed him.

"Wasn't it?" He turned to her. "I certainly made a call that day, to save a civilian over my best friend."

"Isn't that how you were trained?" she asked, her eyes searching his. The pain was like lightning in his eyes, intermittent flickers of darkness and blinding, searing light. "Didn't you do exactly what you'd been taught to do?"

"I could have ignored my training." His tone was shattered now. Jagged like a cliff face. "I could have put that all aside and kept my family together. I could have . . ."

"No, you couldn't." She reached up to touch his face and he flinched, causing her to draw her hand back. "Because you're not the kind of man who does the selfish thing, are you? You try to act like you're this impenetrable wall of stone—this emotionless *robot*—but you're not."

She'd seen it in his eyes, the panic when he thought she'd been hurt. The indulgent way he looked at Digger when he thought nobody was watching. The care he poured into his café on a daily basis. This was a man capable of great feeling. Of great love.

"I wish I was," he said. "It would be so much easier that way."

The air had grown so thick, Juliette wondered if he might need to swim through the front door to leave. But she didn't want him to leave. She didn't want to be in her cold, empty apartment on her own. She wanted this, here. With him.

She tried again, slowly raising her hand to touch the sharp

angle of his jaw. This time he didn't flinch. She could feel the tiniest pricks of stubble pushing through his skin, the warmth of him suffusing her fingertips.

"Juliette." He closed his eyes, the sound of her name like a plea and a prayer. "I don't . . . God."

What the hell was she doing? Indulging fantasies of a man she knew was wrong for her. Or rather, would be oh-so-right if it wasn't for the weight of his past. Because she knew that deep down, Joel *was* the kind of man she wanted. A man of morals, of integrity, of kindness and compassion . . . even if he tried to hide it.

Joel opened his eyes and the lightning was replaced with fire. It was like something had been unlatched in him. Untethered. A barricade smashed down with a wrecking ball. He reached out and brushed a strand of hair from her forehead, neatly tucking it behind her ear in a way that was so tender it made her want to sigh. She pressed up onto her tiptoes, placing both hands on his chest. God, he felt good. Hard and work-honed, covered in a sweater so soft it was like someone had spun the yarn from a cloud in heaven.

He drove his hands into her hair, his fingers curving around her skull as he tipped her back. A shiver rippled through her and before she had time to think about the consequences, his lips were on hers. The kiss was confident, like there was no turning back. She'd wanted him to open up and he had. Now there was nothing left between them—no secret pasts, no cover-up stories.

He slid one hand around the side of her waist, finding the small of her back. Then he was walking them backward. She bumped against the back of the couch and Joel hoisted her up, nudging her knees apart so he could stand between her legs.

This was the man she thought he would be—passionate, fiery, *connected*. Not remote and definitely not cold. He was almost rough, like an unpolished diamond. Perfectly, naturally beautiful.

His lips trailed down her neck as his hands fumbled with her cardigan, popping the buttons open one by one until he palmed her beneath it. When his hand connected with her breast, covered only by the soft lace of a bralette, he brought her body sharply to a pleasurable hum with a speed that was both terrifying and soul-soothingly satisfying. She arched into his touch, thighs clamping around his hips. Somehow, he *knew* her. Knew her body, knew what she needed, knew exactly how to ride the line of hard and soft that hit her in all the right places.

It was like they were meant to be.

"Take me to bed, Joel." Her eyes darted over to where Digger had crawled into his bed and curled up in a kidney bean shape, chin on his paws, his eyes mercifully drooping. Thank goodness. "Now, please."

The transformation in his face—the darkening of his pupils, the parting of his lips, the tightening of his grip—made her feel all gooey inside. But he stilled. She looked up at him, pleading with him not to clam up. Not to flee. It had been so very long since she'd felt like this—liquid and desirable and free.

"Are you sure?" The question came with teeth scraping against her neck and the brush of burgeoning stubble that sent a ripple of excitement through her. "Because if this is just adrenaline—"

"It's not." She cupped his face, forcing him to look right at her. "It's nothing to do with what happened tonight."

He pulled her forward, sliding his hands under her backside, and hoisted her up with ease. She locked her ankles behind his back as he led her through the house, down the hallway and to a door right at the end.

"Wow, you know exactly where to go," she said, surprised.

Joel's cheeks reddened. "When I was looking after Digger the night you got the call about Bonnie, we had a little game of chasey because he stole your bookmark."

*Bookmark? Not the one in the . . .*

Juliette's eyes widened. She had been reading a really enjoyable smutty romance novel that she'd borrowed from Alexa. It was a great book but it was *graphic.* Like, do-not-read-in-public graphic.

"Yes, *that* book," Joel said, as if reading her mind.

"Oh God. You didn't read it, did you?"

"I may have caught a glimpse." His lips pressed to the side of her neck. "And here I was pegging you for the innocent Disney princess type."

"I'm full of surprises," she whispered.

"I don't doubt it for a second."

He walked her across the threshold to her bedroom and nudged the door closed behind them, so there would be no interruptions.

When he placed her on the bed, soft fabric cushioned her back and he came to his knees over her, one either side of her hips. It was like being in the sexiest cage ever. He unbuttoned her cardigan the rest of the way, pushing the soft pieces aside to look at her.

"Holy shit, Juliette." He traced one fingertip over the curve of her breast, following the scalloped edge of butter yellow lace. "You've been hiding these curves away under that uniform of yours."

"Don't want to distract the dogs," she teased.

He reached for the tie at the waistband of her pants and undid the bow she'd knotted there. There was something so sensual about it, this slow undressing. Like she was a gift being unwrapped. Or a statue being carved. A piece of pottery being molded by firm, experienced hands. Everything that held her back was chiseled away. Joel was divesting her of her insecurities, one by one, replacing them with confidence.

She was wanted.

She was treasured.

She belonged.

He tugged her pants down over her hips and legs, tossing them aside while she sat up and wriggled her arms out of her cardigan. Juliette was *not* a seductress. Not a practiced one, anyway. She was the good girl, the rule follower, the try-hard. Never the woman men lusted after. Never the one who commanded attention. But she had it now, from him.

And it felt more powerful than if the whole world had appreciative eyes on her.

She reached behind herself to unhook her bralette and by the time she slipped it loose, Joel had jammed his hands into his jean pockets as if trying to physically restrain himself from touching her. It felt good to put on a show, to lean into a role that had never been hers before. She dropped the bra over the side of the bed and came up to her knees, thumbs finding the waistband of her underwear.

For a moment neither of them moved, and the only sound was their labored breathing. His eyes roamed her body, lingering on her breasts and then the fabric riding low on her hips. She peeled the last thing on her body away and lay back for him, bared.

*I'm all yours.*

He reached forward and gently grabbed her wrists, bringing her hands to his lips so he could kiss her knuckles. Then he released her to let his hands roam—over her shoulders, her arms, her hips, her waist, her ass.

"Your turn," she whispered.

He reached for the hem of his sweater and pulled it up and away, before lifting it over his head and taking the T-shirt underneath along for the ride. Muscles flexed—his body built and strong. She knew firemen needed to be in good shape, and it seemed Joel hadn't let that part of his life slide since becoming a café owner. Juliette felt a small surge of insecurity at her own softness. There was a subtle roundness to her belly, a little extra thickness in her thighs, hips that had those violin dips in them.

But she whisked the insecurities away. This wasn't about being perfect—it was about connection. Intimacy. And the way Joel was looking at her right now said he didn't give a hoot about any of her so-called imperfections.

The click of metal on metal echoed in the quiet bedroom as he gave his belt a yank, and Juliette's gaze flowed further down to where the hard length of him pushed against the fabric of his blue jeans. Joel discarded them and his underwear. Then he was gloriously naked—all sharp angles and smooth skin. A fading tan colored his arms and legs, though his chest was pale. He looked like a real man, rugged and tough yet tender.

"I was so worried, Juliette," he said, coming closer and sweeping her loose hair back over her shoulders. "When you called tonight . . ."

"I didn't mean to frighten you," she said.

"Well, you did."

He wrapped her up in his arms and drew her back to the bed with him, lips coming down to hers. Juliette let herself melt into the moment. She'd called him when she'd needed help and he'd been there for her without hesitation—that was the sexiest thing a man could do. She curled into his warmth, her lips seeking out his as her hands began to explore all the areas she'd only imagined before tonight.

It felt real, all of a sudden. More than a fleeting moment born out of circumstance. More than a pointless fantasy she played in her head each morning as she waited for her coffee. More than a stroke of luck.

The way he was holding her, it was like he really cared.

"I don't . . . uh . . ." He shook his head. "I haven't carried a condom on me in a long while."

"I have some."

There was a box shoved to the back of her underwear drawer, long unopened. She'd placed it there one time after declaring she was going to try dating again—but nobody ever made it this far. There just wasn't the right connection. The right feeling.

But Joel was different.

She opened the box and handed him a foil packet. He pressed a quick kiss to her lips and left her to scoot beneath the covers, burrowing into the soft, cozy bed while he sheathed himself. Then he pulled her close, dragging her body on top of his.

"Ready?" His eyes were hungry, and her heart fluttered in her chest.

*I was ready the first time I saw you.*

She nodded.

He trailed kisses down her neck. Then he pushed into her, slowly. So very slowly. She clamped her eyes shut. My goodness, she'd forgotten how good this could feel. How intense and perfect.

She pressed one hand to the center of his chest, letting her head loll backward so that her hair tickled the small of her back. Undulating, she dug her knees into the soft mattress on either side of him and rocked her hips back and forth, growing accustomed to the feeling. With each sensual rock of her hips, she met him. Joined with him. It was impossible to do anything but ride the waves since her mind blanked everything that wasn't this very moment.

"That feels so good."

She felt her muscles tighten as her mind narrowed to a pinpoint of euphoria. Release broke like a champagne cork popping—sudden and sharp and wonderful. She gasped, arching against him as she rode the ripples of pleasure, her cries uncensored and her nails scraping against his skin.

Then his hands were in her hair, his mouth hot on hers, body solid beneath her. He moaned against her neck, the vibrations skittering through her body and fracturing at the last second in a billion glittering shards as he followed her over the edge, clutching her tight like she was his only tether to earth.

# *Chapter Twenty-One*

**JOEL STIRRED IN** the middle of the night with Juliette's warm body pressed against his. A sliver of moonlight filtered into the room through a gap in the curtains, highlighting the curve of her hip and the ribbons of dark hair spilling across her pillow. It was silent, save for the rise and fall of breath.

After making love once, they'd both been starving and had ordered pizza for dinner, ending up back in bed afterward for round two. It was slower the second time. They indulged in exploration, uncovering and delighting in the details—a hidden freckle, a tender, ticklish spot, an unexpected sensitive zone. Eventually Digger had gotten tired of being left out—either that or something had spooked him—and he'd scraped at the door. Now the three of them were in bed, Juliette's body curled into him and Digger trying to "big spoon" the back of his calf.

He could feel the thump of Juliette's heart against his side, where her breasts were pressed into him and her arm was slung over his midsection. The steady beat lulled him into a state of utter contentment, and he gently stroked her back, brushing her dark hair out of her face when it slipped across her eyes.

A thought struck him out of nowhere—this was the happiest he'd been in a very long time. *Years.*

But he'd been here before.

"What are you thinking about?" she murmured. "I can hear your brain cogs turning from here."

"Nothing. You turned me to mush," he whispered back.

"I did good, then?"

"More than good." He stroked her hair and a content smile lifted her lips momentarily before she drifted back to sleep, her breathing even and smooth. How did she trust like that? So easily, so freely, so willingly? After all she'd been through, her heart was still an open door. An invitation.

Outside the rain pattered against the windows. He used to love that sound and found it soothing to lay in the dark and listen to the drumming of it, the gentle natural percussion. But one day had ruined the rain for him.

It had been pouring *that* day. The day he came home and found his house empty. No pitter-patter of paws. No singsong *hello* from Marissa's home office. The sinking feeling that love had been ripped from his life yet again.

Digger let out a big sigh and stretched against Joel's calf, digging his paws in for leverage. Then he rolled over, popped onto his feet and jauntily trotted up the bed so he could flop back down, plopping his furry little chin on Joel's shoulder. He let out a happy sigh.

Joel's heart jolted.

He remembered this feeling—being wrapped up in love, both the animal and human kind. He remembered the feeling of being embraced, of being warm and welcomed and cared for. And the biting chill when it was all stripped away, leaving him alone and isolated. Stuck in the molasses of grief.

Life had taught him that joy was fleeting. So fleeting that getting used to it was only setting yourself up for more pain in the long run. His mother had suffered when his father died, Marissa had suffered when her parents died in that car crash and when her brother didn't come out of that burning house, and Joel had suffered when Marissa left him because he was broken and couldn't be put back together.

Life was loss. It was heartache. It was full of terrible shocks and devastation and bitter disappointments.

So what the hell was he doing *here*, with *her*, with *them*?

"You're setting yourself up to be hurt again," he whispered. He ground the heels of his palms into his eyes, feeling a migraine coming on. The telltale waviness at the edges of his vision and the start of pressure in the right side of his head always made his stomach tip and turn. "Everyone leaves. Every single one."

He pushed up into a sitting position and gently moved Digger, lifting him up and placing him next to Juliette. But the little dog trotted right back over to him, tail wagging, tongue lolling out of his mouth.

"We're not playing." He frowned, wincing at the throbbing in his head.

Digger headbutted him on the thigh. *Oh come on, man. You want it too! I'm so much fun and you know it.*

"No." He stood, swaying as the disturbances in his vision made it hard to find his balance.

"Joel?"

Juliette was awake now and sitting, her long dark brown hair tumbling around her shoulders, almost covering the little white tank top—the kind trimmed in lace with a small pink rose sewn at the bust. He'd made a mistake about her, he realized. She didn't look like a Disney princess. She looked like a goddess. Like a siren. A temptress. An otherworldly being who had the power to draw him down a dark path, right back to the edge of the pit that was his pain. To make him face it.

But he didn't want to face it. He couldn't.

"I can't do this." Panic twisted inside him. If he left it much longer the migraine would truly set in and he wouldn't be able to drive himself home.

He was already feeling nauseous. That wasn't a good sign.

He grappled for his clothes and started dressing himself, head pounding, vision swimming. He almost toppled over trying to get his foot into the leg of his jeans, and suddenly Juliette was at his side, steadying him with a caring hand. Thank God he'd already had his underwear on, otherwise this would have taken twice as long.

"Joel, what's going on?" Her brows were knitted. "Are you sick?"

"I shouldn't . . ." He swallowed against the nausea. "I shouldn't have stayed last night. I'm sorry. It's not . . . It's not what I want."

Her lip trembled, but she sucked it under her teeth as if to hide how she was feeling. But there was no hiding the hurt shimmering in her big, brown eyes. "You regret what we did?"

"We want different things." He finally got his other foot into the leg of his jeans and he yanked the waistband up over his thighs and hips, jamming the button through the hole and dragging the zipper up with a shaking hand. "You want happily ever after and romance and Prince Charming and I want to be unencumbered and alone."

"You don't know what I want," she replied, frowning. "You've never asked me."

"Why would I ask when I already know?" He hunted around for his T-shirt and found it tangled inside his sweater from where he'd peeled them off in one piece last night. The image of her naked across the bed flashed in his brain. The warmth of her as she'd circled her arms around his neck, the press of her lips to his.

*Stop it. You need to get out of here.*

"You *don't* know, Joel. You don't know because that would require having a conversation about something real, and every time we get close to that it's like . . ." She tossed her hands in the air. "It's like you think I'm going to latch on to what you tell me and hurt you with it."

He did think that, didn't he? Maybe not actively, but subconsciously. Because that's what Marissa had done to him. She'd taken his fear—losing the people he loved—and skewered him with it.

"I don't want people or dogs in my life anymore." He growled as he struggled to flip the sweater and T-shirt the right way, the pain of his migraine swelling and swelling. It was like someone had taken his brain in their hands and was squeezing, dull throbbing becoming sharper and more insistent. It stopped him from thinking properly. "It's not worth it."

"You think people and dogs are not 'worth it'?" She shook her head. "What does that even mean?"

"People are selfish, Juliette. You know that, don't you? Look at how everyone treated you after they found out what your father did—they took pleasure in casting you and your sister aside. The ugly part no one wants to admit is that *everyone* has that in them."

"I don't." She looked appalled. "And I don't think you do, either."

"Then you definitely don't know me." He let out a humorless laugh as he pulled the T-shirt and sweater over his head. "I let two people die because I was scared. That's the fucking truth of it. I didn't rush out of that house simply to save the little girl in my arms. It was because I was scared of dying myself. I wasn't strong enough to go back for him!"

The words came out harsh, like a cracking whip, the truth he'd been guiltily harboring these past years rushing out of him like screaming ghosts.

"I was selfish," he finished, pressing his hands to his eyes again.

"Joel, my gosh. That's human instinct. We're biologically compelled away from things like that. You did the right thing." She touched his arm but he flinched and she drew her hand back.

"You don't understand, Juliette. I'm not some fixer-upper for you to bring back to shiny, new condition. I'm broken. I will stay broken." He walked toward the door of the bedroom, but she followed. "Nothing will change that."

"You're right," she said.

He stopped dead in his tracks. He'd expected her to protest—to say he wasn't broken or that he could be fixed. Saved. But hearing his own sentiment played back to him was almost shocking.

"You won't change if you don't want to," she continued. "Because change is hard and it takes multiple failed attempts before it sticks, and then it's an uphill battle to maintain your new version. So if you put zero effort in then you're right, you definitely *won't* change."

He didn't know what to say to that. Nobody had ever called him on his bullshit before—not like this, anyway. He'd been either wrapped in cotton wool or silently judged, with nobody daring to tell him to his face that he was being a stubborn asshole.

"But I think you're lying to yourself when you say you don't want to change. I *saw* you playing with Digger when you thought I wasn't watching, how sweet and caring you were. How much fun you were having. I *witnessed* a man last night who is open to connection, who came running to help me because he cared. You can deny it all you want, Joel. But I know you're capable of love and I know you're lonely without it."

"Lonely is safe. Lonely doesn't turn around and leave you high and dry because life got hard. I'd take that any day over serving my heart up on a platter for someone ever again."

His voice had risen a little more than he'd realized, because Digger came over, tail between his legs, head swinging from Juliette to Joel as though he was frightened and unsure what was going on.

*See? This is what you are now. Someone who scared a small dog because you're an asshole.*

"I have to go." He walked down Juliette's hallway but a bout of dizziness hit him so hard that he swayed on his feet, steadying his hand against the wall so he didn't topple over.

"What's going on, Joel? You don't look well." Even after all he'd hurled at her, here she was caring for him. "You're pale."

"It's nothing."

"It's something," she insisted.

"After the fire . . . I get migraines sometimes." More, lately. It was the stress of having Marissa contact him and his fear of the feelings he was developing for Juliette.

Because he *was* developing feelings for her. He *had* developed feelings for her.

*You're an idiot. You should never have gotten involved.*

"God, Joel, if you would stop being so damn stubborn for a second, people might be able to help you," she said, worry flashing across her face. "Why don't you lay down? I'll get you a glass of water."

"No." He tried to forge forward, but she stood in front of him like a mouse standing in front of a lion with a thistle in its paw.

"You might regret coming here last night and you might regret . . . being intimate with me, but I don't regret it. Not one bit." Her eyes were shining. "I've faced a lot of rejection in my life and I hate it, but I won't let it stand in the way of doing the right thing. You're not well and you shouldn't be driving. If you don't want to stay here, then fine. But at least let me call you an Uber so you can get home safely."

He could tell she wasn't going to budge and the pounding in his head had reached a point where he wasn't sure himself that he could drive anymore. And he might be a stubborn asshole, but he wasn't a *dangerous* stubborn asshole.

"Okay," he relented, dipping his head forward because his eyes were already becoming sensitive to the light.

She let out a big sigh, as if she'd been holding her breath. Her eyes searched his face and her lips parted, like she wanted to say more, but she must have decided it wasn't worth it. Because she guided him to her couch and then left him to find her phone.

While he waited, Digger followed him to the couch, his tail finally lifted again now that the humans were talking at a normal volume. Joel reached down and ruffled his head.

"Sorry about before," he said quietly. "I didn't mean to scare you."

The dog looked back at him, eyes trusting, and Joel could swear he saw Myla looking back at him.

"I fucked up, didn't I? But it's better for her. She's a good soul and she deserves someone who won't be waiting for disaster to strike every moment of the day. She needs a happily ever after, not a cautionary tale."

Digger plopped his butt down on the floor and cocked his head, looking at Joel with what he could only interpret as stone-cold judgment.

"She doesn't want a screwup like me, I promise," he said. But the dog didn't budge and didn't stop staring. "You'll understand when you're older."

With that, Digger let out an annoyed huff and trotted away to find his bed, where he curled up with one of his toys, gnawing at it and shaking it around. Even the dog thought Joel was being an idiot.

But he knew better than to trust that giddy, warm feeling he'd experienced last night. He'd done that before, and it had turned out to be the most painful decision of his life.

**LATER THAT DAY,** Juliette, Norah and Alexa sat in the waiting room at What The Fluff, watching as Bonnie's lawyer left through the front doors. Digger pressed one paw to the glass as if saying goodbye. Marshmallow, on the other hand, sat by the drawers at the front desk, where Bonnie had always kept her personal items. Could she detect her owner's scent? Juliette's heart sank. The little dog might be a bit of a menace, but she had adored Bonnie.

Tears filled Juliette's eyes again, but she was almost too tired to cry. There had been a *lot* of crying in the last twenty-four hours. Too much. And that was coming from a person who regularly shed a tear. Seriously, if there was a sad movie on the television or someone told her a story about a difficult time they had gone through or if there were cute puppies on a toilet paper commercial and she happened to be in the later part of her cycle . . . boom! Waterworks.

But the tears she'd shed the past twenty-four hours were different. They made her feel wrung out, like she was a dish towel and the universe was twisting and twisting, trying to get every last drop out of her.

Norah reached over and grabbed Juliette's hand, squeezing. "You okay?"

"I don't know what I'm going to do," she said, shaking her head. "Taking on What The Fluff permanently is . . . it wasn't in my plans."

The salon was still closed from the funeral yesterday, and Juliette had no idea when she would reopen it. Thankfully, the broken glass had been fixed right before the lawyer arrived.

Taking possession of Bonnie's legacy felt like a huge weight on her shoulders, especially in light of recent events. But what could she do? Selling the business after it had been gifted to her felt wrong. Leaving it here to rot felt wrong. Opening it back up and driving it into the ground because people didn't like her felt wrong.

"What *were* your plans, Jules?" Alexa leaned forward, two long braids hanging over her shoulders like shiny, strawberry blond ropes. "Like, really? If Bonnie had come back from the cruise and was still running the business, what were your plans?"

"Well . . ." Dammit. Alexa knew her too well and wasn't shy about calling her out. "Nothing, I guess."

"Exactly. Your plans would have been to do the same thing you always do—sit around and wait for permission from other people before you take a chance on yourself. Spoiler alert, folks around here won't change their opinion of you if you stay in the shadows."

It was easy for Alexa to say that, given she was allergic to being ignored. Today she was wearing a pair of dramatically flared blue velvet pants, towering platforms and a tan suede jacket trimmed in long pieces of fringe and studded with shiny silver stars. So of *course* she was telling Juliette to put herself out there more.

But putting herself out in the world *before* she'd managed to win people over . . . well, that felt risky.

*Didn't you scold Joel this very morning for being too stubborn and unwilling to change?*

That was beside the point. That was then, this was now. And right now Juliette wanted to make a blanket fort and hide away with a tub of Cherry Garcia ice cream and her smutty romance novel and pretend the rest of the world didn't exist. Especially the part of the world that existed where Joel was, because it would take a long time to forget how good she'd felt in his arms and how shitty she'd felt waking up to see him desperately trying to escape her.

*Joel: 1. Juliette's Ego: 0.*

"Alexa's right," Norah chimed in. "And really, Bonnie had been slowing down for at least two years. You'd *already* taken over the day-to-day running of this place, even if you didn't have the official title. I know you'll miss having her here—we all will—but you know this business. You know grooming and you know dogs and you know how to keep Bonnie's memory alive."

"It's a lot of responsibility," she said softly.

"Don't talk to me about responsibility," Norah said, eyeing Marshmallow across the room. The dog turned around and pointed her ass right in Norah's direction, as if telling her what she really thought about this situation. "At least your inheritance isn't trying to kill you."

There was a lot of paperwork and waiting ahead, with probate likely to take a few months. But the kindly lawyer assured them he would guide them through every step of the process and ensure they received what Bonnie had intended.

Juliette would give it all back and more to have Bonnie around. She missed the older woman's raucous laugh and the way she used to tell dirty jokes and how she seemed to be able to get any animal to be calm and compliant. Juliette was no Bonnie. She never would be.

"You can do this, Jules. I believe in you." Alexa got up and came over to give Juliette a big hug. "Whatever help you need, I'm here for you. We can talk business strategy and marketing—I've been doing it all with Glow Up for years now, so if there's any way I can help, just say the word."

"Thanks Alexa." Juliette hugged her friend back. "That means a lot."

"I have to get back to the shop so Holden can have his break. But I'll see you girls tomorrow night, right?"

"Absolutely."

After Alexa left, Norah stood and slung her bag over one shoulder.

"I should get going, too. I've got to get Marshmallow back before I head off to work tonight." She cocked her head, looking right at her twin. "Everything will be okay. You know that, right? It's going to be hard to grieve losing Bonnie, but we'll get through it together. We always get through shitty things together."

It wasn't like Norah to get all up in her feelings, but she must be able to tell Juliette needed reassurance.

"You're a good sister," Juliette said, leaning her head on Norah's shoulder. "I'm just scared I'm going to mess things up."

"Hey, don't go trying to steal *my* crown as family screwup. That's not fair. Get your own crown."

Juliette laughed in spite of the pit in her stomach. "I'd feel better if this whole thing with Maurice's and Patrizia's murders was cleared up. It's hanging over me and I keep waiting for Detective Dooley to turn up and arrest me."

"I can't believe whoever did it got to Patrizia as well." Norah shook her head. "Drago has to clean out her locker at work, so he can get everything to her family. It's terrible."

That's when Juliette realized she hadn't told Norah about what'd happened late yesterday. Between spending an amazing night with Joel, their argument this morning and then meeting the lawyer, she'd almost forgotten that the attack even happened. And Norah had rung after work, when she'd seen Juliette's missed call, but by that time Juliette had been . . .

*Naked and unavailable to come to the phone.*

What was the point of telling Norah now? She'd only get stressed right before she had to go to work, and then Juliette would need to explain the Joel thing and . . . nope. No headspace for that right now. They'd talk tomorrow, after Juliette had gotten a good night's sleep. In the meantime, she was going to stick to busy public areas and only be out during the day. The killer wouldn't try to attack her in the middle of the town square, right?

*You should have been arrested by now. Then I could have everything I wanted.*

Remembering the killer's words made her shudder, but she said goodbye to Norah and Marshmallow anyway and locked the door behind them. At least there was only one way in and out of this place and a whole lot of windows to ensure that nobody was able to sneak up on her.

"I should probably go through Bonnie's things and start sorting out what to keep and what to . . . not," she said to Digger. He was currently shaking a rope toy in his mouth, growling and having a grand old time. So at least he was occupied for the moment. "Then we can go to the dry cleaners to drop off my suit that got all muddy."

That's when she remembered the scrap of fabric. Frowning, she went to the canvas bag she'd bundled the suit into and fished out the Barbie pink jacket. Digging her hand into the pocket, she pulled out the small scrap of fabric that Digger had torn from the killer while defending Juliette. It was stretchy and small brown hairs were stuck to it.

Juliette went to grab a Ziploc bag from the stationery drawer behind the front desk. They didn't have much use for stationery these days, since everything was digital. About a year ago, Juliette had transitioned What The Fluff's appointments to an online system—though many of the older customers still liked to call—and all their receipts were sent via email, too. But they still had a small drawer where they kept a carbon credit card imprinter for times when the system was down, any flyers for promotions they were running, and . . .

Marketing samples.

Juliette opened the drawer where the rejected What The Fluff branded leash samples had been kept after Bonnie decided not to go ahead with a full order. Only now, there was a different leash in the drawer. A *broken* leash.

It was thin, made of woven pink-and-yellow fabric, totally frayed around the part that secured the collar clip to the leash. If a strong-willed dog had yanked on this leash, it might have come apart and the dog would have been able to run away from its owner. Dangerous, especially near busy roads.

Juliette picked up the leash and noted a small charm dangling from the handle. It was a gold letter N.

There was also a Post-it note floating around in the drawer, the sticky strip dulled with debris and fuzzy pink-and-yellow fibers, which made it clear it had been attached to the leash. Bonnie's swooping cursive in pink glittery pen read: *Loaned promo leash. 9–29.* It appeared she might have written the name of the person to whom she loaned the leash, but the ink had smudged.

Juliette, however, had a sinking feeling she knew what name had been written down.

It was all coming together—the brown hairs on the stretchy fabric, the dangling *N* charm, the woman she'd bumped into right before finding Patrizia's body . . .

With shaking hands, she brought up What The Fluff's booking system and navigated to the appointments that occurred on September 29. There it was: the name she had been expecting to see sitting right in the 10:30 a.m. slot.

*Serenity McFarlane.*

Juliette shook her head. Serenity had the What The Fluff leash that was used to kill Maurice . . . but why? And what did she mean when she said, *"You should have been arrested by now. Then I could have everything I wanted."*

A wave of nausea washed over Juliette. There was only one thing that Serenity had shown any interest in: Joel.

She had to warn him.

But before Juliette could dial Joel's number, there was a pounding on the front door and Detective Dooley stood on the other side, his meaty fist beating against the glass. A victorious smile stretched eerily across his face.

"Open up, Miss Macintyre," he said. "You're under arrest for the murders of Maurice Allsop and Patrizia Pisano."

## *Chapter Twenty-Two*

**JOEL LAY ON** his couch, lights off, listening to the quiet. Every so often a car went past and for a moment the sound of rushing tires covered his breathing and the house foundations creaking. It seemed like the rain had paused, the wind making a tree out front scratch gently against his windows.

*This is the sound of your life.*

Other people's cars going somewhere. The weather. The shifting of the building. No laughter. No conversation. No joy.

For the past year he'd thought this was the sound of peace and safety, of his good decision to keep to himself and build a life that was a protective cocoon. But today it felt hollow. Like he was subsisting instead of living, with thriving so far out of the equation he couldn't even grasp the concept. Before his panic had set in, waking up with Juliette and Digger wrapped in his arms was . . . God, it felt good. Warm and comforting and perfect.

But then what had he done? His broken ass had freaked out, of course. Because it felt meaningful. Sex with Juliette wasn't about scratching an itch. It wasn't even about blowing off steam or releasing pent-up attraction. It was about the relief he'd felt when he finally arrived at the dog park and could see with his own two eyes that she was okay. Shivering and muddy and shell-shocked, but okay.

He'd wanted nothing more than to protect her forever.

A sharp rap on his front door knocked Joel out of his thoughts. He pushed up slowly, given the remnants of his migraine. Was it Juliette? Something warm and fuzzy stirred in his chest, a red flag that despite everything he said to her this morning, part of him still wanted the forbidden fruit. Part of him still wanted *her*.

He got to the door as more knocking came, insistent. But when he pulled it open, he was surprised to see that it wasn't Juliette on his doorstep. It was Serenity.

"Hi, Joel." She had her arms wrapped around herself and she bounced on the spot, clearly not warm enough in her mint green workout attire. She had a white nylon bag with some sporting logo slung across her body, which matched the white sneakers on her feet. "Can I come in?"

"Uh . . ." He hesitated. Post migraine his bullshit tolerance was basically nonexistent and he really didn't want to have to deal with her antics—or unwanted come-ons—right now. "Is everything okay?"

"I have information you might be interested in." She looked up at him, her blond hair tousled in that way he was sure took *far* longer than she wanted people to think. Like everything else with Serenity, it came off a little forced. A little too perfect. "It's about Maurice's murder. I know you've been looking into what happened with Juliette, and I thought this might help."

"Oh." He nodded. "Sure, come in. Thanks."

As Joel stepped back and flicked on some lights, Serenity entered his house and he noted that a bandage stuck out the bottom of her leggings. "What happened to your ankle?"

"Nibs got a little overexcited when we were playing," she said, something flashing across her face. For a moment, she looked angry but it melted away like wind parting clouds. "It was just a little nip. Nothing serious."

Something about the way she brushed it off seemed odd—surely it was more than a little nip if she'd needed a bandage. He shoved his hands into his pockets, trying to ground himself. His migraine had been reduced to a dull, but still insistent, throb and he really wanted to get back to the couch and darkness.

"So, what do you know?"

"Aren't you going to offer me a drink first?" She came closer, fluttering her eyelashes at him.

He *really* didn't have the energy for this right now. But if she had information that might help Juliette, he would make her a drink and put up with her flirting and it would be worth it.

"Sure. What can I get you? I've got some fresh pressed orange juice from the market."

"Wonderful." She followed him into the kitchen and took a seat at his dining table, her head swiveling slowly around. "Nice place."

"Thanks." Joel retrieved the bottle of juice from the fridge and poured some into a glass, the smell making him slightly nauseous. Everything smelled like it was dialed up to eleven right now.

"You're not having one?" she asked, looking disappointed as he handed the glass to her.

"I had one not long before you arrived," he lied. And there was no way he wanted to encourage her to hang around any longer than necessary.

"You haven't done much decorating, huh?"

"It's not my forte," he admitted, putting the juice bottle back into the fridge.

"Was it more your wife's forte?" she asked.

Joel stilled. "Excuse me?"

"Detective Dooley told me you're married."

Shit. So the detective *had* been flapping his gums about Joel's past to people other than Juliette. He scrubbed a hand over his face. That guy was a menace, and Joel hadn't taken his threats seriously enough, it seemed.

"I'm separated," he clarified, taking a seat at the table.

Serenity looked relieved, though he wasn't sure why. "I told the detective there was no way you were *actually* still married. I mean, legally married but not, like, still in a relationship with that person."

It was a curious response and it made something tingle at the back of his neck, like a small vibration of intuition alerting him that something wasn't quite right. "Why were you so certain of that?"

"Well, because you're always flirting with me, *duh*." She giggled in a way that seemed a little unhinged. "You wouldn't do that if you were still with your wife."

He was so gobsmacked he wasn't sure how to respond. Flirting? Him? A friend had once said Joel was such a terrible flirt the only way he could catch a woman's interest would be to shut his mouth and hope for the best. So why the hell did Serenity think he was flirting with her?

"You know, I thought you and I would end up together the first day you came to Labrador Falls. We both come from somewhere else, we're more worldly than other people here. And I knew you would understand me." She let out a happy sigh and sipped her juice. "And look at us now."

Was this woman having a complete break from reality? A prickling sensation crawled over his skin, like an invisible beetle was tracking across his arms and legs. Desperate for something to do with his hands, he pulled his phone out of his pocket to check the time and at that moment it started to ring. With unexpected speed, Serenity snatched the phone out of his hands.

"Ugh, Juliette? Again?" Serenity looked like she'd tasted something awful. "That girl is worse than a bad smell! She just won't quit."

"Can I have my phone back, please?" He held his hand out. The uneasy feeling was building with every second Serenity was in his house.

*Ironically, she does not create much serenity.*

"I'm not sure I can trust you, Joel. First, I find out you're married, and now it looks like you're still talking to Juliette. Are you sleeping with her, Joel?" She held his phone out of reach, the ringtone continuing to peal out into the air. "Should I answer and tell her to leave us alone?"

"No." The reply came out too instinctively, too quickly.

Serenity's expression darkened in an instant. "To which question, Joel?"

"I think there might have been some kind of misunderstanding—"

"I will *not* be the 'other woman,' okay? I can't. It's like the one thing my mom actually taught me in life, you know? Never be someone's side piece. It doesn't work out well." She shook her head. "I'm not a number two kind of woman, Joel. I'm number one."

"Your mom sounds like a smart woman," he said, keeping his voice even. Escalating the situation by pissing her off was not a good idea.

The phone went silent as Juliette's call was routed to voicemail, but Serenity didn't relinquish the device.

"She wasn't, like, book smart, you know. But she was smart in other ways." Serenity nodded. "She always said to me: find the right man in life and don't fall for a married asshole. I know you're technically married but you're not an asshole, are you, Joel?"

*Depends on who you ask.*

"No," he replied. "I try not to be."

"So you're not one of those men who screws his way around town? Do you have kids that I should know about? Do you have a whole family hidden away somewhere? A daughter you choose to ignore because you don't want everyone to know you knocked up your secretary?"

What an oddly specific question.

"I don't have any kids," he replied, trying not to be obvious as he looked around his kitchen for something to defend himself. "Secret or otherwise."

"That's a relief! Do you have *any* idea what it's like growing up knowing that you were a sordid secret? It's not fun, let me tell you." She shook her head. "My dad told my mom she had to keep her pregnancy secret and that he would never acknowledge me as his child, so my mom moved us away before I was born. But I wanted to know who my dad was and after she died, I tried to reconnect with him. And do you know what he said?"

She looked at him, as if waiting for an actual answer.

"I have no idea," Joel replied.

"He said I was after his money. Can you believe it?" She made a noise of disgust. "His own flesh and blood! You would never do that, would you, Joel?"

He didn't like her tone, nor the direction this conversation was taking. It was almost like she wasn't quite in the room with him, her voice having a far-off, detached quality. Then a strange thought trickled into Joel's brain. Didn't Corinne say Maurice supposedly had an illegitimate child with another woman while he was married to his first wife? And hadn't Juliette told him that Serenity Hope Rainbow McFarlane wasn't her real name, and that she'd changed it at some point?

Holy freaking shit.

Was Serenity the illegitimate daughter of Maurice Allsop?

"I believe family should stick together," he said, his calm tone belying the manic whirring happening in his brain as all the puzzle pieces came together.

If Serenity was Maurice's daughter, she might have had access to his house. Maybe her dad had talked about the significance of the Bob Dylan album or the value of it. Maybe she'd been in his house and seen where he kept it. She also had a dog, and Juliette had mentioned she came to What The Fluff with her long-haired dachshund, Nibs. So she could have stolen the leash.

"See, I knew you and I would be on the same page." She beamed at him.

"I thought you had information about Maurice's murder." He tried to act casual by leaning back in his chair, not wanting to alert her to his suspicions.

"I do. But it's information for *you*, not for Juliette. You really should be done with her, Joel. She's no good for you." She still had a grip on his phone, and it didn't look like she was about to release it anytime soon. "And everyone's about to know it."

A droplet of ice slithered down his spine. "What does that mean?"

"Let's just say that the police received an anonymous tip and now the good people of Labrador Falls won't need to worry about a murderer running around town." She looked proud as punch, like a kid who'd won first place at the science fair. "Detective Dooley will be *so* pleased. You really want to stay on the right side of him, I think. He can be so helpful if you know how to help him back."

"What did you do, Serenity?"

"Oh nothing." She giggled again and looked like she wanted to spill a big secret. "But the cops are going to find an important piece of evidence at Juliette's house."

"The Bob Dylan record."

Her eyes lit up. "Oh you're a smart cookie. How did you know?"

"We—I—heard it was stolen. It's worth a lot of money."

"Uh-huh." She nodded. "I mean, it would be silly to plant the *actual* vinyl in Juliette's possession and forfeit the chance to make thirty grand. But Detective Dooley won't know the difference, especially since the album title is the same."

"You bought the officially released version and planted it instead of the rare one."

"I didn't do anything," she said with a wink. "I'm just saying, that's probably what *someone* did."

Okay, so there was a killer in his house. How many people did one need to kill before they attached the "serial" part of the title? Probably more than two. But two was certainly a strong start, an indication that one might *tend* to kill again.

*Stop panicking. If you freak out and blow this, then Juliette will end up going to jail. Or worse. You might not be alive to know what happens next.*

His eyes dropped to the little bag slung across her chest. It was the kind he saw on women decked out in expensive workout gear, with their branded water bottles and fancy sneakers back home in Cali. But it sat lower on her body, as though there was something heavy inside.

"How do you think *someone* got hold of the vinyl?" he asked, hoping to keep her talking until he could determine the best way out of this situation. She had his phone and, like most Millennials, Joel did not have a landline. So there was no calling for help.

He could overpower her, sure. Unless she had a gun hiding in that bag of hers.

*Think. You can't sit on your ass right now. You need to act.*

"Someone probably got themselves invited inside for a cup of coffee," she said, raising her eyebrows in a way she probably thought looked coy. "And someone might be pretty deft with their hands, enough to drop some liquid laxative into said coffee. Maurice might have been obsessed with security on the outside of the house, but not so much on the inside. Men like him are arrogant, assuming that no one will get past the walls they put up."

"But you did."

"Someone did," she corrected.

"Right. *Someone.*"

"Juliette."

"Juliette didn't kill Maurice." He probably shouldn't be countering anything Serenity said, but Joel could *not* die with another thing on his conscience. "You made that pretty clear with your theories about *someone*."

Serenity's face darkened again. Her moods were like the pendulum on a grandfather clock, swishing from one extreme to the other. This time, it appeared, Joel had pushed her too far.

"What do you see in her anyway?" She shoved back her chair and stood, pacing across the entrance to the kitchen, effectively blocking Joel's exit. "She's so . . . mid."

"Mid?"

"Yeah, like basic. She's always trying to make everyone like her. It's kind of cringe." She pulled a face. "Like, get a backbone already."

Joel should probably have continued to be alert to what Serenity might do next. Instead, his blood boiled.

"Is that why you're trying to frame her for murder? Because she's a good person in an unfortunate position and she keeps trying to hold her head up high and do her best, even when people beat her down?"

"Ugh, can you *stop* talking about her like that? You're supposed to be interested in me, Joel. That was the plan. I always saw her coming into the café and trying to butter you up so I knew I had to get Juliette out of the way. Then you wouldn't be distracted by her anymore. Just like how I got rid of my dad when he said he wouldn't write me into his will."

The room went silent. Even though they both knew it was Serenity who'd killed Maurice, now she'd said it out loud. Something about that shifted things. And not in a good way.

Serenity juggled Joel's phone as she unzipped her bag, pulling out an item that made Joel freeze in his chair.

"I really didn't want to have to do this," she said with a sigh, pointing a handgun in Joel's direction.

It was a Glock 19. He'd seen plenty before—they were lightweight, easy to hold, readily available. It was a popular enough gun that *maybe* she wasn't a gun enthusiast, per se. Maybe she didn't know how to shoot and this was just for intimidation's sake.

As if reading his mind, she said, "I would show you that the safety is off, but this one doesn't work like that. As soon as I pull down on the trigger, the safety will release and I'll be able to shoot."

Shit. She knew more about guns than Joel had hoped.

"And I could shoot you dead in the eye from across this house, so don't try anything." Gone was the giggling, flirting, girlish appearance from earlier. Her eyes were like steel, her voice like flint.

The change was truly bone-chilling. Joel had no difficulty seeing the killer instinct in her now. He could easily imagine her strangling her absent father or attacking Juliette at the dog park.

"What are you trying to achieve here, Serenity?" he asked. Now the gun was out, he *definitely* had to keep her talking. He tried to stand but she waved the gun, so he sat back down.

"I want to find out whose side you're on," she said, as though it were the most obvious answer in the world. "Because this whole thing has turned into a fucking mess. I never set out to kill him, you know. I'm a good person, Joel. I didn't *want* to kill my father."

"Then why did you do it?" This time he wasn't stalling—he was genuinely curious. Maybe it was because the last piece of the puzzle needed to be clicked into place so the world made sense.

*Since when does the world make sense?*

"I wanted to have a relationship with him. I wanted to be like father and daughter. Jeez, I even *moved* to this tiny, stupid town because of him!" Serenity gestured with the gun and Joel found his gaze tracking the weapon, watching to see if her finger was still nestled around the trigger. "After my mom died, I had nobody. Both my grandparents are long dead and she didn't have any siblings. He was the only family I had, and I wanted to know if I had aunts and uncles and cousins and . . . maybe the big family I'd wanted all my life was waiting for me here."

For a moment, he felt a pang of empathy for her. As someone who'd lost many people close to him, he understood that pain. The loneliness and isolation. The need to *do* something about it.

*Yeah, but not homicide. She could have done something else. Literally anything else.*

"When I first came to Labrador Falls, I kept my distance. I watched him and Corinne for a while and tried to understand how I might approach him." She let out a sigh. "My first meeting with my dad didn't go well. He said my mother was a liar and blah, blah, blah. I hated him for a minute, but I decided to give him another chance. You know, I can be very forgiving."

Joel stayed glued to his chair, no solution mercifully bubbling up in his brain. She had his phone, she had a gun, and she stood in front of the only exit.

"The next time I said I just wanted to talk and he agreed, but only if we could meet in secret. He even made up some story about planning a surprise birthday party for Corinne to keep people from wondering what he was up to. You know, since he had a reputation for not being able to keep it in his pants and all." She shook her head. "Anyway, things were going well and I think he felt guilty about abandoning me, but I wasn't happy with secret meetups. I wanted to meet my half-siblings. I wanted to be *part* of the family. I wanted to be in his will, because it would prove I was legitimate. I shared their DNA. Why didn't I deserve to be included?"

She looked at Joel, almost as if begging him to understand her. But he said nothing, focusing only on the gun being pointed at him.

"But he said if I told anyone I was his daughter, he would deny it until his dying breath and use the full force of his wealth to bear down on me legally. Direct quote." She let out a humorless laugh. "Then he said I was the biggest mistake he'd made in his entire life and if he could do things over, I'd never have been born."

Joel winced.

Those words said to someone with a stable grip on the world would be hurtful. Traumatic, even. But said to someone like Serenity, who seemed to view the world through a very specific lens of her own making . . . it would be like taking a match to dry grass.

"I knew then that I didn't have a father. I didn't have a family. I was alone in the world because a selfish man decided that his pride and his lies were more important than his own flesh and blood. Now I'd have to spend the rest of my life alone because of him." Anger crackled across her features. Her eye twitched and her lips parted to reveal her teeth. It was almost like she was transforming into a feral animal. Yet tears shimmered in her eyes. "He'd stolen the only dream I had in the whole world. So, I thought, if I can't have what I want, then neither can he. Neither can his stupid children who squabble over his money. But

I wasn't going to rush, oh no. I wanted to take my time so my father understood what he'd done to himself."

She was like a cat wanting to play with the mouse before she killed it.

*Is that what this is? Is that what she's doing now?*

"I turned up at his house, pretending like I wanted to apologize. That's when I spiked his coffee. I knew he had a sensitive stomach, so he wouldn't suspect anything. While he was indisposed, I helped myself to a few things I knew would be worth something—the record, a pair of Tiffany cuff links, one of his fancy watches. I don't even think he noticed anything but the Bob Dylan record." She made a sound of disgust and shook her head. "He had *so* much stuff. So much money. And do you know what I had growing up, huh? Nothing. My mother worked two jobs, bagging groceries and working at the car wash to keep us afloat. All the while my father is living in the lap of luxury in his big house, showering his other kids with gifts and college educations!"

"How did you get him to come to the dog park that night?"

"He suspected Corinne was having an affair and I told him I had a photo of her and the mystery man leaving their house. I didn't, of course. But he believed me." She looked almost proud. "Then I got there early and waited in the shadows so I could surprise him from behind."

"What about Patrizia? Why kill her?"

"She figured it out. My father blamed her for the theft and she was furious. She saw us together one time—when she turned up early for her cleaning shift—and my father made her wait in the lounge while he shoved me outside. At first, she thought I was screwing him, but then she worked out who I looked like. I'm a dead spit for my mom, and Patrizia went to school with her." For a second, Serenity looked sad. "I didn't want to kill her, either. But she was trying to blackmail me. She wanted the vinyl to sell in her eBay shop. She knew how much it was worth. I couldn't have anyone around who might rat me out to police."

"Yet here you are, telling me everything," Joel said, feeling strangely numb.

Something told him this was the end.

"I came here because I thought . . . maybe I could make a family of my own. Maybe *we* could make a family. It's all I've ever wanted, Joel. Just a noisy house to come home to and a full stack of presents under the Christmas tree. That's not wrong, is it?"

"It's not the desire that's wrong," he said. "More the method of attaining it."

"Sometimes you have to crack a few nuts to get what you want." She sighed. "That's the problem with so many people—they're not willing to do what's required to make their dreams come true. But I am. And I thought you could help me. But all I see is Juliette Macintyre getting in my way. I thought making her a murder suspect would ensure you kept your distance from her! But no, somehow it brought you two together."

As if someone had cued it from the heavens, Joel's phone started to ring again. Serenity looked at the screen and shrieked. The sound was high-pitched and almost inhuman. Then she threw the cell phone through the doorway into the living room, where it bounced off the arm of the couch and clattered across the floor, continuing to ring.

Serenity now had two hands on the gun and was holding it steadily at Joel's face.

"What are you even doing?" he asked her. "The more bodies you rack up, the harder it's going to be to get away with it. You're taking on more risk than you need to."

"I can't let you live after I told you everything, duh. You could send me to jail." She looked at him like *he* was the unhinged one. "And I'm in my selfish era, Joel. I've earned the right to be a little selfish, okay? All these years I went without, I went unloved and unrecognized, now *I'm* the one in control. And since you're not on board with my plans, then you're just another task on my to-do list."

Fuck. She wasn't joking around. He could hear it in her voice.

This could very well be the day he died.

And what did he have to show for his life? A career he'd loved that he walked away from, a failed marriage, an empty house and a loveless, friendless life that was a void of his own making. It was pathetic. And the one person who'd tried to connect with him despite all his huffing and puffing and grousing . . . he'd pushed her away. The memory of waking tangled in Juliette's sheets, her body pressed into his, the small furry form of Digger wrapped around his calf filled him with an ache so bad it was like someone had gouged his heart out with a teaspoon.

Those moments were the point of life. Being. Living. Connecting.

*Loving.*

Of course his dumb ass had to have a breakthrough right as someone was about to put a bullet in him.

*Fight back. Instead of fucking running away and giving up like you always do, fight for your life. Fight for Juliette. Fight like you've never had the courage to fight before.*

Joel stood and Serenity's eyes widened. She was strong—he knew that much, having attempted one of her Pilates classes.

"Sit down," she said.

"No."

"You're going to regret this." She gritted her teeth and steadied herself.

At that moment there was a pounding on the front door.

And the gun went off.

## *Chapter Twenty-Three*

**JULIETTE WATCHED FROM** the back seat of the police cruiser, her wrists in cuffs, as Joel's front door was kicked down. A loud bang brought neighbors onto the street and faces poking out of windows. She plastered herself to the door, trying to see what was happening. Two officers rushed into the house, followed by Detective Dooley.

Juliette's heart was in her throat. What was going on in there? Was Joel okay?

In front of the cruiser, a small blue Hyundai with a dent in the bumper was parked crookedly against the curb. On the back window was a sticker that said *Life happens. Pilates helps.* It was definitely Serenity's car. Juliette had seen it at the dog park on many occasions. What was she doing here? Had she tried to hurt Joel?

Why didn't her calls go through? She tried to get hold of Joel before letting Detective Dooley into What The Fluff after he announced he was arresting her. But there was no answer. If only they hadn't fought that morning . . . he might have picked up. She might have been able to warn him. But in seconds the police were in the grooming studio, her rights were being read and cuffs encircled her wrists. The detective had evidence—Maurice's missing record had been found at Juliette's apartment. An anonymous tip-off.

She *was* being framed.

But when he'd shown her the vinyl—bagged in plastic to preserve its integrity—Juliette noticed something. It *wasn't* the same album! It was the official version released after those four songs, including "Rocks and Gravel," had been removed. The killer was trying to have their cake and eat it, too.

*Serenity is the killer. That's no secret now.*

Juliette had begged the detective and his subordinates to look this information up and they found she was telling the truth. She'd showed them the leash in the drawer with Bonnie's note, proving that Serenity had possession of the murder weapon. And Joel *still* wouldn't answer his phone. On the way to the police station, she'd begged them to go past Joel's house and when Juliette saw Serenity's car there . . .

Suddenly, two police officers had Serenity McFarlane in cuffs and were leading her out of Joel's house. She thrashed against them, short blond hair tossing in the wind, and a sound coming from her that was pure fury. The neighbors watched, agape.

*Where's Joel? Oh God, please be okay.*

Their special night might have ended with bitter disappointment, but she still cared for him. A second later the wail of ambulance sirens sounded further down the street and flashing lights came into her vision as Juliette twisted in her seat to look out the back window.

"No . . ." She shook her head, willing the ambulance to drive past to some other house. But she knew it wouldn't.

The ambulance pulled up behind the police car and three EMTs piled out with a stretcher.

"Oh my God."

Tears welled in her eyes as she watched them head inside, moving with practiced efficiency. It was lucky there was a hospital so close, in times of emergency. But what had happened to Joel?

Seconds stretched on for hours, minutes felt like days. Eventually the EMTs reappeared at the door, pushing a stretcher with a Joel-sized lump on top of it. Juliette pressed her cuffed hands to the window. As they came past, she could see it was him. There was something pressed to his shoulder. Gauze? Bandages? It was hard to make out. As they got closer, she caught a glimpse of his face. He was pale as a sheet, but his eyes were open, teeth gritted. Relief flooded through her and she slumped against the door.

Joel turned to the police car and made eye contact with her through the window, lips moving.

*Thank you.*

She let out a long breath and leaned shakily back against the seat as they moved Joel to the ambulance. He was alive. Possibly thanks to her.

*Two weeks later . . .*

**JULIETTE STOOD IN** the reception area of What The Fluff, hands laced in front of her. The grooming salon sparkled, the appointment log was no longer full of blank spaces, and Joel had fully recovered from a bullet grazing his shoulder.

Oh, and Juliette had been officially cleared of murder.

To say the last few weeks had been a rollercoaster of emotions was putting it lightly. It was a whole damn amusement park!

She glanced down to the basket behind the front desk where Digger usually curled up whenever she brought him to work. There was a near identical one at her apartment, too. Both empty. In fact, everything felt a little empty. Taking Digger back to the animal shelter was bittersweet—there was a family interested in him and, therefore, a potential fur-ever home in his future. But she missed him. And What The Fluff was a strange place without Bonnie's raucous laugh. Plus Norah would be moving into Bonnie's apartment permanently with Marshmallow, so home would feel empty now, too.

She was officially alone in the world.

The realization felt like a boulder pressing on her chest—it was the opposite of everything she wanted in life. Juliette had grown up dreaming of getting married, making a family and having the kind of home where loved ones dropped in without warning because everyone was welcome. In that image there was always a dog running around her feet. Ironically, one of the police officers had told Juliette that she and Serenity had shared that dream. But now Juliette's fantasy featured a very specific dog—a little scruffy white-haired comet flying this way and that.

*And Joel? Where does he fit into this image?*

She swallowed. Joel could have been right at the center of it all, standing next to her, one strong arm around her waist while she leaned against him. It could have been *their* home that was welcome to all, their family growing into something beautiful. Their love that healed the wounds of the past.

She'd seen Joel at Brewed Awakening a few times, but hadn't gone in. She couldn't face him. Because she knew the second she saw him, she'd want to throw herself into his arms with relief that he was okay, and she'd end up making a fool of herself for a guy who was happy to have sex, but not happy to have more.

"You can't be with someone who doesn't want the same things as you," she said to no one. "No matter how much you care about them."

And care about him she did.

In body and mind and soul. She saw the goodness in him. The life he was capable of, if only he would take a leap. Joel could have been her forever. Instead, he chose the safety of isolation over the high risk, high reward of love.

*Aren't you being a massive hypocrite, though? You talk a big game about choosing "forever" and yet you choose fostering over adoption because you're scared it's too much commitment.*

The truth of her own duality smacked into her like a wave.

Holy shit. She was no different than Joel. But instead of pushing people away, she chose to stay on the sidelines, waiting for permission, waiting for someone to say "yes, you belong." When, in fact, she didn't need *anyone's* permission to be part of the community here. She *did* belong. She *was* worthy of putting herself out into the world.

Juliette glanced around What The Fluff. This was *her* business now. She owed it to Bonnie and herself to give it her best shot.

"I don't want to let you down," she said, looking up at Bonnie's picture, which she'd hung on the wall last night. "And I know what you'd say: *just be yourself and stop waiting for other people to validate you.* You're right. I'm ready to listen now."

It was time to step out of the shadows, come what may.

Juliette stuffed a woolen hat on her head, slipped on her coat, snatched her purse from the cubby behind the front desk and flew out the front door.

**BY THE TIME** she pulled her car up in front of the Labrador Falls Animal Shelter, she was fully committed. Digger was "the one" for her. Well, the *furry* one for her, anyway. Ever since she'd returned him to the shelter, she'd felt the terrier-shaped hole in her life. How was it possible that she missed him waking her up at 4 a.m. to play tug-of-war or to jump on her bed like a bouncing ball? But she did. She missed his happy little tail wag, his constant excitement for whatever she had planned and the adorable way he curled up on the couch next to her at night. She especially missed that he lived his entire life with everything dialed to 11.

People could learn a thing or two from Digger about living a full life.

She certainly had.

Juliette hurried into the animal shelter like she was the hero at the end of a rom-com movie chasing down the heroine who was about to marry the wrong guy. She burst through the front doors, breath coming fast, and everyone turned to look at her. A couple stood with a young boy of about five and they were jittering with excitement, clearly about to meet their potential adoptee. They must be here for Digger! The woman who'd asked her to bring him in said it was a couple with a young son.

Behind the counter, a woman with bobbed hair and thick-framed glasses looked up in alarm. Until she saw who it was. "Juliette, is everything okay?"

"Please, you can't adopt him." Juliette rushed toward the family. They weren't local, she was sure of it. They wore matching kitschy sweatshirts with lobsters on the front and the mother pulled the son close against her hip. Juliette must look a sight—dark circles, bloodshot eyes. She hadn't slept properly since Joel got shot. "I know you probably think Digger would fit right into your lovely family, and I'm sure he would. He's the most wonderful little guy. He's caring and sweet and energetic as all get out. He'll make you laugh so damn much with all his antics, even when he's causing chaos and trouble. He does it in this way where you can't possibly be mad. He's the perfect canine best friend. But the fact is, he's *already* part of a family. *My* family. Well, just me, really. Me and him."

The family stared at her. They didn't appear moved by her impromptu speech, or by her passion and pleading. Instead, they looked at her like most folks looked at Juliette—with distrust, and more than a hint of judgment. Shame prickled along her skin. They were strangers—she shouldn't care what they thought of her.

She shouldn't care what anyone thought of her.

But if there was one thing she'd realized about being cleared of murder, it was that people didn't magically change their opinions overnight. Knowing she was innocent didn't suddenly make people like or accept her. She *still* bore the mark of her family name, that black streak of badness. Nothing would ever change that. Nothing would make it go away.

But that didn't matter to her anymore.

People could only shame her if she allowed herself to feel shamed by them. And she had, for years and years and years. She'd tried everything to win people over when really she should have been spending that energy on living her best life regardless of what people thought. She'd been wholly focused on the wrong thing.

Now it was time for her to take the life that she deserved. Screw anyone's opinion.

"I won't let you leave with him." She folded her arms across her chest and braced herself for an argument. "He's my dog and I want to take him home . . . please."

Okay, so maybe some habits still died hard.

"Juliette." Megan, the woman working at the shelter, came around the front desk and gently clasped her by the elbow, leading her away from the family. A second later, another shelter worker appeared from the back holding a cat carrier with a young ginger cat inside. The family broke into excited gasps. "They're not here to collect Digger."

"Oh." Well, her declaration was a dry run for standing up for herself, right? Nothing wrong with a little practice.

"He was adopted yesterday."

"What?" The air left her lungs and her shoulders sagged forward, grief striking her in the gut. "He's been adopted?"

Megan nodded, brow furrowed. "I know it's hard when you foster—"

"It's not that." She shook her head. "He was different."

He was The One. The dog for her. Her furry best friend, different to all the others she'd brought into her home and her care. And now, like Joel, he was gone and she was alone.

"There are other—"

"It's okay." Juliette's eyes filled with tears and she turned away, mortified. Crying in public was a step too far. Learning to give less fucks was going to take baby steps, and she'd maxed out on those with her speech. "Thank you for letting me know."

She exited the animal shelter as quickly as she'd entered, hurrying toward her car as her vision wavered and she swiped at her eyes with the sleeve of her coat. Maybe this was supposed to happen. Maybe it was the lesson she needed to learn—to be okay with being alone. Because maybe that's what life had in store for her.

But even as her brain tried to rationalize this situation, Juliette knew in her heart that it wasn't true. She had too much love to give to be all on her own. And she wasn't going to give up now. She would go home, have a cry in private and then pick herself back up and keep going.

Life had taught her *that* lesson, at least. No matter how bad it seemed, she could always move forward.

## *Chapter Twenty-Four*

**ON HALLOWEEN,** Juliette, Norah and Alexa gathered to hand out candy at Alexa's place. It was tradition. Each year they picked a costume theme and competed to come up with the best execution. Alexa, being the creative one and the person with the best sewing skills, often won, although last year Norah had excelled at the "D-Grade movies" theme when she came as *Sharknado*, complete with wire tornado wrapped around her body, studded with cotton ball clouds, a dozen shark toys glued on and lights that simulated lightning.

This year's theme was "7 deadly sins" and they'd randomly drawn their sins from a baseball cap. Juliette had selected "envy" and chosen to come as the Evil Queen from *Snow White and the Seven Dwarfs*, complete with long purple dress, cape and cardboard crown spray-painted in metallic gold paint. She'd even found a plastic apple from the fall decorations section at the dollar store and covered it in glitter to hang from her belt . . . which had seemed like a good idea at the time. But now she left a sparkly red trail wherever she went.

Alexa had drawn "greed" and had come in a pinstripe suit with a mug shot sign hanging around her neck that read: *Billionaire CEO. Crime: paying less than a living wage*. She also had fanned notes of Monopoly money sticking out of her sleeve cuffs, a fake Rolex she'd found in a thrift store, and a patch sewn onto the breast pocket of the jacket that said "Nepo Baby."

Norah had drawn "sloth" and had come as . . . you guessed it, a sloth.

Marshmallow had come as a mini sloth.

She sat quietly in the corner, her fluffy white legs poking out of the costume in a way that made it look like she was wearing old fashioned pantaloons. The sloth head sat like a cap on Marshmallow's head, the double sets of eyes more than a little unnerving, especially when one set of eyes were crossed and the other were filled with murder.

"This might be the most comfortable costume I've ever had," Norah said, grinning. The furry onesie came complete with sloth claws, which made it almost impossible for her to hand the candy out. "Remember last year? I couldn't even sit down in that stupid tornado outfit."

"I was picking fluff off my floor *forever*," Alexa groaned.

Norah held up both hands. "Jules is worse than me this year. I'm sure I've got sparkles on my ass from using the bathroom after she went in there."

Alexa chuckled. "You know what they say, glitter is the herpes of the craft world."

"I didn't realize it was going to shed everywhere." Juliette frowned. "Sorry, Alexa."

"It's all good. What would Halloween be without a little mess?"

"Maybe we should go for a walk," Norah suggested, slipping her sloth claws off and rummaging through a shopping tote to retrieve Marshmallow's leash. "Feels like things have slowed down, and we can go see some of the decorations all lit up. Might help that apple shed the rest of its glitter *outside* the house."

Juliette raised an eyebrow. Since when did Norah suggest getting outside and doing anything social? Or worry about cleaning up? Especially since it wasn't even her house.

"Great idea." Alexa beamed. "I could use a walk."

Juliette shrugged and followed the other two and the dog outside, picking up the hem of her purple velvet dress as she went down the stairs in front of Alexa's place. As the wind cut through the polyester layers of her costume she shivered and wrapped her cape around herself. The streets had quietened down some with smaller kids back in their houses, leaving the teenagers to run around, shrieking and getting into character.

A vampire couple was out walking their dog, a little pug whose roly-poly body had been stuffed into a bat costume complete with velvet wings. A group of girls were all dressed as different Taylor Swifts—the "Shake It Off" cheerleader, country era Taylor with her curly hair and a guitar, a fairy tale-esque "Love Story" Taylor and another in a Chiefs jersey, each in long blond wigs. They saw the traditional Halloween staples—zombies, ghosts, black cats and witches—and some more modern things—a hilarious group of moms dressed as one of the *Real Housewives* franchises complete with bad fake tans and faux bling jewels.

They strolled down the street, admiring the decorations and pointing out funny things to one another, and Juliette felt like her heart was lighter than it had been in weeks. Even Marshmallow seemed less murderous than she had been half an hour ago, so that was saying something.

"Remember Mom would always make us go to Mrs. Bouchard's house, and all she ever handed out was little bags of candy that were ninety percent candy corn." Norah wrinkled her nose and made a gagging face. "So gross. I suspect she actually hates kids."

"What's wrong with candy corn?" Alexa asked. "I like it."

Juliette and Norah looked at one another, aghast. How did they not know this about their friend?

"You *enjoy* eating the love child of classroom chalk and candle wax?" Norah asked. "Candy corn are tiny, flavorless morsels of pure sadness, and anyone who stuffs their candy bags with them is in league with the devil."

Alexa laughed. "It's not *that* bad."

Norah rolled her eyes. "Next thing you're going to tell me is that you like Peeps! Or worse, Rockets."

They turned a corner, skirting around a house with huge glittering cobwebs dangling from the porch overhang, while a ghostly figure illuminated the front window. Every few seconds, an eerie red light flickered and the sound of an evil laugh filled the street. Juliette remembered running around the neighborhood as a kid, Norah and Alexa in tow, as they filled their little jack-o-lantern buckets with as much candy as they could get their hands on. Juliette always made sure that everyone ended up with an equal share, giving up her own treats to her twin and friend if someone's haul was lacking.

"Wow, look at that place." Alexa pointed.

Juliette followed the line of her friend's finger, blinking when she realized that it was Joel's house. Gone was the perfectly tidy but sterile front yard that featured not even a single pumpkin. Gone was the sense of it being a rental home, rather than a permanent landing place. Gone was . . .

"Did Joel move?" she asked, shaking her head. "Because this can't be him."

The front of the house was . . . well, it looked like someone had taken a credit card to Party City and gone buck wild. Glowing Jack-o-lanterns bracketed the entrance, which was lit with flickering fake candles and had garlands of black cats and ghosts draped like curtains either side of the front door. Several bats dangled from the eaves and his mailbox had been covered in cobwebs and plastic spiders, and had a raven perched on top that cawed when you got close. At the heart of it all was a scene featuring two skeletons on the front lawn, one standing and the other down on one knee. The standing skeleton wore a tiara and the kneeling skeleton held a cup of coffee and a paper bag in one hand—the words *cinnamon roll* were written in black marker on it—and there was a speech bubble above the kneeling skeleton's head that said, "Will you be my sunshine?"

Juliette gaped at the scene in front of her. Nothing was computing right now. Had hell suffered an extreme blizzard she didn't know about? Had she tripped on her own cape and knocked herself unconscious? Had she eaten too much candy and this was some kind of sugar-induced fever dream?

Then she saw Norah texting furiously on her phone. Juliette tried to see what she was writing, but Norah snatched her phone away. At that moment, the front door swung open and a figure, backlit from the indoor lighting stepped forward. A few seconds later a smaller, four-legged figure appeared next to him.

It was Joel . . . and Digger.

"Go." Alexa gave her a shove forward, an excited grin stretched across her face, which looked really at odds with the mug shot board around her neck. "Talk to him."

"Did you two . . ." She turned toward her twin and friend. Both women shrugged innocently.

"We're going to walk around the block," Norah declared. "See you in a bit."

They left her standing there, head shaking, mind whirring, body trembling. What was even happening right now?

Digger bounded toward her, mouth open and a happy little tongue lolling out, his ears flapping with each energetic step. He was wrapped in a furry piece of fabric made to look like a log with a cardboard ax sticking out of it. Joel was dressed in a plaid shirt, worn jeans and his usual boots. It wasn't much of a costume, but given all the effort he'd put into his yard decorations she would let it slide.

Speaking of his yard . . . Juliette noticed two distinct holes that had not been there when she'd visited previously. She crouched to give the dog a cuddle, laughing as she immediately got a tongue swiping up her cheek. Out of her peripherals, two boots came into view.

"*You* adopted him?" she asked, standing and dusting the fur from her palms. "Mr. I Hate Dogs Because They Smell."

Digger trotted right back over to Joel and raised one paw as if asking for a fist bump. Joel obliged.

"Turns out I don't hate dogs that much . . . or at all," he said. "I just hated having mine taken away and I hated grieving the things I'd lost. But a wise woman once said that I wouldn't change unless I wanted to, because change is hard and it takes multiple failed attempts before it sticks, and even then it's an uphill battle. And I've decided that I'm okay with an uphill battle. I *do* want to change."

She looked at him, wondering where on earth this had come from. *Could* someone change on such a level?

*Is he really changing, though? Or is he simply turning into who he was meant to be? Who he* was *before life ground him down to dust?*

Because Juliette knew how far people would go to protect themselves, the layers of armor and shields and masks to turn themselves into the person it was safe to be, instead of who they truly were. She had done that. Only her masks were brittle smiles when she should have been standing up for herself. They were restraints that made her smaller, quieter, more palatable when she should have been living her biggest, boldest life like Bonnie always said. They were the things that bound her to the sidelines of life, waiting for permission. Waiting for the safest opportunity, the option with the least chance of failure or embarrassment.

So while she had said Joel wouldn't change until he wanted to change, the same was true of her.

"Step one, bringing this little guy into my life." Joel looked down at Digger, who appeared to puff his chest out as if to say, *I am totally the chosen one. Best dog ever, that's me!* "Step two, start participating in things around town. Like Halloween."

"Were you handing out candy?" she asked.

"Yeah. Turns out these kids are weird and they hate candy corn, though." He shrugged. "I love that stuff."

"Oh that is a red flag!" She held up both hands.

"Reminds me of being a kid, before everything got so complicated." He ran a hand through his hair. "But that wasn't the end of my plan."

"There's a step three?"

"Yeah. Step three, apologize to the Disney princess for being a scared asshole when she was only trying to help."

"I'm a villain tonight," Juliette said, looking down at her costume.

"You're never a villain. Maybe a little misunderstood, but never a villain." He swallowed. "You saved my life, Juliette. If it wasn't for you . . . I could be dead now."

A lump clogged the back of her throat. No matter how frustrated she'd been with him, the thought that something terrible might have happened was something she couldn't even wrap her mind around.

"I did what anyone would do," she whispered.

"No, Sunshine. You did what *you* would do, which is to speak up for what's right even when people might not believe you or even if it might cause you problems. Not everyone would do that."

"So, that's what this is? An apology?" She gestured to the skeletons on the lawn. "Because it looks like . . .

"A proposal?" He scrubbed his jaw. "Yeah, someone did point

that out to me after I was already done. And Digger and I spent, like, two whole days getting this place ready, didn't we, buddy?"

The dog made a begrudging snort.

"You can't propose to someone if you're still married, anyway," Juliette said.

"I won't be married for much longer," he replied. "I sent the paperwork off to the lawyers a few days ago. Then I called Marissa and . . . we cleared the air a bit."

Juliette's eyebrows shot up. "Really?"

"She's getting married to someone else and I gave her my blessing. It's better for both of us to move on."

"And Myla?" Juliette asked.

"We did a video call. I got to see my girl." For a moment it looked like there was a tear sparkling in his eye, but then it was gone. Was it a trick of the light or something more? "She's happy in her new home. Got lots of space to run around and a new puppy brother to play with."

"Oh Joel." Her heart melted. "I know that must have been hard."

**DIGGER BUMPED HIS** head against Joel's calf. That wasn't all there was to say to Juliette. Because, yes, this wasn't a proposal of marriage. But it *was* a proposal of sorts. A proposal of friendship. Of companionship. Of romance.

*Of something meaningful and lasting, whether or not there's a ring involved.*

Joel had contemplated chickening out at least ten times since he'd gotten the text from Norah that the women were on their way over. It was a miracle she'd even agreed to help him tonight. Lord knew what Juliette had told her. But to his surprise, she'd said that if anyone could understand taking their time to come around to people, it was her. So she'd brought her sister here. And now it was like the universe was pushing him toward destiny.

*Bump.*

There was another headbutt against his leg.

Okay, maybe it wasn't the universe. He looked down at the little white dog at his feet. Digger stared up at him, tongue lolling out of his mouth, warm brown eyes full of love. His face was so expressive Joel would *swear* he could communicate his thoughts.

*Come on, man. You can't chicken out now. That's what* old *Joel would do. You're* new *Joel now . . .*

Maybe new Joel was simply old *old* Joel. The guy who charged into burning buildings to save people because he valued human life. The guy who put himself on the line every day by going after the things he wanted. The guy who wasn't afraid to say "I love you" with his whole chest. With his whole heart.

Because *that* guy was the one Juliette deserved. Not the grumpy dude who ran a café and walled himself off from the people—and dogs—around him.

*Say it, man. Stop hiding behind your walls and say it.*

Juliette was watching him, her eyes wide and sincere. Even after what he'd done—what he'd said—she was still willing to listen to him. To give him a chance to say his piece. It was more than he'd given her.

*Tell her. Now.*

"It was hard," he said, hating the way his voice sounded raw and rough. "But not closing that chapter was even harder."

"What do you mean?" she asked.

"Having to make the choice not to save Chase that day was . . . it was the worst decision I ever had to make. He was like my brother. He *was* my brother. And then losing Marissa and having her take Myla away from me . . . it broke me."

"Of course it did," she replied with a sad smile.

"And I know I said I wasn't a fixer-upper project for you to bring back to shiny, new condition. And I'm not. I *am* broken. But I thought . . . I realized that . . . maybe . . ." He swallowed. God, this was tough, being vulnerable, saying these things out loud. "Maybe I don't have to stay broken."

She looked so beautiful, standing there in front of him, a sheep in wolf's clothes. A princess in disguise as a villain. But anyone who took a moment to listen to her, to get to know her, would know that she was far from a villain. People had judged her for years, and yet she still stood strong, still put on her best face and tried to bring good into the world.

He wanted to be like her. Like how he used to be.

"I thought love meant pain and loss. It's what the last five years has taught me. Watching my mom grieve my father planted that seed years ago, and that fire made it into a whole fucking tree. To love someone is to cut yourself open, I thought. It's too risky. But there you were all light and hope and so full of determination it's like staring into the sun."

"It was too much." Her eyes glimmered. "*I* was too much . . . as usual."

"No." He stepped forward. "It was exactly what I needed."

The air was thick. They were both wounded, both wary of trusting, both hurt by what other people thought of them. But he wanted to put his feelings into words, even if they were halting and inelegant and rough around the edges. Like him. Joel knew that love wasn't smooth. It wasn't a perfect linear progress like in the movies. It wasn't a filtered, edited, perfected picture or a clearly cut path. It was unpredictable and inconsistent and gloriously, wonderfully complex.

The old Joel shunned those things. Who the hell wanted complex when he could live safely in his bubble, alone?

But now he knew that safety could be a cage. It could hold you in one place until you withered from the inside. Was there risk in loving again? Absolutely. Could Juliette crush him if she wanted to? Hell yes. But was being with her worth all that and so much more?

He'd never know a truth stronger in his entire life.

"I want us to be each other's sunshine," he said. "Instead of letting that always fall to you. I want to bring light into your world, instead of rain clouds. I want to encourage you with your business and help you to see what a wonderful person you are, screw what anyone thinks. I want to tell this whole fucking town I think you're amazing."

Her eyes shimmered and her lips trembled for a moment. "Really?"

"Until I'm hoarse, Juliette. I don't want to hide in the shadows and I don't want you to, either. Neither one of us deserves a life like that." He held out his hand, hoping with all his heart that she would take it. "So I'm asking you, Juliette Macintyre, if you'll give me another chance to show you who I am. The *real* me."

"Does this mean you'll start making pumpkin spice lattes?" she asked, a mischievous smile blossoming on her lips.

"Absolutely not." He shook his head. "I might be trying to change but that's a step too far."

"What about mochas?"

"No."

She laughed and took his hand in hers. "Good. I don't want you to change *that* much."

"I'm sorry I pushed you away," he whispered. "It won't happen again."

"It might," she said, cupping his face with her hand. "And that's okay. Change doesn't stick overnight. But how about we promise to always talk about it after, okay?"

"Deal."

Joel leaned forward, his nose nudging hers before his lips brushed hers in a whisper-light kiss. They hovered there for a moment, as if wanting to capture this memory forever. He certainly did. She smelled like candy apple and cinnamon spice and crisp, fresh air, and her eyes were as dark as ebony.

"And after we talk about it, we have to kiss," she said. "That's the rule."

"You don't need to tell me twice."

The soft, yet firm pressure of her lips melted any fears he had as he kissed her. Deeper, harder. More intense than before. And filled with so much love he thought he might burst. Her hands smoothed over his chest, catching the fabric of his lumberjack shirt and curling so she could tug him closer.

Behind them came a whooping cheer, and when they broke apart, Norah and Alexa stood on the sidewalk clapping and setting off some party popper thing. He hadn't even asked them to do that. It was all on them.

The joyful moment was broken by a sound of disgust as Ruth Goldstein and her shih tzu, Robert, walked past. She waggled a finger at them as she and Robert marched on their nightly walk, neither one of them dressed up or appreciating the festivities.

"Get a room!" she said, revealing a smear of pink lipstick on her front teeth. "We don't need to see that filth here."

Robert snorted in their direction and the pair moved on, to chuckles from everyone watching. That's when Joel realized they'd drawn a bit of a crowd—snickering teenagers, giggling girls and some of his neighbors. It was the very opposite of what he'd wanted when he came to town, which was to hide away. To fade away. To be invisible.

And now, he was the center of attention with the one woman in town who always knew how to attract it, for better or worse.

"Nothing to see here, folks," he said. "Just a lucky man and the woman who's going to change his life."

Norah and Alexa cheered again, and surprisingly, the other people joined in. There were cheers and claps and a *good for you* from someone next door. Another person threw a handful of candy corn at them as if it was confetti and Juliette looked on with eyes wide and shining.

"This is your town, Juliette," he said. "No matter what's happened in the past, it's time for a fresh start. What The Fluff is going to thrive. I'll do anything to help you make that happen."

She wrapped her arms around him and looked up, resting her chin against his chest. "Thank you."

From below, there was a not-so-subtle snort and they both looked down to see Digger staring at them intently. *Like, excuse me. Don't I get to be included in this happy moment? As if I didn't basically make this whole thing happen. Jeez!*

Laughing, Joel bent to scoop Digger up and cradle him along with Juliette. She pressed a kiss to his head and nuzzled her nose against his fur.

"I thought you were long gone, little buddy," she said. "I thought I'd never see you again."

*Nah. I wasn't going anywhere.*

Holding his new canine best friend and the woman he couldn't even have conjured in his wildest dreams, Joel looked out over the street that was now his home and felt, for the first time in years, like he didn't want the moment to end.

# *Epilogue*

*Four months later . . .*

**IT WAS FUNNY** how much things could change when a woman finally had the right mindset. In the past few months, Juliette had been doing her best to live Bonnie's legacy—not only by running What The Fluff but also by giving less fluffs. And now, things were really turning around.

"I'm so sorry, Mrs. Carver, I'm afraid I won't be able to squeeze Cookie and Butterscotch in on Friday." Juliette wanted to be the better person, but it *did* give her a slight buzz of satisfaction to hear the older woman trying to beg her way into an appointment after believing, for a moment, that Juliette was a dognapper. "We're fully booked."

"Oh really? Because you know, I've been coming to What The Fluff ever since it opened. I'm a very loyal customer," Mrs. Carver said, her voice like honey. "Bonnie was always able to fit me in, bless her soul."

The old Juliette would probably have caved, agreeing to stay late one night to keep Mrs. Carver happy because she believed that was the only way to get people to accept her. But new Juliette was learning the value of setting boundaries and being herself, regardless of whether people liked her or not.

And a wonderful, strange thing had happened: people actually warmed up to her more when she *wasn't* trying to convince them to like her. It turned out, relaxing and simply being yourself was a much better approach.

"I know Bonnie really appreciated how loyal you've been, Mrs. Carver. One of the things I love most about What The Fluff is how great our customers are. So many in fact, that I'm looking to hire another groomer to help me keep up with the work!" she replied cheerily. "Now, how about next Friday? I can fit both Cookie and Butterscotch in at four o'clock if that works for you?"

She cradled the phone between her ear and her shoulder, tapping the appointment into the booking system as Mrs. Carver begrudgingly agreed to wait until the following week.

After she ended the call and rang back the other people who'd left voicemails during the busy workday, Juliette took a moment to finish her end-of-day cleanup, pumping some of Bonnie's favorite music through a portable speaker—David Bowie's "Let's Dance"—and bopping along as she mopped the floor.

It was hard to believe that only a few months ago she had been too terrified to even think about taking this business on herself, and now she was thriving. In addition to hiring some new staff, Juliette had also started posting on social media (yet another way she was putting herself out into the world), making entertaining yet educational content about pet grooming and running your own business. Alexa had helped her set the accounts up and Joel often helped her film the funny videos, with Digger always wanting to make a cameo.

The days of Juliette feeling like an outcast in her own hometown felt strangely far behind her, even though it really wasn't that long ago. That was another important lesson Juliette had learned: time didn't necessarily heal all wounds, as the saying went. Rather, it was action and belief that healed. And love, of course. Joel's love had helped her to see who she could be if she stopped focusing on the wrong things and bet on herself for a change.

Speaking of which, it was time to do something for the number one man in her life.

*Don't say that in front of Digger. He thinks he's everyone's number one.*

Juliette grabbed her bag and keys and threw on a light trench coat before heading outside into the crisp early spring air, locking the salon up behind her. It was Joel's birthday and she'd decided to throw him a surprise party—something she would have initially guessed he'd hate. But it turned out the man loved a surprise. When his defenses weren't up all the time, he had a spontaneous, playful streak . . . when he wasn't grousing about people's coffee orders, that was.

Juliette had roped Alexa and Norah into helping with the party, luring him to Alexa's place under the guise of a chill dinner. But they were, in fact, putting on a spring-themed party, complete with treats from the local farm-to-table restaurant, Harvest, a tiered cake from a talented local baker and wine from one of Juliette's favorite wineries further up the coast.

But she would have to boogie if she was going to make it on time.

**JOEL WALKED SLOWLY** up Alexa's driveway from where he'd parked his car, Digger almost dragging him toward the house. Joel considered himself a pretty fit guy and he'd kept up with his strength training since leaving his job as a firefighter. But running around after a Jack Russell was a *new* level of energy expenditure. Digger didn't seem to have an off switch and would happily play and do puzzles and games for hours.

And Joel loved it.

"Please tell me you're not going to terrorize Marshmallow tonight," he said as they walked up the steps to Alexa's front door.

Digger turned to look over his shoulder.

*Are you kidding? If anyone is going to be terrorizing anyone, it'll be her doing it to me. Comprende?*

Joel knocked on the door. When it swung open, Juliette was standing there, looking more radiant than he'd ever seen her. She'd recently cut her hair shorter and it grazed her shoulders, looking shiny and full, and there was a fun pink streak running along one side, which April had helped her dye. It was something she'd always wanted to try but never had because of how it might draw attention.

It matched the pink dress that wrapped around her body, highlighting her curves and tying into a sweet bow at her waist that would be decidedly less sweet when he took it in his teeth later that night.

"Wow," he breathed, giving a slight shake of his head. "Best birthday present ever."

She flushed and pressed up onto her toes to kiss him. It started as a peck but deepened into something more until there was an annoyed little *yip* at their feet.

"Sorry Digger, I'm happy to see you, too." She crouched to ruffle his fur and unclip his leash so he could trot into the house ahead of them. "Come on in, the girls are setting the table."

The house was eerily quiet. He'd expected the clatter of cutlery and glasses, maybe some music. At the very least, the kind of chatter that happened when three women got together. But there was nothing.

Juliette wasn't acting like anything was amiss and he followed her through to the living room. The second he set foot inside, however, the lights flicked on and a chorus of *surprise!* washed over him.

Joel was surrounded by the people with whom he'd started to build his community—Norah and Alexa, of course, and there was April, too, and her new girlfriend, Rita. Plus two guys from the dog park he'd recently become friends with and with whom he had a group chat labelled "LF Dog Dads." But even more exciting . . . both his sisters, Alyssa and Faith, were standing there, big grins on their faces and a colorful banner that read "Happy Birthday Joel" hanging over their heads.

"Happy birthday," Juliette said, squeezing his hand.

"I can't believe it." He shook his head, his heart so full of emotion it felt like it was going to burst. That feeling was coming to him more and more, lately. The feeling of a withered organ being flushed with new life, brought back from the brink of death to once again beat as hard as it should.

"I know the last few birthdays haven't felt like anything worth celebrating, but I wanted this one to make up for that. Last year is a year worth celebrating. *You* are worth celebrating."

He drew her into his arms and crushed his lips down to hers, inciting an enthusiastic cheer from the group. Public kissing was another thing that was becoming more common. For Joel, a man who'd tried so hard to hide his emotions away where even *he* couldn't see them anymore, it felt good to be authentic. To be free.

"I love you." The words came out of his mouth for the first time, though he'd felt them on the tip of his tongue for months.

He'd been thinking about the right moment to say it, because he wanted it to be special. To be right. But now it had come out of him so naturally, he knew there would never be a more perfect moment.

"I love you, too," she said, looking up at him, eyes glimmering. "Are you happy?"

"Happier than I ever could have imagined was possible."

She beamed. "Good. Now go say hi to everyone, we've got dinner to eat and a cake to cut."

"And then?" He rubbed his nose against hers, a surge of hungry heat flowing through him.

"And then you get your other present." She smiled slyly up at him. "But that one's just for you and me."

"I'll say it again," he said, kissing her softly. "Best birthday ever."

And when he broke away from the woman he knew without a shadow of a doubt was the love of his life, to embrace the people here—family old and new—Joel knew he had truly found his home in Labrador Falls.